In the past three yea...
Sherrilyn Kenyon ha...
This extraordinary b...
she writes. With more than...
in print in over 100 countr... include:
The Dark-...
Belador. Since 2004, she has placed more than 50 novels on the *New York Times* list in all formats including manga. The preeminent voice in paranormal fiction, with more than twenty years of publishing credits in all genres, Kenyon not only helped to pioneer, but define the current paranormal trend that has captivated the world.

Visit Sherrilyn Kenyon's websites:
www.darkhunter.com | www.sherrilynkenyon.co.uk

www.facebook.com/AuthorSherrilynKenyon |
www.twitter.com/KenyonSherrilyn

Praise for Sherrilyn Kenyon:

'A publishing phenomenon...[Sherrilyn Kenyon] is the reigning queen of the wildly successful paranormal scene'
Publishers Weekly

'Kenyon's writing is brisk, ironic and relentlessly imaginative. These are not your mother's vampire novels'
Boston Globe

'Whether writing as Sherrilyn Kenyon or Kinley MacGregor, this author delivers great romantic fantasy!'
New York Times bestselling author Elizabeth Lowell

SHERRILYN
KENYON
DREAM WARRIOR

piatkus

PIATKUS

First published in the US in 2009 by St. Martin's Press, New York
First published in Great Britain in 2009 by Piatkus
This paperback edition published in 2012 by Piatkus

A CIP catalogue record for this book
is available from the British Library.

ISBN 978-0-7499-5687-5

Printed and bound by CPI Group (UK) Ltd, Croydon, CR0 4YY

Papers used by Piatkus are from well-managed forests
and other responsible sources.

MIX
Paper from
responsible sources
FSC® C104740
www.fsc.org

Piatkus
An imprint of
Little, Brown Book Group
100 Victoria Embankment
London EC4Y 0DY

An Hachette UK Company
www.hachette.co.uk

www.piatkus.co.uk

PROLOGUE

THEY WOULD BE COMING FOR HIM.

Cratus stood on top of the highest point of Olympus, staring out at the beautiful setting sun. Ribbons of warm color split the darkening sky, reminding him of a brilliant fire opal glistening and twinkling. Nowhere else was it more breathtaking than here, and he wanted to watch it set one last time before he submitted himself for his well-deserved punishment.

He wouldn't ask for clemency. There was no need. He knew better than anyone the wrath of Zeus. For centuries, he'd been the Olympian god's hammer, carrying out his justice.

Now that justice would come for him.

"Run and I will run with you."

He glanced down at the small form of his sister Nike. Where his wings were black, hers were a pure white. Her dark curly hair was wrapped with a white ribbon that matched her gown. The personification of victory, she'd been his accomplice throughout his entire life.

They, along with their brother and sister, had been

the sentinels of Zeus. Beloved guardians, they had been treasured by the father of the gods even above Zeus's own children. Until Cratus had committed an unforgivable sin—he'd spared a life he should have taken. It wasn't his place to question his master, only to do his bidding. He still couldn't understand why he'd done it. The gods knew compassion was an alien emotion to him.

Yet here he was . . .

Time to die.

Cratus sighed wearily. "I can't ask that of you, akribos. You still have Zeus's favor. Don't jeopardize that for me. Besides, no one can run from Olympian justice. You know that as well as I do. No matter where I hide, they will find me."

Nike took his hand and held it to her cheek. "I know why you did it and I respect you for it."

And that changed nothing.

What was done was done. Now there was nothing left except the punishment.

He glanced away from the sun to see her there by his side, her beautiful face still tucked into the palm of his numb hand. In all eternity, she was the only one he'd ever really trusted. His sister with the haunting pale blue eyes, whose courage and loyalty was without equal. For her, he would do anything.

But he would not sacrifice her for his stupidity.

"Stay here where it's safe."

She tightened her grip. "I would rather be with you, brother. To the end as always."

He stroked her cheek tenderly before he dropped his hand away and looked down to where the gods' temples were nestled like jeweled eggs among the evergreen foliage. "Stay here, Nike . . . please."

She nodded, but he saw the reluctance in her eyes. "For you only."

Giving Nike his golden helm to keep as a memento of their battles together, Cratus kissed her brow before he headed down the mountain toward the hall of the gods. His embossed shield as heavy as his conscience, he leaned on his thick spear to keep him steady on his path.

As promised, Nike stayed behind, but he could feel her gaze on him as he walked. Her offer to run haunted him. But it wasn't in his nature to run from or submit to anything. He was a warrior, and it was all he knew. All he lived for.

He would fight to the end.

More than that, he refused to give his enemies the satisfaction of dragging him before Zeus in chains. He'd lived his life standing on his own two feet, and so would he die.

Alone. Without flinching, begging or fear.

It was a fitting end, really. After all the lives he'd callously taken for Zeus, this would be his penance.

He paused before the doors that led to where the gods would be gathered. He'd walked here among them a hundred thousand times.

But today would be his last.

His head held high, he threw open the huge gold doors. As soon as he did, silence rang out in the hall as everyone held their collective breaths, waiting to see how Zeus would punish him.

Zeus froze in place before his throne, his eyes dark

and threatening. Cratus's gaze went to the right side of the dais, where his post had been for all these centuries.

It would be his post no more.

Taking a breath for courage, he dropped his shield just inside the door. The hollow, metallic sound echoed loudly in the silence and mimicked the emptiness inside Cratus's heart.

Still, no one moved.

Not even the gowns of the women rustled.

His gaze locked determinedly on Zeus's, he hefted his spear above his shoulder and threw it hard to bury it in the wall right above Zeus's head—a last act of defiance that made every god present gasp in shock.

Cratus pulled his sword over his head and tossed it to the feet of Ares. Next he removed his quiver and bow, which he handed to Artemis. With every step he took toward Zeus, he peeled a piece of his armor off and dropped it to the marble floor, where it clanked loudly. First vambraces, then his greaves, his cuirass and finally his armored belt.

By the time he reached Zeus, he wore nothing but his brown loincloth. He tucked his wings down and lowered his head in silent submission to the king of the gods.

Zeus's curse rang out before he pulled a lightning bolt out of his glowing quiver and used it to slash across Cratus's face.

Cratus tasted blood as his eye and cheek erupted with throbbing pain. Covering his face with his hand, he felt the warm blood from his wound pouring between his fingers.

"How dare you come here after what you've done! No one defies me!"

The next blow knocked Cratus off his feet and sent him skittering across the floor. The cold marble peeled at his skin and bruised his muscles.

He came to rest at the feet of Apollo. Looking down in repugnance, the god sneered at him before he moved back, out of Zeus's line of fire.

Cratus wiped at the blood on his cheek, which dripped from his face to the floor, before he pushed himself up.

He didn't get far.

Zeus planted his foot on his spine and held him down on his stomach. "You have disobeyed me. I want you to grovel for my mercy."

Cratus shook his head in denial. "I beg for nothing."

Zeus kicked him over and drove a lightning bolt through his shoulder, pinning him to the floor. Cratus screamed out at the piercing agony that pulsed with every beat of his heart.

"You insolent dog. You dare defy me even now?"

"I will not—" His words broke off in a growl as Zeus planted another lightning bolt in his side and then in his other shoulder.

Curling his lip, Zeus stepped back. He swept an imperious glare around the gathered gods. "Is there one among you who will speak up in defense of this defiant maggot?"

With his one undamaged eye, Cratus looked to his brethren.

One by one, they turned away. Hera, Aphrodite, Apollo, Athena, Artemis, Ares, Hephaestus, Poseidon, Demeter, Helios, Hermes, Eros, Hypnos . . . et cetera. But the ones who really stung were his mother and his brother Zelos and sister Bia.

They stepped back and looked away, shame-faced.

So be it.

In his heart, he knew Nike would have spoken up for him. But she had done as he asked and stayed behind.

Zeus pierced him with another lightning bolt that would have probably hurt, too, had his body been capable of feeling any more pain. "It appears no one here cares for you."

Big surprise there. Cratus laughed, spitting up blood, as he remembered the day he'd forced Hephaestus to chain Prometheus to a rock for his eternal punishment. The god had been reluctant to carry out the orders and had called Cratus pitiless for his insistence that they obey Zeus's heartless command.

Cratus in turn had mocked Hephaestus's weak-kneed compassion. He'd told the god it was better to be the punisher than the victim.

Now it was his turn to suffer. No wonder no one would speak up for him.

He deserved no better.

Zeus pulled him up from the floor by his throat. His entire body numb from the pulsating lightning bolts that still pierced his flesh, Cratus could do nothing but stare at the father god.

"Will you pick up your arms and fight for me?"

Cratus shook his head. He would never again serve as a mindless dog obeying his master's every whim.

"Then you will suffer for all eternity and you will beg me every day for my mercy."

CHAPTER 1

New Orleans, 2009
6,000 years later . . .
Roughly
(Give or take a few centuries . . .)

DELPHINE PAUSED TO GET HER BEARINGS AS SHE looked around the old buildings with iron-work balconies or elaborate wood trim, many of which had boards over their windows. What a strange city . . . but then she wasn't used to being in the mortal realm except through human dreams. There the world of man looked entirely different.

This extremely loud and bright place baffled her. Not to mention the awful smell of something she thought might be manure of some kind . . .

She jumped as a loud, rude sound startled her while a car went speeding past.

Phobos grabbed her arm and yanked her to stand beside him on the uneven sidewalk. "Be careful. If a car hits you, it will hurt."

"Sorry. I wasn't paying attention."

He nodded before he glanced about the street where several cars were parked in front of a row of houses that were so close together, she wondered if they didn't share a common wall.

"The garage should be that one over there."

She looked to where he was pointing. Landry's Garage, Detail and Repair. "Are you sure he's there?"

Phobos gave her a droll stare. "His presence isn't what's in doubt, his *reception* of us is. We'll be lucky if he doesn't gut us both faster than Noir would." He wiped his hand over his brow to remove some of the perspiration. But it was quickly replaced by more.

She'd never been in a hotter place in her life. Poor Phobos, wearing all black clothes, wasn't exactly dressed for it, either. He looked as miserable in the heat as she felt. She'd always thought of him as one of the more attractive gods with his exceptionally dark hair and sharp features.

Tall and lithe, he moved fluidly and fast. Something that terrified his enemies and made him deadly in a fight. His job was to inspire dread, and at one time he and his twin brother, Deimos, had wreaked havoc on ancient battlefields. In more recent centuries, they'd become warriors for the Furies, punishing anyone who crossed the gods.

Until two days ago when everything had changed . . .

She shivered at the memory. Even though she should feel nothing, her stomach was still knotted over the horror she'd witnessed. They were still trying to piece their world back together after Noir's vicious attack.

"How did we get chosen for this again?" she asked him.

"We weren't there when Zeus banished him and therefore he shouldn't hate us as much as he hates the other gods." He snorted derisively. "Most importantly, we're part of the handful who is neither imprisoned nor dead."

That was comforting . . .

Not at all.

And it didn't mean Cratus would listen to them, never mind actually help them. "You think we stand a chance?"

"Like an icicle on the equator. But Cratus pulls his powers from the same primal Source that birthed Noir. Without him on our team, we're completely screwed."

She still wasn't sure about this. Zeus had sent them here to beg a favor from an ex-god who most likely would gut them as soon as they appeared. She'd never met Cratus, but his nasty reputation was legendary.

He had mercy on no one.

His brutality had only been matched by his single-minded determination. Even though Zeus had bound his god powers, the other gods continued to fear him. That alone said it all about his winning personality. Hephaestus himself had warned her that there was no reasoning with Cratus.

The man was angry and mean.

And that was before his punishment had driven him insane.

"Are you sure there's no other way?"

Phobos's features darkened. "Half your brethren are dead, and every time mine go out, they get their hides kicked back to the Stone Age. Believe me, belly-crawling to this asshole is the last thing I want to do."

But it was a necessary evil.

"Zeus is the one who should be doing this," she groused as she wiped the sweat from her own brow.

Phobos snorted. "You want to tell *him* that?"

Hardly. The father god tolerated no one to question him. She narrowed her eyes. "This was your bright idea, Phobos. You lead the way."

"What are you? Scared?"

She gave him a nasty glare of her own. With her half-human blood, she did have more emotions than most of her Dream-Hunter brethren, but they were muted compared to mankind's. "If I were capable of hate, I would probably hate you."

He sucked his breath in sharply between his teeth. "You know, you get the best sex from a woman when she's angry and hating."

"Since I've never had sex with a woman, how would I know?" She shoved him gently on the shoulder to move him forward. "We're on a mission, Dolophonos. Remember if we fail, your twin dies."

"Believe me, I haven't forgotten." He crossed the street with purpose.

Delphine followed in spite of the bad feeling she couldn't shake. This wasn't going to turn out well. She knew it.

They entered the office of the garage to find a small girl who was doodling on a sheet of paper and a woman around the age of thirty sitting at a dinged, metal desk. The woman was pretty enough, with small brown eyes and dark hair. Her smile was bright when she saw them. "Can I help you?"

Phobos stepped past Delphine to approach the desk. "We're looking for a guy named Cratus."

She frowned. "I don't know anyone by that name. Sorry. Maybe he's at the garage down the street."

Phobos scratched his head, obviously as baffled as Delphine was. "I know for a fact that he works here in this garage. Believe me, my sources are beyond reproach."

The little girl wiped her nose and pushed a pair of glasses back with her knuckle. "Did they lose their friend, Mommy?"

"Do your homework, Mollie." She turned her attention back to Phobos. "Look, I'm really sorry, but I've never heard the name Cratus before. I've worked here for five years and I assure you that none of our guys are named that. It's not exactly a name you'd forget—you know?" The phone started ringing. She put her hand on it. "Is there anything else I can do for you?"

"No." Phobos stepped over to the large window that looked out from the office into the garage area where men in gray and blue coveralls were working on various cars.

Delphine followed his lead and froze as she saw the man they sought.

Holy gods . . .

No one could miss *him*.

Little wonder he was the god of strength and the son of Warcraft . . . That power and formidableness bled from every pore of his body. Standing well over six feet tall, he rippled with well-defined muscles. As she watched him, he wiped grease from his hands with a dark blue cloth. His gray coverall suit had been unzipped, and the sleeves wrapped around his lean waist, leaving his torso covered by a black tank top that only made those muscles more apparent. Black tribal tattoos decorated both of his arms from the wrists to his shoulders.

But it was his face that made her gasp. She'd never seen a man more beautifully made, except for the jagged scar that ran down the right side of his face, hairline to earlobe. His right eye was covered with a black patch and from the depth of the scar, she wondered if he'd lost the eye completely to whatever injury had caused it.

Yet it in no way detracted from his handsomeness. If anything, it added to it and made his face all the more rugged. His jet-black hair was sweaty and curled slightly around a face that was chiseled from steel and dusted with dark whiskers.

Fierce power emanated from every inch of him. Strong and lethal, it said he should be on a battlefield, sword in hand, killing and maiming his enemies, not stuck in a garage, working on cars.

He was everything she'd heard and more.

May the gods help them . . .

If he didn't kill the two of them, she'd be stunned.

Phobos glanced at Delphine over his shoulder. "He is definitely here."

The secretary frowned as she hung up the phone and saw Cratus through the window. "You're looking for Jericho?"

Phobos faced her. "You mean Cratus."

She pointed at the man Delphine had been ogling. "That's Jericho Davis. He's only been here a couple of weeks. Is he in trouble with the law or something? If you're here to serve process—"

"No. Nothing like that." Phobos gave her an almost charming smile. "We're old friends."

She narrowed her eyes suspiciously. "Well, if his name isn't Jericho Davis, we need to know. Landry is a stickler about his people toeing the line. We don't take in convicts or riffraff here. This is a respectable business, and we intend to keep it that way."

Phobos held his hands up. "Don't worry, I'm sure he's not a felon. I just need to talk to him for a minute."

The secretary snorted. "I thought you said you knew him."

"I do."

"Then how are you going to talk to a man who's mute?"

Phobos snapped his attention to Delphine, who was as shocked as he was by that disclosure.

Surely Zeus wouldn't have been that cruel . . .

What was she? Insane? Of course he would.

Sick at the thought, Delphine looked back to where "Jericho" had his head under the hood of another car. What exactly had been done to him? Zeus had taken his godhood, his life and most likely his voice and eye.

Getting his help was looking less and less likely by the second.

"You stay here," Phobos said as he put his hand on the knob of the door that led from the office to the garage.

No problem there. She'd rather confront a rabid lion than try to gain a favor from a man the gods had screwed over so badly. Why on earth or beyond would *this* man ever help them?

Hoping for the best, she walked to the window to watch Phobos. She closed her eyes and opened herself up to the ether so that she could hear their conversation.

The shop was loud with mechanical noises and a radio playing "Live Your Life" by T.I. Several of the men were chatting and joking while they worked. One was singing along, off-key, while he added air to the tires of a red Jeep.

Phobos paused beside the white Intrepid where Cratus stood.

Cratus glanced up, and his face froze an instant before he looked back down and continued working.

Phobos stepped closer. "We need to talk."

Cratus ignored him.

"Cratus—"

"I don't know what you're doing in here," an older man in a coverall matching Cratus's said as he stopped beside Phobos, "but you're wasting your time trying to talk to old Jericho there. Boy can't speak." The man shook his head. "Not that he needs to. The way he works on a car is magic." The man looked at the others and laughed. "Trying to talk to Jericho . . ." More laughter joined his before he walked off to work on the Jeep where the man was singing.

"Jericho," Phobos tried again. "Please give me one minute of your time."

If looks could kill, Phobos would be a distant memory. Jericho flipped the wrench in his hand before he walked over to another car.

Phobos glanced at Delphine, who shrugged in response. She had no idea how to persuade him.

Sighing, Phobos followed him. "C'mon, I—"

Jericho spun on him so fast that Delphine didn't even realized he'd moved until he had Phobos slung over the hood of a car and pinned in place by a tight hold on this throat. "Fuck off and die, you putrid bastard," he snarled in the ancient Greek language of the gods as he banged Phobos's head furiously against the hood.

Every mechanic who heard his deep growl paused to stare at him.

"Be damned," a tall, lean African-American man said. "He can speak after all. Anybody know what language that was?"

"Russian?"

"Nah, I think it's German."

"Dude," a younger guy said, pulling at Cratus's arm. "You're going to dent the hood and when you do, *that* will come out of your paycheck."

Grimacing, Cratus slung Phobos off the hood like a rag doll. Phobos rolled halfway through the bay before he caught himself.

His features looking shaken, Phobos pushed himself to his feet. When he spoke, he continued to use their language so that the humans wouldn't understand them. "We need your help, Cratus."

As he moved past Phobos, Cratus drove his shoulder into Phobos's, making Phobos grimace in pain and rub his arm. He went back to the Intrepid. "Cratus is dead."

"You're the only one—"

Cratus growled at him. "You're dead to me. *All* of you. Now get out."

Delphine projected her thoughts to Phobos. "Should I come in?"

"No. I don't think it'll help." Phobos turned to Cratus. "The fate of the entire world is in your hands. Don't you care?"

The feral look Cratus gave him said no. Well, that, and for him to go to Tartarus and rot.

Delphine sighed. What were they going to do now? They needed the god of strength. One who could pull power from the primal Source to combat the most evil of beings. Without Cratus, they didn't stand a chance of winning against Noir and his army of Skoti.

The older man walked over to Cratus. "So what country are you from, anyway?"

Cratus ignored him as he returned to his work in silence.

Phobos moved to stand by his side. "Zeus is willing to forgive you for what you did. He's offering you your godhood back. We need you desperately."

When Cratus still refused to respond, Phobos let out a frustrated breath. "Look, I understand why you're mad. But my brother's life is on the line here. If you don't help me, Noir *will* kill him."

Cratus didn't even twitch as he worked.

A muscle worked in Phobos's jaw. "Fine. When the world ends and everyone here is dead, remember you're the only one of us who could have stopped it."

Cratus continued ignoring him.

Phobos turned and headed back to her.

Delphine kept waiting for Cratus to reconsider and stop Phobos. But he really appeared to have meant what he'd said. He didn't care.

Even she, who had nothing save muted emotions, had more feelings than this man showed.

"We're so dead," Phobos said in a dire tone as he rejoined her. "Maybe we ought to join the other team before they pound us into hash."

Delphine cast a hopeless glance back at the man in the garage. "Maybe I should try."

He shook his head. "There's no reaching him. He's past help."

"I can try to contact him in his dreams tonight. He won't be able to run from me then."

He didn't tell her no, but his look reiterated the fact that he thought she was wasting her time. "You want backup?"

"I think I'll be more effective alone."

Phobos snorted. "Good luck. If you need me, I'll be on standby."

Delphine glanced back at Cratus. He was working, but she saw the agony in his one eye. It was so deep and biting that it made her ache for him. . . .

How strange to have those feelings. But they meant nothing. She had a mission to fulfill.

I'll be seeing you tonight. And she definitely didn't intend to fail.

JERICHO PAUSED AS HE SAW THE GREASE ON HIS HAND covering the tattoo he'd used to hide the words of condemnation his own mother had burned into his skin at Zeus's command. Old memories tore through him anew as he thought about the way the Olympians had turned on him.

And all because he'd refused to murder an infant. Closing his eyes, he remembered that one defining moment so clearly. The small hut . . . the goddess's screams as she begged him for mercy.

"Kill me, not my baby, please! For the sake of Zeus, the baby's innocent. I'll do anything."

He'd tightened his grip on the child, fully intending to fulfill his duty. The baby's father had gone at his back. But the god of pain, Dolor, had caught him and cut him down before the goddess who'd tried so desperately to save her family.

That baby's only sin had been its birth.

And as he'd looked into that small, trusting face and the baby had smiled up at him, unaware of what was going on, he'd faltered.

"Kill it," Dolor had snarled.

Cratus had pulled his dagger out to slice its throat. Laughing, the baby had reached for him, its eyes twinkling with fire and joy as its tiny fingers wrapped around his large hand.

So he'd done the only thing he could. He'd used his powers to put the baby to sleep, then smuggled it out and given it over to peasants to raise.

One moment of compassion.

An eternity of shame, abuse and degradation.

Now they dared to ask him for a favor after all they'd done to him. They were out of their collective minds.

And he was through with them.

"Hey, man," Darice said, coming up to him. "Why didn't you ever tell us you could speak?"

Because talking to Darice might lead to friendship. And if he made that mistake, Darice would die right before him. Brutally and mercilessly.

Zeus had taken everything from him.

So he ignored Darice while he unbolted the alternator that needed to be replaced.

Darice made a sound of disgust. "Whatever. Guess you're too good to associate with the rest of us."

Let them think that. It was much easier than trying to explain a truth they would never accept. He was alone in this world. As always.

Darice wandered over to work on the Toyota that had come in earlier. He and Paul joked good-naturedly while they set about flushing the radiator and putting in new plugs.

Jericho had just pulled out the alternator when a shadow fell over him. Looking up, he found the shop owner, Jacob Landry. Short and pudgy, Landry had salt-and-pepper hair that was receding and a pair of greedy blue eyes.

"I heard there was some trouble here with you earlier."

Jericho shook his head no.

"Um-hmmm. Charlotte done told me that you can speak, too. Is that true?"

He nodded.

"Boy, why you want to lie to me? I done told you when I hired you that I don't play that bullshit. You want to work here, you come to work on time, keep your personal life at home and give me no lip and no lies. Comprende?"

"Yes, sir," he said as he tried to keep the hostility out of his voice. He hated that he was reduced to belly-crawling to assholes like this just so that he could eat. "It won't happen again, Mr. Landry. I promise."

Landry poked him sharply in the shoulder. "It better not."

Jericho tightened his grip on the wrench in his hand, wanting to give Landry a taste of what he was capable of. There had been a time when he'd have gutted anyone who talked to him like that. Never mind someone who'd actually dared to touch him uninvited. Before his human life had begun, everyone who came into contact with him quivered in fear of his strength and sternness.

But Landry was a bully. He enjoyed his minuscule power over the people who worked for him. He only felt good about himself when they were groveling for their livelihood.

And as much as it sucked, Jericho needed this job. As the world became more modern, it was getting harder and harder to find people who could make fake IDs at a reasonable price and who were willing to let him live off the grid.

Other immortals were allowed to accumulate wealth, but that, too, was beyond him. Any time he tried to save even a dollar, Zeus cleaned him out. One catastrophe after another.

So had been his existence for so many centuries that he no longer even bothered to count them.

He was nothing and he would never have anything again. Not even dignity.

Sighing, he went back to work, hating himself and this life.

You could change that. . . .

It had to be bad for Zeus to send someone to ask for his help.

You could be a god again. . . .

The dream of that thought tormented him. It was tempting except for one thing. He'd have to look at the very beings who'd turned their backs on him and left him to this pathetic state. Every one of those bastards had ignored him.

Every one of them.

Or worse, they'd tortured him.

Every single night. For thousands of years, the Dolophoni—the children of the Furies—and the dream gods had come to him and killed him. And every morning, he was resurrected to live this miserable existence right where he'd left off the night before.

Over and over. Bloody and violent. No matter how hard he tried to fight them off, he held no powers against them. They gleefully held him down and beat him or carved him to maximize the pain of his sentence. Every organ in his body had been torn out of him so many times that the pain was seared into his DNA. He dreaded every night and the horror it would ultimately bring.

Just last night, two of them had cut his heart out . . .

Again.

At the end of the day, he would never forgive what had been done to him. So what if something was threatening the world? If the world was to end, then at least he'd have some peace.

Maybe this time he'd actually stay dead.

DELPHINE RETURNED TO OLYMPUS SO SHE COULD spend the rest of the day researching her latest target. For hours, she watched him work in solitude. While the other men joked and laughed with each other, he kept to himself. Bitterly alone. Every now and again, she'd see him look up at the others and their camaraderie with a glint of longing so potent it made her ache.

They ignored him as if he were invisible.

At six-thirty, he washed up after the others were finished and leaving. He pulled his coveralls off, tucked them into a beat-up black cloth backpack that he slung over his shoulder and headed out on an older-styled motorcycle.

He stopped briefly to go into a small grocery store on a corner where he grabbed a loaf of bread, chicken salad spread, a paperback novel, and a six-pack of beer. Without speaking to a single person, he paid for it, tucked it into his backpack and went home to a tiny one-room efficiency apartment. The place was so run-down even the scuffed, chipped linoleum floor dipped in the middle. She wondered how the building kept from falling down around him.

It had to be the most depressing thing she'd ever seen.

There was no furniture whatsoever. Not a single piece, or even a TV or computer. Worn blankets were pinned to the windows for curtains, and his bed was only a threadbare sleeping blanket on the floor with a single pillow that was so old and flat he might as well not have it. Next to that, he had one additional pair of shoes and a small stack of clothes and one old wool jacket.

That was it.

Her heart clenched as she watched him open a beer, then wash the coveralls in the sink before he hung them up to dry in the rundown bathroom. Brushing his hand through his dark hair, he went back to the kitchen—which had no stove and only a filthy old refrigerator—to make a single sandwich out of the bread that had been flattened in his backpack. He ate it in silence while sitting on the sleeping blanket, reading his book.

Every now and again, he'd look up expectantly at any sudden sound. Once he was sure it was nothing, he'd return to his reading.

Just after midnight, he sighed and stared up at his ceiling. "Where the hell are you, assholes? You scared or something?"

He waited as if he really expected an answer. Glaring furiously, he put the book on the floor and pulled his tank top off to show her a chest rife with horrendous scars. She would think them battle wounds, but they were so jagged and torn that they appeared to be where his vital organs had been viciously ripped out of his body.

"Fine," he said, his tone filled with disgust, "just don't leave too big a mess in my place. I'm sick of having to clean up blood first thing in the morning and don't fuck up my book. I'd like to finish it for once." He turned out the lights and went to sleep.

Alone and in total solitude.

Who had he been talking to?

He's gone insane from his punishment. . . . Hephaestus had warned her of his delicate mental state. Obviously the god was right.

Delphine sat in the darkness, waiting for Cratus to reach the dream state—which took forever, since he seemed to be fighting sleep. It was as if he was waiting for someone to attack him and he wanted to be alert when they did.

As she waited, all she wanted to do was comfort him and she didn't even understand why. She'd never felt a compulsion like this before.

Probably because she knew what it was like to feel isolated from the world—granted, not as much as he was, but she still remembered the desolate feelings of her former life. As a young woman, she'd lived among the humans and had thought herself one of them. Even then she'd known something wasn't quite right with her. She'd never felt emotions the way other humans did.

It hadn't been until her teen years that her powers had fully manifested. She'd been so afraid of rejection or hostility from her family and friends that she'd held it in and told no one about her vivid dreams and frightening powers.

Until the Dream-Hunter Arik had shown up in her dreams and explained to her who and what she really was. Explained that her mother had been seduced by a sleep god, which had resulted in her birth.

To this day, she owed her sanity to Arik. He alone had explained to her how the Oneroi—the gods of sleep—had been created to help mankind with their dreams. Night after night, he'd visited and trained her until she had control of her powers. And once she was able to channel them, he'd taken her to the Vanishing Isle, where her kind lived, and had introduced her to the other gods.

There for centuries they'd been friends.

Even though Arik had eventually gone Skoti—turned into the evil dream gods who preyed on humans as they slept—she'd still been grateful to him for his guidance. So much so that she'd never pursued him in the dream realm to fight against him as she'd done other Skoti.

But Cratus had no one to protect him . . .

A fact that became brutally apparent an instant later when the air around him surged. Delphine started to go in, but an inner sense told her not to.

Something bad was about to happen.

She could feel the evilness of it. The fierce power went down her spine, painfully, and it froze her to the spot.

In the blink of an eye, one of the deadliest of all creatures materialized over his sleeping form. At first glance Azura appeared small and frail. But appearances were most deceiving. The very heart of evil, she was deadlier than any creature except for her brother and sister. Her skin was blue to mirror the icy coldness of her heart. Her hair, eyes, eyelashes and lips were snow-white. Dressed in a black leather halter top and pants, she knelt down by Cratus's side.

Delphine tried to transport in, but couldn't.

Azura looked back over her shoulder and smiled as if she knew Delphine could see her. "You will all perish," she said softly before she reached out to touch Cratus on the arm.

He came awake ready to battle.

Azura dodged his hands. "Calm yourself, Titan. I'm not here to harm you."

Cratus froze as he found himself in the presence of one of the original gods of the universe. The only problem was, she was concentrated evil. Granted, she wasn't quite as sinister as her brother, Noir, or sister, Braith, but she gave him a good run for his money.

"What are you doing here?"

She smiled. "You know what I'm here for, baby. I've come to make you an offer you won't want to refuse."

He sneered at her. "I'm not interested in fighting for the gods."

She patted him gently on his face. "Sweetie, you so greatly underestimate us." She dropped her hand to his arm.

Cratus hissed in pain as the words his mother had placed there burned like fire. The agony was so fierce that he couldn't move. Couldn't breathe. He wanted to shove her away, but even that was impossible.

She whispered in the first language of the universe and as she did so, he felt his will slipping. His sight dimming.

Then the pain was gone, and his heart was as empty as the sty he called home.

"Follow us, Cratus, and you will serve at the right hand of the masters. No one will ever be able to turn you again."

He wanted to tell her no, but the part of his heart that resisted was closed and sealed. Instead he saw all the centuries of his suffering. Felt all the degradations he'd been through, starting with Zeus pinning him to the floor with his lightning bolts.

As the son of Warcraft and Hate, he wanted revenge.

No, he burned for it.

"Come with me, Cratus, and we will make Zeus beg you for mercy."

"I live in a world where if something seems too good to be true, it always is."

She gave him a sweet, placating smile. "Not this time. You will have all the power you want. All the money you could ever imagine. No more crawling to a boss you loathe. No more being tortured on the human plane. No more having to fight with the gods who cursed you to this." She leaned forward to whisper in his ear. "Revenge . . ."

Revenge.

She nuzzled his cheek with hers. "Take my hand, Cratus, and I'll take you far away from this misery to a place where you will never again want for anything."

Don't do it. There was more to this than what she told him. There always was. He knew it deep inside and yet as he lay there, all he saw was the past. The unending cycle of misery that Zeus had given him.

If nothing else, at least Azura would kill him and put him out of this suffering.

He had nothing to live for. Nothing.

Dying was easy. He'd done that every night for thousands of years. But to have one minute free of what his life had been . . .

He would take it.

His gaze burning into hers, he nodded. "I'm yours."

Laughing, Azura took his hand. "Then come, my precious warrior. Let us rain fire and destruction on the Olympians and humans. The final war has begun."

CHAPTER 2

DELPHINE STAGGERED BACK IN HORROR. SHE TRIED her best to flash into Cratus's room to stop them.

She couldn't. Azura had her blocked and wasn't about to let her in.

"No!" she shouted at them. But it was too late. They were gone from his apartment, and he was now in the hands of ultimate evil.

What were they going to do?

How could this have happened?

Most of all, why couldn't she have stopped it from happening? She shouldn't have waited for him to go to sleep. She should have let him know she was here and stayed on him no matter his protests. They should have kept him in their sights until he caved.

But that was neither here nor there. Would'ves, could'ves, should'ves didn't change the fact that Cratus would now fight against them.

Damn.

There was only a tiny handful of gods who could draw power from the Source and most of them had already defected to Noir's side. Out of the ones left on their side, none could touch Noir's skill. Only Cratus had been strong enough to fight against them. Worse, she'd now have to face Phobos and Zeus with her failure.

She'd be lucky if they didn't kill her.

But she wasn't a coward. Things had unraveled and she needed to let them know as quickly as possible so that all of them could adequately prepare for the war that was coming.

And their inevitable defeat.

Look on the bright side. You'll most likely be dead in a few minutes instead of imprisoned for eternity.

Swallowing, she wanted to run and hide. To find one place of safety in the world.

If only she could. But there was no safety now. Noir and Azura were back, and they wouldn't stop until they had all of them in chains.

Until they had the world of man conquered.

Her heart thundering in fear, she left her small room to travel to Olympus. To the hall of the gods, where Zeus and the others usually gathered at this time of day to eat, gossip and plot. As a demigod, she'd mostly avoided the place. She'd never felt welcomed there. The gods had their cliques and she tried to stay out of the line of fire, especially since so many of them had horrific jealousy issues. She'd heard of lesser gods being turned into all kinds of monsters for no other reason than one of the gods happened to look at her while his wife was present. Not wanting to become a gorgon, deformed spider or some other such, Delphine had avoided the place at all costs.

Until today.

Swallowing a fear a Dream-Hunter shouldn't be feeling, Delphine pushed open the doors to see over three score gods gathered there. Apollo played on his lyre while Aphrodite and Ares shared a bowl of ambrosia. Hermes was with Athena, playing a game of chess with miniature live pieces.

Zeus rested contentedly on his throne while Hera sat beside him, talking to Persephone. It was a cozy scene that she really hated to disturb.

As she walked forward, Phobos appeared and pulled her to a stop. "What happened?"

"Cratus defected." She could have sworn she'd whispered those words, but all sound and activity paused in the hall as if she'd shouted.

Zeus stood up slowly, his eyes flaming with the weight of his fury. Tall and blond, he would have been very handsome were it not for his nasty disposition and tendency to kill anyone he took even a minor dislike to. "You are not about to tell me that you've failed to bring Cratus here."

Not while you're looking at me like that, I'm not. She had to bite her tongue to keep that quip inside. Given his mood, he wouldn't be exactly kind and take it.

Phobos's eyes widened to caution her to silence—as if she needed it—before he turned to Zeus and defended her. "Minor setback, my lord. Really."

That did nothing to appease the king of the gods. "Are you willing to take her place beneath my axe?"

"Do I have to?"

Zeus bellowed his anger. "I am not amused by either of you."

As Zeus started toward them, Nike stepped forward. "My lord?" she asked quietly. "Might I have a word with them?"

He looked at her as if she might be the next to get blasted—right after he finished with them. "Make it *very* short."

Nike nodded before she descended the dais where Zeus's throne was set. Apollo sneered at her, but she paid him no attention as she made her way to Delphine's side.

Nike pulled her close. "Tell me what has happened."

Again, Delphine spoke in only the quietest of tones. "Azura got to him before I could. She promised him freedom and revenge if he'd join them."

Zeus cursed. "I shall have you both killed for this!"

Nike stepped in front of Delphine. "My lord, please bear with me. I'm the goddess of victory, and Cratus is my brother. Believe me, if there's anyone in this room who knows how to reach him and sway him, it is I."

Zeus curled his lip. "Then sway him, but that has nothing to do with their lives." He gave a meaningful glare to Phobos and then Delphine.

Delphine definitely didn't like where this was heading, and she wanted to get out from under Zeus's angry countenance. She also had to bite back the question of why Nike, if Nike knew her brother so well, hadn't been sent after him to begin with.

But the point of this was to save her life, not goad them into murdering her.

"What my brother needs, I cannot give him." Nike glanced at Delphine. "But she can. Give us a chance, my lord. Please. I know we can regain his allegiance."

The fury on Zeus's face intensified until Delphine was sure he'd strike out at her.

But after a few horrendous heartbeats, he conceded. "One chance is all you have. Azura and the others will kill their hostages in two weeks and then come for the rest of us. You have twelve days to sway him or kill him."

Delphine shook her head at his order. "Cratus can't be killed."

Zeus laughed bitterly. "Oh, yes, he can. Even if they restore his powers to their full potential, stab him in his heart and he *will* die."

Delphine frowned. "How?"

The pride on Zeus's face sat ill with her. "His immortal heart was ripped from his chest when I cast him out of here, and it is a frail human heart he has now. Pierce it and he dies, plain and simple. And there will be no resurrection for him in the morning as we've done in the past."

She saw pain flash in Nike's eyes. "Come with me, Delphine."

Delphine followed the smaller goddess to the doors that led out onto a balcony overlooking the rainbow falls and the thick green foliage that surrounded the hall. When Phobos started to join them, Nike shooed him back inside.

"This isn't for you, Phobos. Please understand."

He inclined his head before he returned inside and shut the doors behind him.

The moment they were alone, Nike pulled Delphine to the farthest corner of the balcony before she spoke in a hushed tone. "You know what's at stake so

I won't even reiterate it. But what you don't know is the part of my brother that only I was ever privy to. He and I bonded because he protected me from our parents, and I worshiped him for it. He's a good man, but it's not easy to find that part of him that he keeps guarded and that was before his punishment. You will have to remember that he's the son of Hatred and War, and those two things are mother's milk where he's concerned. It's what he does best."

Delphine didn't understand what that had to do with her mission. His birth didn't matter to her, only his surrender did. "And how do I defeat him?"

"You can't. Not if he has his full strength. That's the honest truth. Our own father tried to beat him after he'd reached adulthood, and Cratus left him a bloody heap for the effort. The only reason Zeus was able to hurt him originally was because Cratus didn't fight back. Had he done so, he would now be the king of the gods."

"Then I shall have to kill him."

"No!" The ferocity in her tone made Delphine's eyes widen. "My brother doesn't deserve that. He suffers now because he spared the life of an infant. Those are not the actions of someone beyond reach. When we were children, he took beatings for me that no one should ever suffer. I don't want you to kill him. I want you to help me save him and return him here where he belongs."

"How?"

Nike took a deep breath before she answered with tears in her eyes. "He will fight and he will die to protect what he loves. To the grave. Make him care for you more than he cares for his revenge, and he will join us on our side."

That was ludicrous. "I don't know him and I only have a few days." It was barely enough time to kill him, never mind try to seduce a man she didn't even know. "Why aren't you the one going in since he's your brother?"

Nike shook her head. "He won't listen to me. It's been too long, and I have never gone to see him before. Not in all these centuries. Cratus is the most unforgiving of people when he feels he's been wronged. That's why you must seduce him. You're the only one, I think, who can. Often it only takes a small amount of time—remember, he knew nothing of the infant he saved and yet he destroyed his life for that one tiny being. Please, Delphine. For me, try to save him. He is a great man, but he's not a perfect one. As the goddess of victory, there is one truth I know above all others. You only win when your heart is pure and when the victory is motivated for the right reasons. Give him a reason to live and give him one to fight with the whole of his strength, and we will all win in this."

"And if I can't?"

Her eyes turned even darker as she let out a sadness-tinged breath. "You know the answer, and you know what Zeus will do to you both if you fail."

Delphine nodded. They would lose without him. They needed his strength and his powers to combat Noir and his army. As for her fate, she would be lucky to get off as easily as Cratus did. "Should I get Eros to shoot him?" That would be the easiest way to seduce him.

Nike shook her head. "Those powers wouldn't work on Cratus and the attempt would only infuriate him. Trust me, that's the last thing you want to do. He will have to be won over honestly."

Oh, that was going to be easy . . .

Not.

"How can I seduce him? I have no emotions."

"That's not true and we both know it," Nike whispered. "You have all that you need. You're not completely Oneroi. You still have a human spirit and emotions inside you. They will guide you through this." She lightly nudged her on the shoulder. "Now go and win him over."

Win him over. She made it sound like it was easy. But as Delphine watched her leave, all she could see was her own doom.

And that of all the other gods who were relying on her. This was impossible.

Phobos joined her on the balcony. "You okay? You look more pale now than when Zeus barked at you."

Truthfully, she felt more ill now. More scared. "How do you seduce a man?"

He laughed at her question. "I think I'm offended that you're asking me that. What? You think I have some kind of expertise on the subject?"

She gave him a droll stare. "I'm serious, Phobos."

"As am I," he said, offended. "Seducing men isn't exactly something I have a lot of experience with. Nor is it something I spend time thinking about." He glanced at the door to make sure it was shut completely. When he spoke, it was a barely audible whisper. "You might want to ask Zeus that."

She rolled her eyes. If the stories were true, all a woman needed to seduce Zeus was to be female. They didn't even have to be breathing. "You're not funny, Phobos. I need help here. Real help. What do men like?"

"That depends on the man. I like breasts myself. A nice rack goes a long way in getting me to do just about anything. Even stupid things."

She let out a frustrated growl. "You are so offensive!"

"Oh, please," he said unabashedly. "I'm ten thousand years old. You're lucky I'm not more chauvinistic than I am. Babe, I've come a long way."

And he wasn't helping her in the slightest. "Just go."

Phobos hesitated as if he wasn't sure it was the best thing to do.

She gestured toward the door.

He held his hands up in surrender. "All right. I'm going. But if you need me . . ."

"I'd rather gouge out my eyes."

He took that with a good-natured smile. "As the personification of dread fear, I often have that effect on women. Maybe I should look into changing places with Himerus. I've been told women rip off their clothes the moment he appears. Definitely better to be the god of lust than fear."

She shook her head at his glibness as he headed back inside. How she wished she was more like him. Nothing ever seemed to get to Phobos or rattle him. Honestly, she was scared, and even muted, that emotion was bitter.

Alone, she looked out over the lush landscape and considered her next course of action.

Cratus was with their enemies . . .

And she was charged with seducing him or killing him. What a great conundrum for her.

As she contemplated a way to reach him, Phobos reappeared, his expression furious and worried. "Noir's Skoti are attacking in the hall of mirrors." He grabbed her hand and teleported her back to the Vanishing Isle before she could so much as blink.

Sure enough, there was a group of Skoti smashing the portals they used to monitor human sleep and join the sleepers. The entire glass hall was in shambles. Pieces of glass and mirror were littered all over the floor as a handful of dream gods tried to fight them off.

Delphine manifested a sword to attack the Skotos nearest her.

The Skotos laughed. "Wanna play, little girl?"

She lunged at him, showing him exactly how lethal she was. And it removed the smile instantly from his face. Say what he could, she was deadly accurate and had practiced the whole of her existence to battle the demons who preyed on humans as they slept.

There were very few Oneroi more accomplished than she.

Phobos was fighting two more, trying to protect the remaining portals. While they could technically do their job without them, it wasn't nearly as easy. Nor as effective. The portals needed to be saved.

Just as Delphine was about to run her opponent through, someone grabbed her from behind. A rough hand clutched her throat, paralyzing her entire body.

There was nothing there but a deep, black mist. The aura of evil was tangible.

It was Noir.

And she was in his clutches. Something cold caressed her cheek an instant before he twisted her head and the darkness invaded every part of her.

AZURA WALKED A SMALL CIRCLE AROUND JERICHO AS she smiled proudly.

He closed his eyes, letting the power from the Source fill him again. It had been so long . . .

Too long.

He was whole once again, and it felt incredible. How he'd missed this. The sights and smells of his powers. The feeling of it coursing through him like living fire. Flexing his hand, he watched as his fingers turned into metallic claws that were razor-sharp. Gone were the words his mother had burned into his flesh, and in their place his tattoos glowed brightly in the dim light.

No one would ever control him again. He was back and he was furious.

Ferocious.

And he was ready for revenge.

Azura cupped his cheek in her hand. "Would you like me to repair your face and eye?"

"No," he growled. He wanted the reminder of what being weak had cost him. He would never make that mistake again.

"Very well. You are completely restored to your godhood. Do us proud."

He intended to.

She stepped back so that he could see himself in the mirrored wall. Gone was the grimy human who had to beg for jobs and satisfy himself with scraps of food and ragged clothes, all the while waiting for Zeus's assassins to slaughter him at night.

His hair was no longer black. It was once again the pure white of the gods and it contrasted sharply with his black clothes.

Azura handed him a sword and whip. "Not the ones you were used to, but I think you'll find them to your liking."

He felt the life blood of the universe in the blade. It hummed like a living being. "What is this?"

"It was forged from the pit of the Source. The very essence of the universe is inside it. That blade will cut through anything. More to the point, it will cut through any*one*."

He ran his finger along the edge, appreciating the sharpness of it. Hissing, he saw the bead of blood that welled up. Blood that quickly evaporated as his body healed itself.

Like that of a god.

More to the point, the blade absorbed his blood as if it were feeding on it.

"You will have to feed the sword regularly," Azura explained, dragging one nail down the blade. "The sword requires fresh blood to thrive. With it, you can kill Zeus and absorb his powers." She paused and met his gaze with one as hungry as his soul that begged for justice. "You could be king of the Olympian gods. . . . Imagine, Cratus. All of them prostrate to you."

He curled his lip at her words. "Cratus is dead," he said in a guttural tone. "My name is Jericho."

She laughed. "I could think of no better name for you. Cursed and reduced to ashes. And like the mighty Phoenix, you're rising out of the destruction of your past to rain fury down on those who cursed you."

And he would relish bathing in their blood. The sword in his hand would never go hungry so long as he wielded it.

Azura stepped back. "For now, you will command my army of Skoti. We want to neutralize Olympus and use their gods of sleep to attack the ones we need to control."

"Consider it done." He was more than willing to throw Zeus and his crew to the wolves. They deserved it and more for all their cruelty.

A flash of light almost blinded him. Raising one arm to shield his eye, he frowned as the black mist formed into the only being he knew to be more evil than Azura.

Noir.

Tall and dark with black hair and eyes, Noir exuded supreme merciless power. Even Jericho had to admit he was handsome in a way only the gods were. But this was one of the first beings created.

Or more likely in Noir's case, the first being spawned.

Dressed in ornate burgundy armor, Noir wore a dark red cloak that was trimmed in gold. Noir's cold gaze narrowed on Jericho until it went from him to Azura.

"Congratulations, little sister."

"I told you I could convince him to our side."

Noir inclined his head to her. "And I've scored another haul from the other side."

"Really?"

"See for yourself." He spread his hand to show her in his palm a dark hole where a group of Oneroi were lying in utter misery.

Jericho expected the sight to make him supremely happy. But as he looked at their torture and damaged bodies, an unwanted wave of sympathy went through him.

Why?

He couldn't imagine. The gods knew they'd never had mercy where he was concerned. More times than not, they'd laughed as they killed him. But as he scanned the prisoners, one in particular caught his eye.

Without thinking, he took a step forward.

Azura snapped her attention to him. "You see something you like?"

Jericho turned away from the woman whose face he couldn't even make out. He didn't know why she'd called out to him. It was another stupid move on his part. "No."

"Then I'll have one of my servants show you to your new accommodations. I think you'll find them much more to your taste than the hovel you were living in." Azura snapped her fingers and a young girl around the age of sixteen appeared.

At least that's what she looked like at first. But her tanned skin held an iridescent quality to it that reminded him of a dragon's eye.

She was a beautiful demon.

"Follow me, my lord," she said quietly.

He did and was amazed at the opulence of the golden palace that Azura and Noir called home. Unlike the Olympians, they lived in the darkest pit of the earth's core. Yet it was far from dark or gloomy.

"How long have you been here?"

She glanced back over her shoulder. "I was born here, my lord."

"And how old are you?"

"A little over two thousand years." She opened a black door with gold hardware.

Jericho let out an appreciative breath at the sight of his new room. Lush and rich, it beckoned him inside. Stepping past the demon, it was all he could do not to run to the bed and throw himself across it. It'd been so long since he'd slept in a bed that he couldn't even remember the sensation.

The girl closed the door and moved to the fireplace. Throwing a burst of flames out of her hand, she started the fire. Then she turned toward him with a calculating gleam in her dark eyes. "Is there anything else I can do for you, my lord?"

He understood her meaning immediately and had no intention of going there. At least not with a demon and not right now. "No."

She looked relieved. "If you should change your mind, call my name. Rielle. I will come immediately."

"Thank you."

She appeared baffled by his thanks before she vanished.

Alone, Jericho set his sword down on the dresser.

He moved around the room, running his hand over the finely polished wood of the bedposts. This reminded him of his bed on Olympus. Of the time before recorded history when he'd been respected and feared.

He was back.

And he was pissed. May the Source take pity on those who'd caused his mood.

Because at the end of the day, he would have none for them.

"WHAT ARE YOU DOING?" NOIR ASKED GRUFFLY.

Azura paused as she had her servant lay the body of the Olympian bitch on the table before her. "Did you not see the way he looked at her?"

Noir shrugged. "She's attractive. It's to be expected."

"Yes, but we need to keep our new tool happy. The last thing we want is to have him turn on *us*. Without your Malachai, we will need him when we attack the Source." She dragged her hand over the woman's unconscious body, appreciating her slight stature. "She is a beauty, isn't she?"

"If you like pale, pasty women. Personally, I prefer ones with more color."

Azura smiled as he pulled her close and ran his tongue along her throat. Chills erupted over her skin. Even though they called themselves brother and sister, there was nothing that united them in blood except their mutual quest for power and hunger for death. In that, they were family.

Reality was a different story.

"Not now, lover. I want to present her to Cratus."

"Dump her into his room, then. Or kill her. Either way works for me."

Azura conjured a containment collar for the woman's powers. The last thing they needed was to have her loose in their home. Not that she could do that much. It was merely the principle of the matter.

As soon as she had the Olympian's powers restrained, she undid the woman's pale hair so that it would cascade over her shoulders. "Yes, very pretty."

Satisfied, Azura teleported to Cratus's room. He was looking out the window as if trying to find an enemy of some sort. The moment she popped in, he swung about as if ready to fight.

She had to suppress the urge to mock him for something that was actually admirable. He was intelligent to not trust them. Most people, to their extreme detriment, did. The fact that he alone suspected treachery said much for why he was a valuable ally.

"No need to be so jumpy."

His face was absolute stone. "What are you doing here?"

"I've brought you a gift."

Jericho scowled at her, wondering what game she played—and he knew she was playing something. Her entire demeanor warned him that she was about to make him even angrier. And he wasn't jumpy. It was just that he knew the treachery that lived in the hearts of all creatures. It was all he expected of them.

No one could be trusted.

Actually, that wasn't true. They could be trusted to screw over the people around them when it served their purposes. *That* he would bank on.

"Gift?"

Her smile was wicked and it was colder than ice. "Bon appetit, precious," Azura said as she snapped her fingers. The sound was still ringing in his ears when a small form materialized at his feet.

Jericho gasped at the sight of the tiny woman . . .

One who was completely naked.

CHAPTER 3

DELPHINE STIFFENED AS SHE CAME AWAKE TO FIND herself sprawled face down on a cold marble floor. Naked. Mortified. Terrified.

Rising slightly, she tried to cover herself with her hands, but she lacked enough hands to do it. And if that wasn't bad enough, she was more than aware of the pair of black men's boots she couldn't take her gaze off of. Mostly because she didn't want to see this man, whoever he was, eye to eye after he'd seen her completely naked.

Heat spread over her as she wanted to crawl into a hole, one that hopefully had some clothes in it, and hide.

Cursing so foully he made her jump, the man knelt down. She tensed, expecting the worst and ready to fight him to the death.

But he didn't touch her.

Instead he pricked his finger with a small knife, and the blood from his fingertip wove itself around her to form a warm crimson cloak that covered her completely. She still didn't look at him. She couldn't while she was this embarrassed.

"That was unnecessary," he growled in that deeply masculine tone she'd recently learned belonged to Cratus. His voice rumbled like angry thunder.

It was Azura who answered him. "She's our offering to you to show you our thanks for your loyalty."

Completely covered now and finding some semblance of dignity, Delphine rose to find Jericho glaring at Azura, who stood in the corner by the door. The evil goddess looked entirely too pleased with herself.

Smirking at Delphine, Azura gestured toward her. "She's your slave."

Delphine gaped at her disclosure even though Jericho didn't say anything.

"I've bound her powers and delivered her to you," Azura continued. "Do with her as you please. But you should know she's one of the Oneroi and friend to the Dolophoni you hate so much . . . the ones who have tortured you for centuries. I've restored all of her emotions so that you can take pleasure however you see fit . . ." She started to leave, then paused. "Oh, and you'll probably want to know she's one of Zeus's favorites among the goddesses. I'm told he values her greatly."

Delphine opened her mouth to deny it, but no words would come out. Azura had her voice blocked.

Oh, to have one second of her powers . . .

And a minute alone with that deceitful bitch.

Her features smug, Azura vanished in a cloud of blue smoke.

Jericho glanced at his new "present," intending to

return the woman to Azura immediately, but the moment his gaze met hers, he was frozen in place.

Long, wavy blond hair contrasted sharply with the red cloak he'd made for her. But it was her eyes that held him prisoner. A deep hazel green, they showed him a potent fear that she, as a Dream-Hunter, shouldn't have been able to experience. More than that, they showed her spirit and her fight. She was tensed to hold her own even though she had to know she didn't stand a chance against him. The fact that she was willing to fight anyway said a lot about her.

Her form was slight, her face porcelain smooth with high cheekbones and a small widow's peak. She looked so much like a Dream-Hunter he'd once known that he couldn't help asking, "Leta?"

She frowned at him. "My name is Delphine."

Delphine . . .

She took a step back and again he was aware of exactly how frail she was in appearance. He could crush her and yet, even given her relationship with Zeus, he couldn't bear the thought of harming her and damned if he knew why. Kindness wasn't something he made a practice of. It was his nature to strike the first blow.

As if sensing his thoughts, she put more room between them. "I won't be your slave."

Her defiance amused him. "I don't think you have much choice."

She lifted her chin defiantly. "I will fight you until one of us is dead."

He was consumed by an overwhelming urge to soothe her. It was something he hadn't felt since he'd comforted his sister when they were younger—and he'd never felt that for another person.

Until now.

It made no sense that he'd want to reassure Zeus's pet after what that bastard had done to him, and yet he couldn't stand the thought of her being afraid of him. "I won't hurt you."

Delphine wanted to believe that, but she was having a hard time, especially since the rawness of her new emotions was making her dizzy. They were sharp and so confusing. How did people cope with this? "Where am I?"

"Azmodea."

Delphine cringed at the name, which translated into "furious demon." This was where Noir and Azura made their home and where they gleefully tortured their unfortunate victims. She had no doubt that's exactly what would become of her now that they'd taken her hostage, too.

Her gaze fell to his sword on the highly polished dresser. "You would really fight at the side of such unrelenting evil?"

His one eye flashed with the weight of his anger as he snarled at her. "You know *nothing* about me."

"That's not true. I know you were cursed by Zeus and that you've lived every day since completely alone."

He laughed bitterly. "Only when I was lucky."

She scowled. "What do you mean?"

All the emotion left his face. Still raw hatred bled from his pores with a tangible heat so potent, she could swear it singed the air between them. "I owe you *nothing*."

Delphine couldn't breathe at the fury that glared at her from his one good eye. It was palpable and terrifying. "*I've* never hurt you."

Faster than she could blink, he grabbed her by the throat and pushed her against the wall. Yet for the quickness and ferocity of his action, he didn't hurt her. He merely held her neck in the large paw of his hand in a gentle grip while that one deep blue eye pierced her.

Jericho wanted to snap her neck in two. His pent-up fury begged him to do it. Send her back to Zeus in pieces.

But he couldn't bring himself to kill her.

Grinding his teeth, he released her. "Don't push me."

She met his gaze unflinchingly. "I didn't realize pushing you would involve me stating a simple fact."

He was appalled by her unending temerity that seemed to prevent her from being silent even when it was the prudent thing to do. "Have you no concept of self-preservation?"

"Have you no concept of decent behavior?"

That made him really want to hurt her because deep inside it cut him harshly. There had been a time when he'd been decent. Even courteous. But his past degradations had killed that long ago. No one had showed him mercy, so why should he ever give it to another?

"No, I don't."

Delphine felt a whisper of wind before he vanished out of the room. She looked around, but there was no sign of him. Even his sword was gone. Yet what surprised her was that in its place was a set of clothes for *her*. A pair of jeans, shoes and a pink top.

Why would he bother?

Grateful even though it didn't make sense, she dropped the cloak and reached for them. The moment she did, she became aware of just how cold it was here in his room. Chills ran over her body, making her teeth chatter.

It was absolutely frigid.

Frowning, she touched the cloak that vibrated with warmth. It truly felt like living body heat. . . .

Was it from his blood? She had no idea, but she was grateful for the warmth. And right now, she wanted to have something on besides her skin and his cloak.

With her hands shaking, she quickly dressed. She kept trying to use her powers, but the containment collar was more than effective.

Bloody dogs . . .

Furious with her predicament, she opened the door to leave, then pulled up sharply. There in the hallway was what had to be the largest, ugliest demon she'd ever seen in her life. At least ten feet tall, he had bulbous skin and a stench so foul she had to hold her breath.

She immediately took a step back and slammed the door shut.

His evil laughter echoed outside.

Delphine rolled her eyes. "What are you? Stupid? Of course they have a guard. What part of 'You're a prisoner' did you miss?" she castigated herself out loud.

Feeling ill, frustrated and upset, she wrapped her arms around her chest and wondered what she could do to help the others from here. This had to be where the Skoti were taking them. If she could find their prison, maybe she could set the hostages free . . .

Then she could focus on converting Jericho back to their side. That would be the best of all worlds.

Literally.

But how did one go about seducing someone? She truly had no idea. Most of her interactions with people were through dreams and since she wasn't an erotic Skotos, she'd never been sexually involved with them. She'd gone in only as a warrior to combat the Skoti and free the dreamer from their spell.

As a human . . .

Well, that had been a long time ago. And while she remembered having an appreciation for some of the boys in her village, those feelings had been muted.

Now her emotions were something else. Raw. Hurtful. Painful.

Overwhelming.

Anger burned her over their holding her captive and she wanted to hurt someone. Luckily, she understood that it was only an exaggerated fury inside her and not real anger. She had to calm down and think rationally.

The window . . .

She went over to it and drew the curtains back. Rain soundlessly pelted the glass. Gray skies stretched out endlessly with puffed and ugly clouds. Her view looked out on a sea that boiled and crashed upon black stones. Placing her hand to the pane, she snatched it back immediately. It was so cold that it burned her.

"Calm down," she whispered, trying to remember everything she knew about Azmodea. Honestly, it wasn't much. It was said to be the primordial ooze that had been left over when the universe had been created. Afraid it might taint the beauty of the rest of the universe, the Source had banished it to the deepest part of the earth, never to be seen again.

When Noir and his sisters had risen to power, they had profaned the light and taken up residence here. It was said that the walls of their palace were painted red with the blood of the victims they had tortured.

She looked at the burgundy paint. No, it wasn't dried blood. That was just a story meant to frighten.

It's doing a superbly good job.

Stop it! She was rational and not given to panic attacks even though a chill went down her spine. While the room was large and well-dressed with intricately carved furniture, the austere ambiance made it less than inviting. Honestly, she preferred the hole Jericho had lived in on earth to this place. At least the hovel hadn't been insidious and so icy cold. Creepy. She kept expecting something to jump out of the walls and grab her.

Nervous and out of sorts, she went to the mirror and tried to pry her collar off even though she knew just what a waste of time it would be. It was better than doing nothing. It'd never been in her nature to not fight.

But after a few minutes, her frustration grew and left her snatching at it until she had a bruise forming.

So much for that.

"Where are you, Jericho?" And most importantly, what was he doing?

JERICHO PAUSED OUTSIDE THE DOOR TO THE ROOM where Azura had first taken him. She'd called it their war room, which made sense. But as he stood there, he felt a sharp pain in his chest. It was so hard to breathe. To think.

Images flashed through his mind. Quick and intense, he saw himself as he'd been in the human realm. He felt the hunger and the pain of it.

Bet you wish you'd never turned on Zeus now, huh?

He didn't know the name of the Dolophonos who'd killed him that time, but if he ever found that bastard, he'd bathe in his blood.

He gripped the hilt of his sword, dying to use it on anyone who dared to cross him. Again, he was surprised by the warmth of it. It really was as if it were alive, and he knew this was a sword meant for killing.

Why would Azura have given him so valuable a gift? Such creatures as she and Noir weren't stupid. They wanted something more from him than just a warrior. He could feel it deep inside his soul.

But what exactly were they after? And why was *he* so important to them?

Wanting to find out, he pushed open the door to find Azura alone in the room.

She turned toward him with an arched brow. "Is something wrong?"

"Where is Noir?"

She tsked at him. "We don't answer to you, love. You fight for us and that is all you do. Don't ever forget your place."

Those were not the right words to make him happy. It was all he could do not to tell her to go screw herself.

Her features softened as she jerked her chin toward the door behind him. "Now why aren't you entertaining yourself with your new pet?"

Her tone and attitude didn't sit well with him. But he wasn't about to let her know that . . . yet. He had a few things he wanted to investigate first. "I want to see the Oneroi who were brought in."

She scowled in displeasure. "Why?"

Her incessant questions were beginning to piss him off. "I have a score to settle with most of them."

"Have no fear. They are being made adequately miserable for you. I assure you, you would be impressed with their current conditions."

His suspicions snapped to the forefront at her continued denial. "Are telling me I'm a prisoner, too?"

"I didn't say that. But you have to remember that we are as unsure of your loyalty to us as you are of ours to you. You, Noir and I have only a shaky alliance at present. One that is untested."

"Yet you gave me a rare sword?"

"A token of trust and a hope for our future together."

Something wasn't right in this scenario. Every instinct he had was on guard. There was something more to this sword. Something she wasn't telling him. "Why?"

"I told you. We want you on our side. So long as you're with us, all you desire will be given to you."

And if he displeased them, they would make him pay. It was an unstated threat that hung heavy around him. One he didn't take kindly to. He'd been down that road and crashed hard.

But if she wanted to give him his every wish . . . "I desire to see the Oneroi."

She laughed. "Insistent child. In time we will be open with you and you can do as you please. But not yet. Now return to your pet. Or if you'd rather, I can return you to your garage and remove your powers again."

Tempted to tell her to shove it all up her sphincter, he withdrew from her even though he wanted to attack her for her patronizing tone.

That would be suicide.

Rest now, gain bearings. Attack only when you're in a position of strength. He knew the warrior's code by heart.

Still, he couldn't shake the feeling of dread inside him. Something was seriously wrong here. He just didn't know what.

Unsettled and unhappy, he returned to his room to find Delphine dressed in the jeans and pink top he'd left for her. She also wore his cloak wrapped around her like an armored shield. Little did she know, it was. Nothing would be able to penetrate it.

She sat nervously on the bed, watching the door as if expecting someone to come in and attack her. Which, given this place, wasn't that unlikely a fear.

He stopped halfway to the bed, unsure of what to

say to her. Idle chatter hadn't been something he'd participated in even before he'd left Olympus.

Hell, he'd barely spoken to anyone in centuries.

And especially not to an attractive woman. His cock hardened from need just looking at her. One of Zeus's cruelest punishments had been to make him burn for a woman whenever he saw one, and then the minute he was alone with her, his body went soft. The frustration of wanting sex and never being able to have it had driven him insane. He couldn't even take care of it himself.

That alone was enough to make him want to crush the Olympian god's throat.

So he'd learned to not even think about it. To keep as far away from a woman and her scent as he could lest he make himself ache any worse than he already did. But honestly, he'd missed being touched and held. Missed the softness of a woman naked in his arms.

Yet there she sat, so pretty. So tempting.

One touch . . .

But he couldn't. For all he knew, his body would still go soft on him. And that made him even angrier.

"Are you hungry?" he growled at her.

She frowned. Her expression was one of worry and fear.

Was that the wrong thing to ask her? Instead of soothing her it put her more on guard. Or maybe it was his tone. How *should* he reassure her?

Someone really ought to write a manual. Then again, gods trying to communicate with hostages was probably something so rare no one would think to create it.

"I want this collar off me," she said, her tone stern.

"I can't do that."

"Why not? Are you afraid of me having my powers?"

He snorted. "Yeah, right. Calling me a coward won't accomplish anything. Believe me, you're an amateur in that field and I've been called a lot worse."

Delphine didn't miss the note of pain in his voice that he tried to hide. Given what she'd seen of his life, she was sure he'd been insulted and then some. But it didn't change the fact that she was his prisoner and she hated it.

Most of all, she couldn't understand why he was here. "Why did you join *them*?"

Jericho paused at her question as he considered how to best answer. If she would even understand his reasoning or motivation. In the end, he knew the truth. She'd have had to experience the hell he'd been through to comprehend it.

He raised his hands and created an arc of bright power that pulsed between his palms. For the first time in centuries, he could make and throw a god bolt to fry any and everything. That invigorating sensation . . . knowing he would never be stepped on again . . .

For that alone he'd sell his soul, his life and anything else they wanted. How could he have said no to what Azura offered? But he had no intention of sharing that with Delphine. "None of your business." He dropped his hands down and rested one on the hilt of his sword.

She gave him a frustrated glower. "Noir will destroy the world."

"So what? Who says it's worth saving?"

Delphine wanted to shake him for his obstinacy. She'd never met anyone so dense and so unforgiving. What had they done to him to make him like this? "You would kill or enslave everyone? There is so much beauty in the world that they'd destroy. How do you not see it?"

He scoffed at her as if she were a child. "Spoken like someone who has only lived in the cushioned world of dreams. You have no idea what the real world is like. What people will do to you when they know they can get away with it. People are absolutely cruel and I say more power to Noir for tearing it down."

"They can be cruel at times," she admitted. "But I've seen the best in people. Their hopes and dreams." That was why she fought so hard for mankind.

"And I've lived through their worst." The pain in his eye scorched her.

It also explained a lot about him and his reasoning. But that didn't make it right. "So anything you do is justified, is that it? They were mean to you so it's okay for you to be mean back?"

He shrugged nonchalantly. "Sounds justifiable to me."

She let out a long breath. What would it take to get through to him? To make him understand and most of all *care* about what he was doing? "Were you always this bitter?"

Jericho paused at her unexpected question. No one had ever asked him that before. No one. And it forced him to take a hard look inward.

He'd never really liked himself. Not when he served Zeus and definitely not after his banishment. From the moment of his birth, he'd been a god with a destiny that had been forced on him.

Balance your siblings. Serve your master. Do as you're told. No questions. No life . . .

And so he'd existed until that one moment when he couldn't blindly obey anymore.

All things ended. Birth, destruction, death and rebirth. It was the law of the universe. The code of the Source. Who was he to fight against it?

But the truth was still harsh. "Yes," he said, his tone cold. "I've always been this bitter."

She let out a tired breath. "Then I'm very sorry for you."

"Don't be. I don't need pity from someone who knows so little about living."

Delphine shook her head. "That's not true. Every time I've stepped into a dream, I've seen life. I've seen love and joy in its purest forms. They're beautiful to behold even if they are muted by the dream state."

He made a rude noise of disagreement. "You live like a by-product."

That set her ire off to a level of rage she'd never experienced before. "And you don't? I saw you, too, you know. You didn't interact with anyone. Not even to say good-bye to them when you left. What kind of living is that?"

His nostrils flaring with anger, he sucked his breath in sharply as he advanced on her with a fury so potent, she tried to flee only to have him trap her in a corner. She had to crane her neck to look up at him. He was so incredibly large. So fierce. And that one eye glowed with absolute hatred.

Jericho wanted to tell her exactly why he couldn't interact with people. He wanted to lash out and make her pay for what Zeus had done to him. But as he stood there and the scent of her hit him, it paralyzed his entire body.

Worst of all, it evaporated his fury and it made his cock so hard, he was sure he could use it as a hammer. She became the focus of his reasoning, not his hatred.

She and that soft skin and delicate body that he wanted to taste so desperately . . .

His gaze focused on her lips, which were parted by her rapid breathing. Were they as soft as they appeared? Would they give him the pleasure he hadn't known since he'd been damned and cursed?

He hadn't kissed a woman in centuries. . . . Could he even remember how?

Kill the bitch and get on with your revenge. Deliver her to Zeus in pieces. Let him know what it feels like to suffer. Take from him what he took from you.

But he couldn't. Even with her words and his rage, it wasn't enough to make him hurt her. And damned if he knew why.

Her hazel eyes still had that fire and joy . . . even though she was afraid. He couldn't take that from her.

No, he didn't *want* to take that from her.

Before he even realized what he was doing, he picked up a fat curl from her shoulder. Her hair was so unbelievably soft. It wrapped around his finger, teasing his flesh. Lifting it to his face, he closed his eyes and inhaled the sweet scent of it and imagined what it would be like to make love to her until they were both sated.

His cock jerked with need as he imagined her naked in his arms.

Delphine couldn't breathe as she watched him. Part of her expected him to attack her still. But he didn't.

Instead he rubbed her hair against his lips. Lips that were so close to hers . . .

Never had she been kissed. Until this moment she'd never even thought about it. Since she didn't really feel lust, it hadn't been a problem. Now for the first time, she felt her body flush with heat. Felt her heart quicken along with a deep heaviness she'd never experienced before.

She wanted him to touch her. . . .

He dipped his head as if he'd kiss her. But just as their lips would have touched, he buried his face in her hair and inhaled.

Not sure what to do, she cupped his head in her hand and wrapped her other arm around him. She was unprepared for just how good it would feel to hold him like this. He smelled of leather and sharp spices, of all man. His thick white hair was feather soft as it brushed against her face and made her shiver. She could feel his muscles rippling under her hand, the softness of his blond hair in her palm. . . .

Jericho buried his face in the crook of her neck as he imagined all the things he wanted to do to her. As he tried to imagine how good she would taste. He wanted desperately to breathe her in.

The sensation of her hands on his body right now . . .

It was heaven.

And it was hell.

He didn't want to feel like this. He didn't want to be weak ever again and definitely not for another person. To have someone control him. The last time he'd allowed himself to feel for someone, he'd lost everything.

Even his dignity.

Angry at the thought, he growled low in his throat and tore himself out of her grasp. He didn't need softness or comfort. He didn't need to be touched. Zeus had taught him that. He could survive well enough on his own with no one around him.

He was stronger that way.

"Stay away from me," he snarled at her.

She looked baffled by his words. "You came at me."

"Don't press me, woman!"

She narrowed her eyes. "You know, this whole emotion thing is new to me, too. I don't know how to cope with all these conflicting things, and you yelling at me isn't exactly helping . . . Man!"

"Don't raise your voice to me!"

"Ditto, buddy. Ditto." She hadn't realized she'd drawn near him again until she was looking up at him, toe to toe.

The rage inside him actually hurt her, but there was nothing she could do for him. Nothing at all, and the frustration of that made her want to withdraw to someplace where she could feel safe again. "I just want to go home."

Jericho did a mental flinch at those softly spoken

words. It was a cry that he'd echoed so many times the first century he'd been banished that it was still a raw aching need in his heart. How many times had he closed his eyes and remembered the sound of Nike's laughter? The beauty of being respected?

All he'd wanted was to change what he'd done and to beg forgiveness from them so that he could go home, too.

But over time, he'd learned not to want. Learned not to remember.

At least *he* wasn't degrading or torturing her like they'd done to him.

"You'd better get used to it here. Soon there won't be a home for you to return to."

She was aghast. "You would kill your own mother?"

There was nothing but coldness inside him where the goddess Styx was concerned. "My mother was the one who stripped my powers from me and turned me out into the world. What do you think?"

"I think your mother should be beaten for her cruelty and probably Zeus, too, but the rest of us shouldn't have to die because the two of them were wrong."

Yes, but that wasn't good enough to appease his anger. Not by a long shot. "You know *nothing* about revenge."

"You're right. I don't. All I know is how to protect people. It's all I've ever done."

"Because you're a mindless automaton."

She lifted her chin. "Better a mindless automaton who protects than a rampaging murderer without any regard for others. Just because my emotions were bound, it doesn't make me mindless any more than you were while you carried out Zeus's punishments before your banishment. Hephaestus told me how he begged you not to hurt Prometheus. Yet you stood over Hephaestus, making him shackle the god to the rock so that he could be torn apart every single day for the rest of eternity."

"And you see how well that turned out. Believe me, I have paid dearly for my mindless obedience. If I could go back, I would have driven my sword through Zeus when I had the chance."

Delphine put her hands up and choked the air between them. "But you didn't. You did the right thing, and now I ask you to do the right thing again. Join our side in this battle. Don't let evil take over the world."

He laughed bitterly. "You do realize that the one and only time in my life I did the right thing, I was cursed for it? That fact doesn't really motivate me to repeat the experience. When Zeus asked if any god would stand up for me, they all turned their backs. They're the ones who started this. *All* of them. Now I intend to finish it *and* them. The world be damned."

"And it will be," she said choking on the hopeless grief that welled up inside her. "It will be." She drew a deep breath before she spoke again. "Then what will become of you?"

"Does it matter?"

"If it doesn't matter to you, how could it possibly matter to someone else?"

He curled his lip. "Don't twist my words with your bullshit psychology. No one likes me. Boo-hoo. I really don't give a shit. Now if you'll excuse me, I have an army to meet and train." He vanished.

Delphine expelled a long breath as the air around her cleared. His anger and pain was so thick, it was virtually tangible.

What would it take to reach him?

Was it even possible?

But the saddest part was that she couldn't blame him even a little for his reaction. What had been done to him had been wrong. Unforgivable. How would she have reacted in his place? To save a life and have it ruin yours . . .

The trade-off seemed so unfair.

And the clock was ticking. Time would be up soon.

If he can't be turned, he must be destroyed. . . .

There was no other way.

CHAPTER 4

THIS TIME JERICHO FOUND NOIR IN THE WAR ROOM with no sign of Azura. Dressed in his burgundy armor, the primordial god was sitting in a chair with his legs propped up on the table and his ankles crossed. His eyes were half-opened, his fingers laced as his hands rested on his stomach.

If Jericho didn't know better, he'd think Noir had been napping.

"You want something?"

Jericho paused at the gruff words. Even though Noir hadn't added an insult to the end, they were said with enough contempt that it was more than implied.

"Azura told me I was to lead an army. I would like to meet those soldiers."

Noir smirked at him. "Do you understand what we're asking you to do?"

"Kill Zeus and bring the Olympians down."

Noir's face was impassive and cold. "You think you can do that?"

Jericho wasn't one to be intimidated. While he knew

Noir was the more powerful of the two of them, he really didn't give a shit. "I'm a Titan and I fought with Zeus to imprison my brethren for him. What do you think?"

"I think if you stand by those brave words, you'll be a worthy ally."

"You doubt me?"

Noir shrugged before he yawned as if the conversation bored him. "I doubt everyone. I have yet to find one person I can't corrupt and/or own. Everyone is for sale. It's just a matter of negotiating the right price."

"Then I probably should have asked for more."

Noir laughed. "Yes, you should have. I expected you to be harder to sway, but then I didn't take into account your immense hatred of Zeus." He took in a long, savoring breath. "I so love the smell of hatred and revenge. It's the headiest of concoctions."

Jericho disagreed. "I personally feel that way toward blood. No better smell in the universe than when it's combined with the aroma of those fearing death."

Noir sucked his breath in sharply as if he was getting a sexual thrill from Jericho's description. "Oh, I do like you. True kindred spirits are hard to find."

"You forgot who and what birthed me."

Noir nodded as he twiddled his thumbs. "I pity those born of the lighter side. They have no understanding of how seductive cruelty is. The music made out of screams and pleas for mercy. Mmmm. Nothing better."

Jericho swore he could feel the blade at his side tremble, but whether in approval or fear, he couldn't tell.

"Asmodeus!" Noir shouted suddenly. "Show yourself."

A dark cloud formed at Noir's side. It slowly solidified into a being that reminded Jericho of a tall elf. His sharp features leaned toward pretty, yet his dark gray eyes showed nothing but cruelty. Dressed all in black, the demon looked sinister and emotionless. "You called me, Master?"

Noir gave him a cold stare. "I would never call *you* master, slug." He jerked his chin to indicate Jericho. "This is our newest ally. I want you to show him to Zeth and the rest of the Olympian dogs who fight for us."

Asmodeus bowed low in true sycophantic form. "Anything else, Master? Lick your boots? Wipe your ass?"

Noir shoved him roughly, but didn't rise from his seat. "Piss me off, worm, and it'll be the other way around."

Asmodeus's eyes widened as he straightened. "And on that note, Master, I'll be taking him to Zeth." He paused beside Jericho. "Come with me, Minor Master. I'll show you the way." The demon headed for the door.

What an absolutely bizarre creature. Jericho hesitated in his place for a moment longer as Noir continued to stare at nothing.

"Is there anything else?" Noir asked from his half-lidded repose. Even though it looked as if he were oblivious, Jericho had a feeling nothing escaped Noir's attention.

"Just curious. When you rule the world, what do you plan to do with it?"

"Enjoy it. It's been too long since we were last revered by the masses. Once you get a new taste of it, you'll understand. And you'll remember. We are over-lords. It's mother's milk to our kind."

Noir was right. Jericho couldn't remember the last time someone had shown him any kind of respect or even common decency. He'd spent years of his past locked in prisons, in dungeons and other hell holes Zeus had dumped him in. No part of him had been left unviolated.

It was why he wanted to be sticky with the blood of the Olympians. Why he wanted to lick it from his fingers . . .

Inclining his head to the ancient power, Jericho turned and followed Asmodeus out of the room and down the hallway that seemed to glow. How very strange.

"Where does the light come from?" he asked the demon.

Asmodeus glanced up, then looked back at the floor as they walked. "Um, I don't think you want me to an-swer that, Minor Master."

"Why not?"

"It might upset you."

"Then upset me."

Asmodeus hesitated another few seconds before he finally answered. "It's from the blood of *the* Cali, not the goddess Kali, 'cause let's face it, bleeding her would just anger her and that's not a smart thing to do since she's pretty damn powerful—you probably knew that. Rather it's from the little harmless Cali demons who were created when she pricked her finger on a rose. *Those* Cali. Apparently their blood glows. Who knew, right?"

Jericho paused as he looked up. The Cali were a benevolent race of demons who helped mankind. Since he'd never fought them, he'd had no idea their blood was blue or that it glowed. The blood flowed through the tubes, reminding him of a glow stick. "How many did it take to illuminate the hallway?"

Asmodeus visibly cringed. "Well, you see the problem with blood is that it often dries out, and so you have to keep a constant supply of it, which is really not something we're supposed to talk about and why I said you didn't really want me to answer your question. I was right, huh?"

Jericho's stomach churned at the thought of the cold brutality of killing a species just to use their blood for light. Then again, humans pulled fireflies apart for the same exact reason. He couldn't count the number of people he'd seen who had smeared the poor insect's abdomen over their skin to make it glow and then laughed about it.

He supposed it was basically the same principle, really.

Jericho continued after Asmodeus. "How many demons and people are enslaved here?"

"Define slavery." Asmodeus hedged.

"Kept against their will."

"Good definition." He scratched his chin in thought. "Counting me?"

"Why not?"

"Probably a couple of million . . . you know it's really hard to count to a million, plus they're always dying and new ones are coming in. I tried to count once, but it got really depressing so I stopped. The constant adding and subtracting. Not my forte, really."

It made Jericho wonder what the demon's forte was. Then again, it was probably best not to ask. "How long have you been here?"

"Don't know. Again, tried to count once, got depressed so I stopped. I find it easier to just go with the flow. Ease with the peas."

Jericho frowned. "Ease with the peas?"

"Yeah," he said slowly, "that's not a happy memory, either. Let's forget I mentioned it." He stopped outside a door. "Here we are. Maybe I should warn you before we enter."

Jericho stepped past him and threw open the door.

"Or maybe not. Let's just barge in and be surprised, shall we?"

Jericho was definitely surprised by what he found. There were drunk Skoti everywhere. Some entwined in scenes the *Kama Sutra* would appreciate. He had to pause at one couple. The sheer flexibility required to do what they were doing was amazing . . .

Damn, they would both need a chiropractor later.

If it didn't kill them first.

"They're blood-drunk," Asmodeus explained as he tugged on Jericho's arm. "Appears they've never celebrated their victories before. Personally reminds me of a bunch of drunk frat boys, but what do I know? I've only seen the movie *Animal House*. At least none of them are pretending to be zits." Asmodeus shuddered.

Jericho scowled at the rambling demon. "Are you always this random?"

He nodded glibly. "Mostly. It really irritates Noir, which is just an added bonus for me. At least so long as I can outrun him."

Jericho gave him a hard, unamused stare. "Add me to that list of people you annoy."

"Oh." He looked a bit stricken. "You're not going to singe my testicles over it, are you?" Jericho admired the even, dry delivery of a question that was obviously near and dear to the demon's heart.

"No plans to."

Asmodeus cheered up immediately. "Good. We can be friends, then."

Friends? Given the demon's personality, he wasn't so sure about that. But Asmodeus seemed rather harmless and a font of information. Perhaps it wouldn't be too bad to keep him around.

Provided he could calm down. There was something about the demon that reminded him of a wound-up Jack Russell terrier.

Jericho turned his attention back to the horny, out-of-control Skoti. "So who leads them?"

"That one." Asmodeus pointed toward a couch where a male Skotos was entwined with two half-naked females. "I think they're having trouble adjusting to the emotions they have outside of their dreams. At any rate, they keep acting like demented teenagers from a porno version of a John Hughes film."

Jericho frowned. "How are you so up to speed on pop culture?"

"You ever been trapped in a hell hole? When not being tortured by psychos, there's not much else to do. Besides, I like Molly Ringwald. She has this demon look about her that really turns me on. Wish I could get her out of her panties for a few minutes."

Yeah . . . well, at least it explained much about the demon's insanity.

Jericho watched the Skotos, who was oblivious to the fact that there were unwanted guests here as he kissed his way down the female's body. "Head guy is Zeth?"

Asmodeus grinned. "Oooh, someone was paying attention in class. Yes. Zeth. I would introduce you but he doesn't like me, either. And since he's one of those kids who likes to pull the wings off demons—"

"You don't have any wings," Jericho reminded him.

"Anymore. Key word there."

Jericho winced in sympathetic pain. He wasn't sure if he still had his own wings or not. As a human, they'd been taken from him. And since his powers had been restored, he had yet to try them out.

Not wanting to think about that right now, he made his way through the floor of passed out or entwined bodies to the couch where Zeth appeared as drunk as the rest of them.

He didn't look up until Jericho cleared his throat.

Zeth pulled his head back from the woman's throat to stare up at him.

Jericho frowned. Instead of the trademark blue eyes of the Skoti, Zeth's were jet black. So black, he couldn't even see the man's pupils. Were they that dilated or did something else cause it?

Zeth looked him up and down. "Who are you?"

"Your new commander."

Zeth snorted. "Got one. Don't need another, so piss-off."

"Too late." Jericho looked around to get an idea of how many Skoti were in the room. It appeared to be several hundred and none looked to be sober. "Are all of your soldiers here?"

Zeth leaned his head back so that one of the women could suckle his neck. "I don't know. Maybe."

Jericho pulled the woman off of Zeth, then grabbed him by his shirt and hauled him to his feet. "Focus, asshole. What is wrong with you?"

Zeth's head lolled back. "I can't focus. There's too much sensory overload." Zeth laughed as he patted Jericho on the shoulder. "You need to get laid."

Jericho had to force himself not to slap some sense into the man. But it was hard to maintain his control. "You need to sober up. How can you fight the Oneroi like this?"

"We don't need to fight them. We convert them."

Disgusted, Jericho let go of him and Zeth sank back to the couch. Without a word, Zeth rolled over on top of the other female while the first one draped herself across his back so that they could resume necking.

Ridiculous.

"Asmodeus!" Jericho called, summoning the demon again.

He appeared instantly. "You rang, Minor Master?"

"I'm looking for a god called Deimos. Is he here?"

Asmodeus screwed his face up before he answered. "Define *here*."

"Asmodeus!"

"Okay, fine, don't yell at me. I don't like being

yelled at. He's not here in this room, obviously, but he is in the realm, if you know what I mean."

"Take me to him."

Asmodeus looked around sheepishly. "Am I supposed to do that?"

"If you don't, you're going to have something a lot more painful than your wings pulled off."

He gaped and then cupped himself. "You're a mean, mean man."

Jericho had no intention of doing that to him, but he wasn't about to let the demon know that. "And you're about to be in pain."

"Fine. I'll take you. But if O Great Evil One comes around, I'm blaming you immediately. This is not my heat. Not my bad. I won't own it, not even for a friend. You're on your own, bud."

This time Asmodeus didn't walk. He touched Jericho's arm and transported them into a dark, iridescent pit. An unbearable stench permeated the place, as did moans and pleas for final death. Noir would definitely call it homey, but Jericho, in spite of his desire for vengeance, couldn't call it anything other than hell.

"Where are we?"

Asmodeus created a ball of light in his hand so that they could see the ravaged bodies that were chained and bleeding everywhere. "Noir's happy place. It's where he brings the beings he wants to play with."

"Punish."

"You say to-may-to, I say to-mah-to. Would you like to see Deimos now?"

Jericho tried not to commiserate with the poor souls trapped in this dismal place. "That's why we're here."

Asmodeus pointed behind him. "He's the fifth victim on the wall. I think. Kind of hard to tell, really. Once they've been beaten enough their features start contorting and swelling, then figuring out who's who is a bitch. But he had blond streaks in his hair when they brought him in. If the blood hasn't matted it too badly, that might help you find him."

Jericho gave him a disgusted look before he started making his way over to the people who were hanging by chains along the wall. Asmodeus was right. He couldn't tell who they were and that honestly sickened him.

Enemies or not, these were people. And they had been tortured to the brink of death. Having suffered enough abuse to last out eternity, he hated to see them in the same shape he'd been reduced to on countless occasions.

As he reached the fifth one, he saw the blond streaks through the dark hair. Deimos hung as if he were dead. His swollen eyes were closed, his head resting against his bruised arm. Black stylized tattoos zigzagged from his forehead down his face to his chin. His clothes were torn and bloody. In between the tears in the fabric, Jericho could see the deep gashes and wounds.

Noir must have had an excellent time with the Dolophonos who currently bore little resemblance to his twin, Phobos.

The moment Jericho stopped in front of him, Deimos opened his eyes and lunged at him, ready to fight in spite of his pathetic state.

Jericho stepped back and almost hit him out of reflex.

Their gazes met and locked. Deimos's snarl faded as he recognized him. "Cratus?"

He inclined his head.

"What are you doing here?" His gaze went down Jericho's undamaged body before he cursed. "Traitor!"

His condemnation set Jericho's fury to boiling. How dare this bastard look at him like that. "Betrayed."

"Fuck you!"

Jericho curled his lip. "Now you know how I felt, brother. Remember the day you turned with them against me?"

"How could you?"

That was laughable. "That's the same question that has haunted me since I looked at you while Zeus held me on the ground and you looked at the floor at your feet." Jericho grabbed Deimos's head and made him meet his gaze. "You held me down while my mother burned her words into my flesh. I can still feel the pain of your arm wrapped around my throat."

"You earned your punishment."

Jericho struggled not to strike out at him and add to his pain. How could Deimos not apologize even now for what he'd done? They had been friends before that. It was why he had no pity for any of them. They had none for him.

Screw them all.

"And you've earned yours," he said pitilessly. "Son of the Furies. How many people have you tortured throughout the centuries for your mother and Zeus? It sucks to be you now, huh?"

Deimos tried to head-butt him, but Jericho moved away. "Noir is going to kill us."

"I'll make sure you have a nice requiem."

Deimos shook his head. "So that's it, then? You have no remorse?"

Jericho held his arms out and shrugged nonchalantly. "We are the products of our past. But if it makes you feel any better, I do feel sorry for you."

Deimos sneered. "You'll feel even sorrier when you're hanging on this wall, too. Don't think for one minute Noir won't do this to you. He's the god who invented betrayal, and I'm sure he already has a space here with your name engraved on it."

Jericho laughed at his warning. "Oh, brother, you all have taught me well. I will *never* put myself in that position again. Believe me. I learned my lesson at the hands of the Dolophoni you command. I have no intention of giving Noir any reason to turn on me. I am his to command. Forever."

"Jericho?"

Shocked that someone in this hole knew his adopted name, Jericho looked to his right at the next prisoner hanging on the wall. Like Deimos, he'd been badly beaten. His dark hair hung around a face distorted by swollen lips and a black eye so severe the entire whites of that eye were red from busted blood vessels.

It took him a full minute to recognize him. It was those eyes that gave him away. One dark brown and one a bright green . . .

Jaden.

Jaden was the one the demons summoned whenever they wanted to barter with Noir or Azura for favors. Jericho had known Jaden lived here with them, but he would have thought the broker would have a lush place to call his own, not be caged with the rest of their victims.

Stunned, Jericho released Deimos and stepped back. "What are you doing here?"

Jaden laughed bitterly. "Do my accommodations offend you? I've grown quite used to them. Though a view of something other than mangled bodies might be nice for a change."

Jericho scowled. "You serve the Source. You're one of them."

Jaden shook his head. "I serve Noir and Azura. Word to the wise, don't ever displease them. For some reason, I can't seem to stop myself. I guess old habits die hard." He looked down at his torn and bleeding body that was barely covered by shredded clothes. "As do I. But don't worry. I'm sure they'll be kinder to you than they've been to me. I held their enmity long before I came here, which is part of the reason they love to gut me every chance they get."

He looked past Jericho to see Asmodeus hiding in the shadows. The light from his hand was muffled and faint. Jaden called out to him. "Mo, long time no see."

"Yeah, you looked better last time, too. I told you not to piss off Noir. One day you're going to listen to me."

"Why start now?" Jaden asked.

Asmodeus nodded. "Ah, you're right. Bled so much now, it doesn't really matter, does it?"

Deimos curled his lip. "You all sicken me." He jerked at his chains as if trying to break them.

Jaden ignored him as he pinned those mismatched eyes on Jericho. "By the way, your infant lived."

Jericho had no idea what the man was talking about. He didn't have a baby. "What?"

"The child you saved all those centuries ago. I just wanted you to know that you never suffered in vain. The baby lived and grew up healthy."

Bully for the brat. "Do you think I care?"

Jaden shrugged. "You gave up your godhood for her. I thought you might."

Jericho's frown deepened. "Her?" Unbelievably enough, he hadn't bothered to check the infant's gender before he handed it over. It hadn't mattered to him back then. All he'd seen was the baby's smile and its warm eyes.

Jaden nodded. "The Oneroi Delphine is the baby you saved."

Jericho was floored by the news. The air left his body as those words seared him. He shook his head in disbelief.

It couldn't be.

"You know it's true," Jaden said, his voice deep and sure. "The moment you saw her, you recognized how much she looked like her mother."

Still, he refused to believe it. What were the odds? "You're lying to me."

"Why would I?"

"Everyone lies."

"I don't."

Jericho winced as he felt even more betrayed by this. And yet as he considered it, he knew Jaden wasn't lying. Somehow he'd known it instinctively.

He'd saved Delphine. . . .

The woman waiting in his room was the same person he'd given all but his life for.

Fury tore through him. Oh, this was rich irony.

And she owed him a debt he more than intended to collect on. Before this day was over, he was going to get satisfaction from her hide.

CHAPTER 5

HIS FURY RIDING HIM HARD, JERICHO STORMED BACK into his room. Then fell instantly still as he found Delphine asleep on his bed, beneath his blood cloak. Her features pale, her blond hair cascaded around her in a soft, tangled mess that made his hand itch to touch it.

She had the faintest of snores that strangely teased his ears and warmed him.

So instead of yelling at her for something that wasn't her fault, he crossed the room to kneel beside her. It was hard to reconcile her with that sweet, happy baby who had wrapped its little fingers around his and held on so tight that it touched him when nothing ever had before.

Now he knew why her eyes had given him pause.

They had touched him then as they touched him now. But why? What was it about her that quieted him? Who in his right mind would destroy his entire life and future to save a stranger?

Granted, he'd known her mother, but not well. They had been passing strangers, really. He'd known Leta's name. That she was a dream god. But honestly, he'd never cared beyond that. Since Leta had never upset Zeus and hadn't run in the same circles he had, there had been no reason for them to be friendly.

Yet that one night when their worlds had violently collided, they had both lost everything.

Zeus, furious over a dream one of the Oneroi had given him, had demanded all the dream gods be rounded up for punishment. Those like Leta, who were married to humans, were to have their spouses and any progeny they'd produced killed. Zeus had wanted no one to survive who could ever harm him again.

Then the Oneroi had been tortured and stripped of their emotions for eternity. Zeus figured if they had no emotions, they wouldn't feel compelled for whatever reason to play in anyone's dreams again.

What he hadn't realized was that in dreams, they'd be able to channel the sleeper's emotions. So much so that some of the Oneroi would become addicted to it, since it was the only way they could feel anything but emptiness.

So the Skoti had been born. Then it became the job of the Oneroi to police or kill their brethren so that none of them would suffer again under Zeus's command.

A part of that vicious cycle, Jericho had harmed Leta even worse than the Dolophoni and Oneroi had harmed him. They had only killed him. He had taken what Leta loved most.

Her husband and daughter.

Leta's desperate screams still echoed in his memories. She had screamed herself hoarse and he couldn't blame her for it. Not given what they'd taken from her.

Maybe the past centuries were justified after all. What they'd done to her had been inexcusable. The least he could have done was let her know that he'd saved her daughter. But everything had happened so fast, there hadn't been enough time. Not to mention had anyone known what he'd done, they would have killed Delphine instantly.

Yet here she was . . . alive. Because he'd hidden her and had never breathed a word of it.

Jaden was right. His suffering hadn't been in vain. She was grown and beautiful.

Placing his hand to Delphine's warm cheek, he cocked his head to study her resting features. She was so similar to her mother. Yet so different. The blond hair made her features softer. Inviting.

His heartbeat raced at the softness of her skin under the pads of his fingertips. He hadn't really touched a woman in countless centuries.

He ran his hand from her cheek to her hair. A part of him wanted to kiss her so badly that he wasn't even sure how he kept from doing it. Perhaps because she was asleep and he didn't want to violate the peace she seemed to have found.

Was she dreaming?

What did Oneroi dream of? His dreams used to be of battle. To his knowledge, he'd never had peace in the dream realm. As an immortal god, he'd been violent and cruel. His dreams had reflected his reality.

As a man, he hadn't dreamed at all since he'd spent the nights as a corpse. No, that wasn't true, he'd dreamed while conscious. And in those, he'd escaped to peaceful havens. A quiet beach. A cabin in the woods. A lone temple in the desert. Places that were isolated from the world where no one could make him feel small or worthless. Where no one could kill him or hurt him in any way.

Where he had his old strength back and no one could touch him . . .

Now he was there at long last. He had power. He had dignity. Most of all, he had a beautiful woman in his bed . . .

The very one who had cost him everything.

He hated her for that. She'd grown up without knowing her life had been paid for with more suffering than she could ever imagine.

He clenched his hand in her hair, wanting to hurt her for that. But he knew it wasn't her fault. She'd been an innocent child.

It had been his own decision to ruin his life. He could have killed her as Zeus ordered and everything would have been fine.

For him.

"Were you worth my sacrifice?" he whispered.

Her eyes fluttered open as if his words had reached her. The moment she saw him, she jumped with a loud gasp. He tried to pull his hand away, but her hair was wrapped around his fingers. She yelped as her movements pulled it.

"I'm sorry," he said, wondering why he bothered since it was her own actions that had hurt her, not his.

"What were you doing?" she accused.

"Nothing."

Delphine frowned at his sullen, angry tone. His demeanor reminded her of a child caught with his hand in a cookie jar. Rubbing the sore place on her head, she stamped down her own anger. "Where do you keep going?"

"I went to see Deimos."

She sat up as a shiver of excitement went through her. "Did you see M'Adoc? Is he alive?"

Jericho felt jealousy flare at the obvious concern and care she had for the leader of the dream gods. M'Adoc had never sacrificed for her. "No, I didn't see him."

She looked crushed, and it killed the satisfaction he wanted to feel. "Is Deimos all right?"

That was a matter of opinion. Personally, he'd never thought the god was all there, but that was a separate argument. "I've seen him look better. Still, he's alive, even though Noir has carved him up pretty good."

"And I suppose that made you happy."

"No," he answered honestly. "In spite of the fact I wanted to beat him myself, I don't like seeing anyone tortured."

"Not even Prometheus?"

He growled at her. "Why do you provoke me?"

Delphine paused at his question. Honestly, she didn't know. It really wasn't in her nature to go after people. Yet the moment he drew near, she wanted his jugular. How out of character for her. "You irritate me."

"*I* irritate *you*?"

She nodded. "You have the power to save people and yet you intend to fight for Noir. That irritates me."

He snorted at her words. "Give me one real, tangible

reason why I should fight for a god who has already shown me how little regard he holds for me. For an entire pantheon that spent thousands of years attacking me."

"It's the right thing to do." That sounded ridiculous even to her.

He arched one brow.

"Okay. So I admit it doesn't make sense, but it is the best reason. You are a good man. I know it."

He laughed bitterly as he moved to put his sword down on the dresser. His hand lingered on the sheath as if he were afraid to let go of it. And from this angle, she had a very nice view of his muscular back. Tall and handsome, he could easily take a woman's breath away and he made her heart race.

"You know nothing about me," he said simply.

"I'm willing to learn."

He turned on her with anger again. "What game are you trying to play?"

She backed up on the bed. Not afraid of him, but concerned that she continued to irritate him even when she didn't mean to. "No game, Jericho. I'm here. I'm your prisoner. Azura gave me to you naked and rather than attack me or hurt me," she picked up a corner of the cloak that was still draped around her, "you covered me up. Those aren't the actions of someone who's innately cruel. I think there's a lot more good inside you than just this." She was willing to bet on it. "Why did you cover me?"

Jericho ground his teeth. *Because no one deserves to be shamed like that.* He knew from personal experience. But he would never say that out loud. He didn't want her to know that he was weak where she was concerned. She'd be able to use that against him, and he'd had enough of the gods playing with his life. No one would ever have control over him again.

"Asmodeus?" he called.

He waited until the demon appeared.

"You rang, oh evil Minor Master?"

"I'm hungry. Where do we find food here?"

Asmodeus's eyes widened as if he thought Jericho insane for even asking. "Truthfully, I don't advise eating in this realm. I mean, you can if you want, but . . ."

"But what?" Jericho prompted after Asmodeus seemed to have sputtered to a stop.

He twisted his hands together. "We have certain demons who are motivated by the smell of food. They tend to get rather violent whenever they smell it. I personally wouldn't be caught eating anything because I would end up dead. You might not. But you'd still have to fight them, and since some of them are rather ugly and really, really smelly, it might spoil your appetite. Then again, maybe not. Doesn't spoil Noir's. I think it makes him hungrier, especially when he guts them. Sick, but true."

Asmodeus looked at Delphine, and his eyes widened again, this time in appreciation and interest. "Oh, hello, me lovely, we haven't met." He flashed her a charming smile as he kissed her tenderly on the hand. "Asmodeus, demon extraordinare, at your service. Any service you may require, especially those that involve nudity and adjoining body parts joining other people's body parts."

"Asmodeus!" Jericho snapped. "You don't see her, do you hear me?"

He jumped back as if something had electrocuted him. "Completely blind, Minor Master. Hearing is intact." He put his hands out as if feeling for furniture. "Is there anyone here besides the two of us? No? Good. I'm leaving now unless Minor Master has another preferably nonpainful task for me."

"You're dismissed."

"Cool beaners." Asmodeus vanished.

Delphine frowned at Jericho. "He's not right, is he?"

"Yeah, I think Noir may have hit him on the head one time too many and way too hard." He faced her. "So would you like to join me for something to eat?"

"As long as it doesn't involve the entrails of demons, I might be persuaded."

"Demon entrails have no appeal for me, either. Zeus's are another matter."

She wrinkled her nose at the mere thought. "Ew."

He held his hand out to her.

Delphine hesitated, wondering if she should be doing this instead of finding a way to M'Adoc and Deimos, but she couldn't get near them without Jericho. Maybe food would predispose him to a better, more amicable mood.

Against her better judgement, she took his hand in hers.

As soon as she did, he teleported them back to New Orleans, to a small dark alley at Exchange Place. It looked to be early evening, but it was hard to say for sure since time on earth moved differently than it did in other realms. What might seem like fifteen minutes in Azmodea might be a year on earth. A slight exaggeration, but . . .

She looked around the deserted alley that had closed and boarded-up shops. What a strange place to choose. She didn't know what she'd been expecting, but this wasn't it.

"What are we doing here?"

He changed his clothes into a pair of jeans, a black shirt and dark hair before he started toward the street. "Going to eat. What? You got Alzheimer's?"

She narrowed her eyes at him. "No, but I don't see a restaurant around here."

He gave her a "duh" stare. "If I put us inside the restaurant, people might scream and freak. Not to mention, it has a Web cam there that makes it even harder to just poof inside. Damn modern people and their wizard's tools," he said sarcastically. "I miss the days when we could just kill and roast a chicken, huh?"

She rolled her eyes. "You really can't help being an asshole, can you?"

"I probably could, but it's not worth the effort. Gods forbid you might actually take a liking to me. Then where would we be?"

"I have no idea, but I might be willing to risk it."

His eye turned dark. "You don't ever want to see what's inside me, Delphine. It's not pretty."

Delphine reached up to touch the scar that ran out from under his eye patch.

He caught her hand in a fierce grip. "I didn't say you could touch me."

"No, you didn't. Sorry." She pulled her hand from his and watched as he walked stiffly to the street and toward a restaurant called Acme Oyster House.

Delphine followed even though her heart was heavy with guilt over eating while her brethren were suffering.

Win him over and you can save them. What else could she do? So long as she lacked her god powers, she was at his mercy.

She winced as she finally understood the true horror of all he'd been through. It was so hard to be without the powers that had been a part of her almost the whole of her life. To be at the mercy of others. How had he stood it?

The world was terrifying like this. And it gave her a whole new appreciation for the humans who inhabited this place. Especially since they were the prey for so many more powerful beings.

She paused at the door while the hostess grabbed their menus and looked around at the gathered people. People who had no idea that Jericho was a god and she his prisoner . . .

The hostess seated them at a table in front of the window that looked out onto the street. Even though there were TVs playing and people talking, she could still hear the music from Bourbon Street, which was just a few feet away.

How she wished Deimos and the others could be here now and not in whatever holding cell Noir was using for them.

"Is something wrong?" Jericho asked.

She glanced at him and sighed. "I'm worried about

my friends. It seems wrong to be eating while Noir is torturing them."

Jericho set the menu down to give her a stern glare. "First of all, you don't want me to get too hungry. Ever. I'm an even worse bastard than normal and having starved for centuries, I'm not about to deprive myself again when I don't have to. Second, let me tell you something about your *friends*. Deimos held me down while I was branded and then took me to the human realm where I was left with nothing. No clothes, no money. Not a damn thing to call my own. Hence the aforementioned starvation."

She cringed at what he described.

But he took no mercy on her. "A hundred years later, M'Ordant"—one of the leaders of the Oneroi who had been her mentor—"dumped me inside a Spartan prison camp and told the commander I was a traitor to their people. You don't really want to know what the Spartans did to people they thought betrayed them. D'Alerian"—the third leader with M'Adoc rounding out the crew—"had me put inside a Turkish prison in the fifteenth century where I was impaled after being tortured for three weeks." His face was stoic, but the pain in his eye was excruciating. "So you'll have to excuse me if I have a hard time feeling too sorry for them right now. At least no one's shoving a sharp spike up their asses."

Her stomach shrank at the horrors of his past. "You were impaled?"

His expression turned to chiseled stone. "You know the worst part about impalement? You don't die immediately. You hang on bleeding and aching as the spike works its way slowly through your body until it pierces some major organ. Pray to the gods you worship that you never know what that feels like."

But he did.

She looked away, unable to cope with the emotions that filled her. How could they have done that to one of their own? Then again, they'd been even crueler to others for reasons every bit as petty. It was why she'd done her best to stay off all their collective radar.

Her throat tight, she felt a tear slide down her cheek.

Jericho froze as he saw the sparkle in the candle-light. Without thinking, he reached out to touch her wet cheek. "Tears?"

She brushed his hand aside and wiped her cheek. "I'm sorry for what was done to you. I really am."

Tears . . .

For him.

No one had ever cried for him before. And when she met his gaze, her hazel-green eyes glistened from the ones yet to fall. Something inside him snapped painfully at that. He made her feel pain. How could that be?

No, it wasn't possible. It was another trick meant to weaken him. Ruin him.

He growled low in his throat. "What are you doing?"

She looked confused by his question. "Nothing. Sitting here."

He grabbed her wrist in his hand. "Are you playing me?"

"Playing you how?"

He tightened his grip. "I swear to you if you're trying to seduce me to your side, I will kill you. And it'll take a lot more than fake tears to sway me."

She snatched her hand away from his hold. "Are you really that cynical that you don't think anyone could feel bad for the way you were treated?"

He didn't answer.

Delphine was aghast at him and his inability to understand compassion. Dear gods, with the lack of emotions he had, he should have been an Oneroi himself. "Fine, then. I'll be a total bitch since that's all you can take." She flipped her menu open and started reading.

Jericho wanted to be angry and offended, yet he somehow felt . . .

Wrong.

He actually had to bite back an apology.

For what? He'd spoken the truth. He didn't want faked emotions that were designed to weaken him.

What if they weren't?

What if she was being honest and they were real?

Don't go there, fool. You know better. The very person who birthed you couldn't feel pity or compassion for you. How could a stranger?

It was true. He was nothing to her, and she was . . .

His reason for suffering.

He glanced at the menu, then looked back at her. Her brow was furrowed as she read and a lock of blond hair fell into her eyes. Her gaze was completely focused on the food. For some reason he couldn't fathom, he had a desire to brush that stray piece of hair back into place.

What is wrong with me?

"How did you grow up?" he asked before he could stop himself.

Her scowl made a deep impression on her forehead. "Pardon?"

"Your family. What were they like?"

Delphine started to tell him it was none of his business, but the sincerity in his eye kept her from it. He seemed to be genuinely curious, and she didn't want to anger him again. She actually liked their more calm discussions. Few though they were.

"I knew nothing of my real father." It was something she'd never really talked about before. Mostly because no one ever asked or cared. "Arikos said my father was one of the Skoti who seduced my mother in her sleep." And a part of her still wished he'd come forward to claim her once she'd joined their ranks. That was the human side of her that at least wanted a face to put with her mysterious procreator. It would have been nice to have known which of the thousands of them had fathered her.

But she didn't want to dwell on that. "My mother was a gentle woman. Lovely." A tiny smile played at the edges of her lips as she remembered the beauty of her mother's face and the tenderness of her touch. She'd truly loved her mother, who had never once raised her voice to anyone. It didn't mean her mother didn't stand up to people. She just did it in a calm, sweet way that Delphine had always admired.

"She used to make these honey cakes that were so good they would melt before you could even swallow them." She closed her eyes as her throat tightened with the part of her heart that still ached over the fact that her mother was no longer with her. "I asked her once what her special trick was to make them like that. She told me it was the love she had for me that she put into them." Delphine blinked away tears at the thought.

How could she still miss a woman she hadn't seen in centuries? And yet there would always be a part of her that missed her mother and her mother's kind heart and gentle soul.

"Did you have a stepfather?"

She nodded. "He was a good man. A blacksmith. I used to take drinks to him while he worked, and he would make up funny stories to entertain me." She even had the crude silver heart he'd made for her when she was a girl that bore his smith's mark. She kept it in a small box in her room on the Vanishing Isle. Even with muted emotions, she had loved them greatly, and that spoke more of them than it did her. The fact that they could make her feel what they did . . .

A part of her was sad that she hadn't possessed a completely human heart to give them all the love they'd deserved in return.

Jericho looked away from her wistful face, wishing he could relate. But the world she described was nothing like his childhood. His parents had seldom been kind and the two of them had fought ferociously.

"And siblings? Did you have any of those?"

She shook her head. "No. It was just me. I think it's why they doted on me the way they did."

"And were they good to you?"

Delphine scowled suspiciously. Not that he blamed

her. He was being nosy, but he had to know if he'd done right by her. *Please tell me I didn't suffer without reason. . . .* He needed to hear that he'd spared her more misery, though he wasn't sure why it was so important to him. All he knew was that a part of him would die if she'd been harmed in any way by his actions.

"Why do you care?" she asked.

"I'm curious."

Still, suspicion hung heavy in those hazel eyes. She wanted a real reason, but he couldn't give it to her. "Yes, they were very kind to me. Even though we were poor, I never wanted for anything. I think since they couldn't have any more children, they lavished all their love on me."

Jericho didn't know why that made his heart lighter, but it did. He'd chosen well for her parents.

Good.

She took a sip of water. "What about you? Did you have a good relationship with your parents?"

He snorted before he could stop himself. But why hide the truth? It wasn't like the whole of Olympus didn't know what kind of family he had. "My mother is the goddess of hatred and my father the god of warcraft. My sisters were the goddesses of force and victory, my brother the god of rivalry. Let's just say those personalities don't lend themselves to a calm, peaceful home. Any time things started to go too smoothly, Zelos was there to stir everyone up and get us going at each other's throats."

And those were the good memories. His father had

spent his childhood making them all "stronger." His mother filling them with hatred because in her words, "Love is fickle and it will betray you. But hatred lasts forever. It gives you strength and it will never leave you cold."

The fact that the other gods, including Zeus, swore on his mother and then were terrified to break those oaths for fear of her wrath, pretty much said everything there was about his mother's "dainty" personality.

Her idea of tucking her young into bed had been to throw him into a lava pit and watch as he almost drowned.

"Why did you do that?"

"It is by your own strength that you will be known. You can never rely on another for help. Everyone sinks or swims by their own effort. Never forget that."

"In a lava pit?"

Her answer had come as a vicious backhand. "You will stand. You will fight and you will never shame me."

Yeah . . .

His childhood had been great indeed.

Delphine shook her head as she twisted the straw wrapper in her hands. "I met your brother Zelos once. He was a total jerk."

"You have no idea." She should have tried growing up with the mean bastard.

Jericho paused as the waitress returned to take their orders.

Delphine hesitated when it was her turn. She looked at the menu uncertainly. "I don't know what to eat."

Jericho leaned back in his chair. "Try the medley.

It has some of everything. If you don't like it, you can always order something else."

"Okay." She ordered it, then handed her menu to the waitress. "So have you eaten here a lot?" she asked once they were alone again.

He glanced out the window at the small line of people that was forming, waiting to come inside and be seated. "No. Darice's girlfriend works here and she used to bring food over to Darice during lunch. It always smelled and looked good so I wanted to try it."

Jericho paused as he became aware of what they were doing. . . . He was eating with a companion. He hadn't done this in centuries.

More than that, they were chatting. Sharing. Something he'd never really done with anyone.

How strange.

Delphine fell quiet as she waited for her food. She kept thinking of M'Adoc and Deimos, along with the others Noir had taken. What were they going through right now? She knew they were in pain and she couldn't stop dwelling on it.

And as she glanced around the restaurant, she wondered what would become of places such as this in the human realm if Noir succeeded with his plans. Would any of it be left standing or would he tear it all down?

It wasn't right or fair. None of the people who were laughing and talking had any idea that evil was around them. That they were on the brink of total annihilation and that one of the people who could stop them sat across from her not even caring.

She watched as a couple walked out the door with their arms draped over each other. Frowning, she couldn't take her eyes off them as they paused outside the window and kissed. They looked so happy and in love.

What would that feel like?

"You look like you've never seen people kissing before."

She glanced back at Jericho. "I've seen it before. Just not in real life."

He watched the couple until they vanished out of sight. Then that penetrating gaze came back to hers. "Have you never kissed?"

She gave him a droll stare. "Arik took me to the Vanishing Isle when I was fourteen. So no, I've never kissed. The Oneroi aren't really big on affection. It goes against that whole no-feelings thing."

Jericho had to concede that point. Zeus had done a number on all of them. "Were you never tempted to go Skoti?"

"It has crossed my mind briefly, but no, not really. I would *never* become one of them."

Her adamant vehemence surprised him. He'd struck a nerve with her. "Why?"

Her gaze saddened as she swirled ice in her glass with her straw. "There was a woman in my village when I was a young girl. Beautiful and sweet, she used to bring fresh bread to my parents and make doll clothes for me. Then one afternoon, I noticed how tired she looked. She hadn't been sleeping for days. Every night her dreams worsened. Within two weeks, she'd gone insane from them, and that was before the Skoti had lost their emotions. Back when they preyed for nothing more than cruelty."

Delphine flinched; the memories were hard for her even now. "I can still remember the wails of her children when they found her. She'd killed herself to get away from the demons in her sleep. It wasn't until Arik came to me that I learned it was the Skoti who'd driven her mad and why it was so important that we fight and stop them. Any time I ever considered allowing my emotions to rule me, I thought of Nirobe. I would never harm someone the way they'd harmed her. It's wrong to prey on people."

Wow, he wished he had those convictions. But truthfully, he felt vindicated for any action he took against mankind.

Still . . .

She shook her head. "I don't understand why people can't be nice to each other. Why someone always has to push someone else around."

Unlike her, he got it completely. "It's intoxicating to feel that power. To know that in your hands is their life or death. That no matter what they do or how hard they fight, they're no match for you."

Her gaze turned harsh and condemning. "Do you really feel satisfied when you've crushed them knowing they were weaker than you? That they couldn't fight back and win? Is that true victory?"

Jericho looked away.

"Tell me," she said, her voice thick with conviction. "I want to understand because I really don't get it."

Jericho swallowed, unable to meet her gaze as he remembered the times in his past when he'd gone after weaker enemies. There was one truth he kept coming back to, and it was one he didn't want to think about. "I was always still empty afterward. The exaltation of victory is momentary and fleeting. By the time it's felt, it's gone."

"So why do it?"

Because it was better than the emptiness inside. At least there for a moment, he had some kind of feelings besides hate and pain. That was all he knew. It was why Nike had been so precious to him. She had made him feel something else.

But even that had always been fleeting. Nothing could take away or soothe the rage and hate in his heart. At least not for more than a few minutes at a time.

It was those minutes he craved.

He sat back as the waitress brought their food and set it down in front of them. Silently, he ate his oysters while Delphine picked daintily at her food. Her nose wrinkled ever so slightly as she bit into her gumbo.

"Is it not good?"

She wiped her mouth. "Yes. But very different. Spicy. I wasn't prepared for that."

He pushed his basket of crackers toward her on the table. "That'll help absorb it."

"Thank you." She started to bite into the wrapped package.

"Wait," he said, pulling it out of her hand. "You have to unwrap the plastic."

"What?"

He shook his head, amused by her confusion. She could be so knowledgeable and yet so childlike. But then, her experiences in the world had been through dreams and not based in reality. It made a big difference.

"You don't eat the plastic part." He opened the crackers and handed them back.

"Oh. Thank you again." She smiled a smile that actually made his stomach tighten. Her hand brushed his as she took it.

That simple, innocent touch seared him. He wanted to take her hand and hold it to his face. To kiss his way up her arm and over her body.

But he didn't dare. Tenderness for her could weaken him. He'd already sacrificed enough for her. He had no intention of giving anything more.

Her eyes sparkled as she continued to eat her meal. She was enjoying it. He didn't know why he took pleasure in that, but he did.

But his pleasure died as he glanced out the window to the street.

There in the darkness, he saw a shadow he recognized. Inhuman and evil, it was after two girls who had just left the Fire of Brazil restaurant across the street.

Damn it! Couldn't he even eat in peace?

What do you care? Let him have them.

He looked down at his plate, telling himself it was none of his business.

Then he looked at Delphine, who hadn't seen what he had. She would be so disappointed in him if she ever learned that he'd sat here and done nothing to help those girls.

And the truth was, so would he.

Cursing, he pulled his wallet out and used his powers to create enough money to put on the table to pay for their food.

Delphine frowned at him as he stood up. "Is something wrong?"

"Yes," he growled. "I'm about to kill someone." Without another word, he headed outside to confront the creature.

No doubt this was going to be the second-worst mistake of his life.

CHAPTER 6

DELPHINE WAS MORE THAN READY TO LAY INTO JERI-
cho for his cruel intentions as she followed him outside the restaurant. Whoever he was going after didn't
deserve to die, and from what she could see, it was
one of two young women.

Or, Zeus forbid, both of them.

What was it with him that he'd forgotten all compassion? What could those girls have done to him to
make him want to kill them? They looked as harmless
as could be.

At least that was her thought until she saw the demon rush into a dark alley to attack the two young
women they'd been following.

She tried to blast the demon, only to be reminded
that her powers were completely gone.

Jericho ran at the demon and grabbed him from behind. No more then five-eight in height, the demon had
dark skin, flashing black eyes and a bald head. Lean
and wiry and extremely handsome, he struggled against
Jericho.

Jericho pulled the demon off the screaming co-ed. "Get the girls out of here," he shouted at her.

She did as he said, knowing he wouldn't be able to fight the demon with witnesses present. Humans really didn't want to know what was out in the world, preying on them.

As soon as she had the alley clear and the crying girls were running toward safety, Jericho let loose the demon, who turned on him with flashing fangs. Jericho caught the demon's shoulders as he came at him and flipped him onto the ground.

In one fluid move, he pulled the dagger out of his boot and held it against the demon's throat. Unable to move now without hurting himself, the demon's eyes turned red and his demon's marks appeared on his bald head.

"What are you doing here, Berith?" Jericho demanded in a cold, lethal tone.

The demon's eyes bulged as he realized who Jericho was. "Kyrios?" he asked excitedly, using the term meaning "master." "It's so good to see you again. I'd heard you were banished. Stripped of your powers."

Jericho kept him in place. "I'm sure my father's filled your head full of bullshit. As you can see, I'm hale and whole, and willing to gut you. Now why were you after those girls?"

"Bidden."

"By?"

Berith shrugged. "Dunno. Some boy-man who says he bought my ring in an antique store. You know the rules. I can't question my orders. I only carry them out."

Delphine was completely confused by what was going on but didn't want to interrupt them.

Jericho pulled his knife away from the demon's throat and sat back on his haunches. "Where is this boy who owns your ring?"

"In something called a dorm room not too far from here. It's a small place. After I bring him the girl he sent me after, he wants me to put him in a house. A big one in something called the Garden District. Not sure what that is. I'll have to do research on it."

Delphine finally interrupted. "I take it you know this demon?"

Nodding, Jericho rose to his feet, pulling the demon up with him. "He was one of my father's generals until he pissed him off. For that aggravation, my father bound him into slavery to a ring. You own the ring, you own Berith."

Berith straightened his clothes with exaggerated jerks. "And it hurts every time they conjure me. I swear it feels like someone peeling my skin off."

She shook her head in pity for both of them. Crossing her arms over her chest, she looked at Jericho. "You must have had such a great childhood with a man like that for your father."

"Yeah. All puppy dogs and rainbows and those weird furry people with padded coat hangers on their heads that look like space aliens on acid."

Berith paused as he brushed debris off his clothes to frown. "You mean the Teletubbies?"

Jericho gave him a smirk. "The fact that you know what they're called, Berith, truly scares me."

Berith shrugged. "As a demon of torture, it behooves me to know all things that are deeply annoying. You'd be amazed how many people in the modern age no longer fear zombies as much as Teletubbies."

Jericho snorted. "Not really. I'd rather battle a brain-eating zombie any day than hear them sing."

"You're both sick individuals," Delphine said, yet she was oddly amused by their conversation.

Jericho ignored her. "So what were you going to do with the girls?"

Berith rubbed his eyes before he answered. "One I was going to eat, the other the kid wanted for his girl-friend. You do know I still have to take her to him, right?"

"No, you don't," Jericho said in a flat tone.

"What do you mean?" Berith's voice was filled with fear. He took two steps back. "You plan to kill me?"

"No. I'm going to liberate you."

Berith backed up another step, his face contorted with suspicion. "That's the demon euphemism for death . . ."

"I'm not going to kill you, Berith."

"Really?" He dragged the word out slowly. "Why not?" The way he said that was comical. It was almost as if he were disappointed.

"Because I need an ally and I can think of no one better."

Berith scoffed. "Sure you can. I can think of a lot of gods with more power than a bound demon."

"Yes, but I know your weaknesses, which means you'll think twice before betraying me."

"Very good point. You get the ring and I'm yours to command."

Jericho looked at Delphine. "Shall we?"

"Have I any choice?"

"Not really."

"Didn't think so."

Berith took them straight to his master, who turned out to be a pimple-faced nineteen-year-old college student. Some master he was. He actually wet his pants the moment they flashed into his room.

"What do you want?" he asked, his voice shaking as he cringed in a corner of his dorm room.

Jericho crossed his arms over his chest in a tough stance as he scowled at the boy. "I want Berith's ring."

"It's mine. I bought it fair and square."

"Kid," Jericho said sternly, "hand it over. I'll reimburse you. Most importantly, give it over without a fuss, and I'll let you live."

The boy swallowed. He looked at Berith. "What about *our* deal?"

Berith indicated Jericho with his thumb. "The man doesn't want me messing with it and, no offense, I wouldn't anger him. I've seen what he can do and it's the stuff horror movies are made of. Body parts flailing, blood. Lots of blood and torture." He leaned forward to whisper loudly, "and the woman with us? Goddess of nightmares. These two can get you sleeping and awake. You might want to let them have the ring so that they'll go away peacefully."

"But—"

Delphine stepped forward. "No buts, sweetie. Give us the ring before someone gets hurt."

Berith cleared his throat. "That someone would be you, just for clarification."

The boy's eyes widened before he pulled the ring off his pinkie and held it out to them. "I just wanted Kerry to notice me."

Jericho took it from him. "For the record, kid, summoning a demon to kidnap her, not the best way to meet a woman. It usually backfires on you."

Delphine arched a brow at that.

Jericho didn't comment on her unspoken sarcasm.

The next thing Delphine knew, they were all back in Azmodea in Jericho's room.

He turned to the demon. "Berith, back in the ring. Now."

Berith saluted him before he complied. Jericho slid the ring onto his finger. Small and gold, it held a single blood-red stone that had a skull etched into it. The ring looked rather creepy, and given the fact that it housed a demon, it was rather apropos.

"What are you planning to do with that?" she asked, indicating the ring.

He shrugged. "It never hurts to have a surprise your enemies don't know about. Even the toughest of us need the cavalry from time to time."

That made sense to her. And Berith would have nothing to gain by working for Noir.

Not to mention Jericho didn't trust Noir. Even though he didn't say it in so many words, she sensed it in the way he was more on guard here than he'd been in the restaurant.

He might talk the game, but he knew the drill. She gave him credit for not blindly following someone she had no doubt would turn on him even worse than Zeus had.

She walked closer to Jericho. His hair was long and blond again—he'd made it short for their brief trip to New Orleans, probably because he seemed to have an aversion to standing out. But now he looked like the god he was, complete with an eye that glowed with color.

He was so much larger than she. Stronger. She should be afraid of him, and yet she had this overwhelming compulsion to rub herself against him. To have him hold her.

In spite of those feelings, she playfully narrowed her gaze. "By the way, I want to revisit that demon comment you made earlier. Isn't that how *we* met?"

He scoffed. "And you see how wonderfully sweet you've been to me as a result of it. You've done all but bite me."

She tucked her hands behind her back and smiled devilishly. "I probably should have done that while I had the chance."

"Well, there's always tomorrow. I'm sure you'll get around to it then." There was no humor in his tone at all. It was deadly serious.

"I was teasing."

"Sure you were."

She caught him as he started past her. "You don't trust anyone, do you?"

"What do you think? I'm sure you'll turn on me just like everyone else has. It's not like we're family or even friends. Like Noir said, we're all for sale. It's just a question of price."

"And I don't believe that. There is nothing that could make me turn against M'Adoc."

His mocking laugh rang in her ears. "Easy for you to say. You've never been tested."

"And there you'd be wrong."

"How so?"

She turned around to give him her back. Lifting her shirt, she showed him the scars that she usually used her powers to conceal. Since her powers were bound, she was sure they were prominent now.

Jericho paused as he saw the scars she held from a past beating. How had he missed them earlier? But then, he'd been so occupied with getting her covered that he'd been trying not to focus on her body, only on concealing it. Because he knew how embarrassing it was to be naked in front of strangers, he'd kept his gaze off her bare skin.

It was routine for the Oneroi to be beaten whenever they broke the rules. But he couldn't imagine Delphine doing anything to warrant such cruelty. He touched the faint scars as a wave of anger consumed him that someone would defile her body so. "What are these from?"

She put her shirt down and turned to face him. "My refusal to pursue Arik when he turned Skoti."

"Arik?" He didn't know that name.

"He was the Oneroi who came to me when I thought myself human. He tutored me and protected me until I was strong enough to fight on my own. You asked if I had a sibling . . . I always considered him a brother for his kindness in helping me. Therefore, I refused to hunt him even after they threatened me and carried out their beatings. I would have died before I betrayed what I felt I owed to him."

That was the kind of loyalty Jericho was desperate for. Just once.

He tried to tell himself that he'd had that with Nike, but he knew the truth. His sister could have helped him. Yet she never had. Not once in all these centuries.

She'd turned her back on him like the rest of them.

And it made his heart clench that Delphine was capable of it. "I commend your loyalty. It's a rare thing."

She shook her head. "I don't think so. And I don't think I'm any better a person than anyone else. So if I can stand by my principles, I know other people can, too. Case in point, Deimos and M'Adoc could turn against the Olympians and join Noir. Yet they'd rather be tortured than betray their people. Is that not loyalty?"

"So what?" he snarled. "I'm a bastard for betraying the Olympians? Is that what you're saying?"

"No. I'm . . ." She paused as if frustrated. "Forget it. You're beyond hearing me."

That set his fury to boil. She was dismissing him, and he couldn't stand it. "I'm not a piece of shit for you to flush and walk away!"

Delphine caught his face in her hands. "Jericho, relax. I haven't accused you of anything."

"You don't have to. Your eyes do it for you." He tried to pull away, but she held him in place.

Those eyes tore at him and weakened him as she gave him a gentle look. "Don't put your insecurities on me. I won't take that from you. I don't condemn you for what you've done. A single beating for disobeying orders doesn't equate to the betrayal you had, and I know that. While I was hurt, I wasn't thrown out, powerless, to survive on my own."

No, she hadn't been, and the fact that she understood the difference weakened him even more.

Then she did something no one had done in centuries.

She hugged him.

Jericho wanted to curse and shove her away, but the softness of her body against his . . . the sensation of her arms around him . . . he couldn't move. Deep inside, in the darkest place of his soul that he'd always denied, he craved this so desperately that all he could do was savor it.

Her blond hair was so soft on his face. Her breath tickled his neck. Before he could stop himself, he cradled her head in his hand and imagined himself inside her. Imagined what it would be like to have her loyal to him and to know he could depend on her to stand by his side no matter what.

What would that feel like?

Wanting to be closer to her, he dipped his head down and captured her lips.

Delphine was unprepared for the ferocity of his kiss. Yet for all the passion, he was still gentle as he tasted her. Her entire body exploded with heat and need. The hardness of him . . . the sensation of his hand in her hair . . . it was a heady mixture. No wonder the Skoti turned into incubi and succubi. If a kiss held this much pleasure, the other would have to be blinding.

His teeth nipped at her lips as his breathing intensified. Growling deep in his throat, he ravaged her mouth.

Delphine melted into him, reveling in the sinews of his body, the power of his desire.

He took her hand in his and slowly led it to the bulge in his pants.

Jericho trembled as she cupped him through his jeans. It'd been so long since a woman had touched him like this. For centuries, he'd craved the ability to stay hard whenever a woman neared him. Until now, that had only been a dream.

And he was desperate to be touched . . .

Needing release, he unzipped his pants and freed himself. Her touch faltered.

"Please," he whispered, pressing her hand against his cock. "Please don't pull away."

Delphine was afraid. What did he want from her? She wasn't ready to have sex with him. They barely knew each other.

But he didn't seem to be pawing at her for that. He wasn't encroaching on *her* body. Rather he used her hand to stroke his. "This is all I want from you," he whispered, his tone deep and heartfelt.

Nodding, she looked down at their entwined hands. This was a man who'd known nothing but suffering, and this gave him pleasure. How could she deprive him of something that wasn't hurting her?

For some reason she couldn't name, she couldn't bring herself to hurt him.

He buried his face in her neck as he thrust himself against her hand. His breathing was so ragged that it worried her. Was he okay?

"Jericho?"

The moment she said his name, he let out a fierce, primal growl as he released himself in her hand. His entire body shuddered violently. When he pulled back and met her gaze, his eye was a vibrant shade of blue as his wings shot out from his back and unfurled. They were black and huge as they fluttered softly, fanning her slightly.

Panting, he held her gaze with his. His cheeks were flushed bright red. He braced one arm on the wall behind her and leaned against it as he tried to calm his breathing.

"Are you all right?"

He answered her with a kiss so tender, she shivered. His lips were a mere whisper against hers. He wrapped his arms around her and held her like a lover.

Like she was precious.

No one had ever held her like this. And something inside her sparked from it. It felt so good to be held. To feel like she was part of him somehow. That they were something more than strangers.

Something more than enemies.

He trailed his kisses from her lips to her neck. Then he looked down at her wet hand. "I'm sorry. I didn't mean to make a mess." He manifested a small towel to clean her.

Delphine wasn't exactly sure what had happened, but there was a profound change in him now. He seemed calmer.

Kinder.

Did sex do that to everyone?

As soon as her hand was clean, he lifted it to his lips and placed the sweetest of kisses on her knuckles.

The way he looked at her made her tremble. She lifted her hand from his lips to touch the patch over his eye. "May I?"

She saw his uncertainty before he gave the subtlest of nods.

Afraid of what she'd find, she removed the patch slowly to see the depth of the scar that bisected his face. It was brutal and harsh. She could only imagine how much it must have hurt when Zeus did that to him.

But he still had his eye. It was milky white, and by the way he focused his gaze on her she could tell he wasn't blind in it.

"Why do you wear the patch?"

"It makes people less uncomfortable. They look away from the patch. They stare at the scar when it's uncovered as if trying to figure out what happened to cause it."

And it hurt him when they did that. He didn't say it in words, but his tone told her the truth.

She traced the shape of his eyebrow before she cupped his cheek in her hand. "I'm sorry they hurt you."

Jericho wanted to curse her for that sympathy, but he couldn't. Her words touched him as deeply as her caress.

"We should rest," he said, his voice thick. He was so sated now after his release that all he wanted was to curl up and hold her. But what killed him most was the knowledge that she didn't feel that way toward him. And he couldn't blame her.

She was a prisoner.

His prisoner.

And she'd given him the first real pleasure he'd had since Zeus pinned him to the floor in the temple hall. For that alone, he'd give her anything she asked. Thank the gods, she had no idea how weak he was right now.

How much power she held over him.

When she didn't protest his desire to go to bed, he closed his eyes and exchanged her clothes for a sleek pink nightgown. It draped like a dream over her slender body, highlighting her curves. Her nipples were hard and more than apparent through the satin.

What he wouldn't give for a taste of them. But he wouldn't take from her. Not without an invitation.

She gasped as the gown appeared and crossed her arms over her chest.

"I won't hurt you," he promised, stamping down the urge to brush his hand inside the deep V of her gown and cup her breast. How could he hurt her after what she'd just done for him? "We're just going to sleep."

She gave him a look that mirrored the suspicion he always held. Ignoring it, he changed his clothes for a pair of dark green flannel pajama bottoms. Normally he slept naked, but he was pretty sure she would protest that.

His patch forgotten, he tucked his wings into the skin of his back as he pulled her toward the bed.

Delphine wasn't sure about this. But she admired

the look of his sculpted backside as he moved away from her. He climbed into bed first, then waited for her.

"I've never slept with anyone in my life," he confessed.

"Neither have I." And she noticed he tucked his sword on the other side of his body as if he were afraid he might need it. The only question was, who did he think would attack him? One of the others?

Or her?

"What are you doing?"

"I'm . . ." A muscle worked in his jaw as he pierced her with a harsh stare. "I'm trusting you."

In that moment, she understood that he was more afraid of her than she was of him. It took a lot of faith to lie down at someone's side and trust them not to hurt you while you slept.

He was extending his hand to her. Deciding to take it, she smiled. "Truce?"

"Truce."

She joined him in bed and rolled onto her side so that her back was facing him.

After a few minutes, she felt his hand in her hair. "What are you doing?"

"Sorry." He immediately put more distance between them.

Tempted to roll over, she refused. She didn't want anything more than this. If she looked at him, he might misread her intentions, and who knew where that might lead.

Jericho lay on his back, watching her from the corner of his eye. It was so hard not to touch her when she was this close to him. The outline of her body under the covers was enough to make his body stir all over again.

The next time he came, he wanted to be inside her for it.

But that wouldn't be tonight. He'd seen the fear in her eyes when he'd pressed her hand against him. More than that, he knew the unspoken truth.

She was a virgin.

Most Oneroi were. At least those who'd been born after Zeus's curse. Since they didn't feel desire or love, they had nothing to motivate them for sex.

The Skoti were a different matter, as he'd seen earlier with Zeth. But Delphine . . .

She'd never been touched by anyone. He'd been the first to kiss her.

That thought brought a wave of possessive tenderness over him. Turning his head, he looked at her. She was completely relaxed and that tiny little snore started.

Smiling at it, he inched closer to her. The heat from her body warmed him even as the smoothness of her skin beckoned him to touch it. Unable to resist, he brushed his hand down her supple arm while he leaned forward to breathe her scent in. As he pulled back, his breath caught in his throat. The edge of her gown had been pushed back, showing him her bared breast.

Like her, it was beautiful. His body exploded with desire as he ground his teeth, wanting to sample it.

Back off . . .

He'd made her a promise and he wasn't about to

break it. Instead, he kissed her lightly on the head. "Good night, Delphine," he whispered, savoring the syllables of her name.

Rolling over, he closed his eyes and forced himself to ignore her.

As if . . .

But the sound of her breathing did lull him. And as he drifted off to sleep, a part of him imagined what it would be like to spend eternity with her by his side.

"DELPHINE?"

At the sound of her name, Delphine jerked up from where she was making a flower garland. She was in a quiet meadow . . . the one she'd played in as a girl. But now dark clouds were rolling in, blocking out the sun.

"Who's there?" she called.

A shadow of Zeth appeared.

She shot to her feet, ready to battle him. This was how they always attacked. He would bring others into her dream, and they would defeat her.

Zeth was a beautiful god, and his blue eyes normally glowed. But he looked sick now. His long black hair hung lankly around his gaunt face. Those eyes, now black instead of blue, were sunken.

"There's something wrong," he breathed.

"You've destroyed us."

"No, it's more than that. There's something Noir is feeding us. Don't . . ." He faded out, then reappeared. "Don't eat." Then he was gone.

Delphine turned around, looking for others. Was it a trick?

But there was no one else here.

She tried to use her powers. Again, they were worthless to her. It appeared that even in this realm, she was trapped.

Lightning flashed, followed by a tremendous clap of thunder. An angry wind plastered her clothes against her.

Delphine headed toward the woods where her house had once been. She didn't get far.

Azura was there on the pathway, blocking her. "What's the matter, child? Are you afraid?"

"Why are you here?"

Azura smiled, but the gesture didn't reach her cold eyes. "I have a gift for you."

"I don't want your presents."

She tsked. "You'll want this one."

Delphine started running. If she could reach the trees . . .

She didn't make it.

Azura appeared before her and caught her. Screaming, Delphine tried to fight. It was no use.

Azura threw her to the ground and shoved something in her mouth. "Swallow."

Delphine shook her head, trying to break free. She tried to spit the bitter-tasting gel from her mouth. Nothing worked.

"Swallow!" Azura shouted in a demonic voice.

Delphine choked, but in the end, she couldn't resist the order. The gel went down her throat.

She cried out as it seemed to slither through her.

Azura laughed. "He'll like you even more now." She pulled back and left Delphine on the ground.

Writhing in pain, she wanted to vomit and couldn't. But after a few minutes, the pain lessened.

And an unbearable heat started deep inside her. One that wouldn't let her sleep another minute.

Opening her eyes, she found herself still in bed with Jericho. Darkness enveloped them, and yet she could see the outline of his body perfectly.

Needing a taste of him, she attacked.

AZURA LAUGHED AS SHE RETURNED TO THE WAR room, where Noir sat feeding one of his ugly black hounds.

He glanced up with a stern frown. "You look pleased."

"I am. I've just guaranteed us a little more time of Cratus being out of our hair."

"Good." He patted the hound on the head. "He's entirely too nosy. I found out from one of my pets that he was downstairs talking to Deimos and Jaden."

She hissed like a cat at the name of Jaden. If there was one creature she hated, he was it. "It seems our little broker hasn't learned his lesson."

"Does he ever?"

She curled her lip. "Such a pity we can't kill him."

"At least he bleeds well. Something the others don't do."

"True." Azura trailed her hand along the back of his chair. "Have you found your Malachai?"

"Only the city. Ma'at and the Atlantean god Apostolos are guarding him so that I can't find his exact location. But I will tear that city apart until I do."

She paused by his side. "Perhaps you don't have to."

"What do you mean?"

"One of my demons told me that there's a group of gallu looking for a haven."

Noir looked up with interest. "Gallu?" Those were Sumerian demons and some of the most brutal of any demons. Best of all, the blood of a gallu was infectious and could turn their victims into zombies.

"Shall we invite them in?"

Noir smiled. "Absolutely. And I know their first victim."

"Cratus."

He nodded and Azura laughed. With Cratus bitten, they would be in complete and utter control of him.

Then, even without the Malachai or their sister Braith, the world would be theirs forever.

CHAPTER 7

JERICHO CAME AWAKE THE MOMENT DELPHINE touched him. For a heartbeat, he thought she was fighting him until he realized just how wrong that assumption was.

Completely naked, she rubbed her body against his. *Oh, gah . . . What did I do right?*

His senses spun as she groped him, and his body begged and burned for more. Her hands were everywhere, stroking, dipping and cupping. His breathing ragged, he groaned in pleasure and ground his teeth.

You're not this lucky. Wake up, asshole!

But that was the last thing he wanted to do. He wanted to be her plaything.

Most of all, he wanted to be her chew toy.

More likely you're her patsy. She's going to screw you over, and not the way you want her to.

When was the last time a woman mauled you like this?

Delphine was a virgin, and unless they were in a porn movie he didn't know about, women like her didn't do this to men who were holding them prisoner.

That reality check went over him like ice water. Shaking himself mentally, he pushed her back. "What are you doing?"

She answered him with a scorching kiss. His senses on fire, he rolled with her, trapping her under him. Still she ran her hands over his body, making him crazy with lust, especially since the hairs at the juncture of her thighs teased his hip bone, making him crave a taste of that part of her.

"Please," she begged, her voice cracking. "I'm on fire. I need you."

Jericho froze as he realized she had the same drugged look in her eyes that Zeth had held in his. And she was every bit as out of control. More to the point, her eyes were jet black and not their normal shade.

What had they done to her?

She nipped at his chin, pulling his hair as she continued to buck against him, making his body hard and heavy. "I need you inside me." It was a raw demand.

He sucked his breath in sharply as she cupped him in her hand. "Stop!"

Are you out of your fucking mind? You want this!

Yes, yes, he did. He really did. But not with a woman who wasn't in control of herself.

Yes, you do. Look at her. She's gorgeous and all over you. Take her!

Just look at that body . . .

No kidding. She was truly a goddess in every sense of the word. With the exception of the scars on her back, there wasn't a flaw on her.

Then do what she asks . . . worship her until you're both limping.

His inner voice was relentless. And it was hard to stay in control, especially since she'd pulled his pants down to his hips and had him in her hands as she massaged his cock.

Damn, she was a quick learner.

He had to give himself a jolt as she tried to guide him into her body. "Delphine!" he shouted, trying to make her hear him. "Stop it!"

She tugged at his cock.

He almost came just from the sheer pleasure of it.

Give her what she wants!

Growling in frustration, he launched his wings and moved far enough away that she couldn't reach him. His heart racing, he stared down at the bed where she lay with her legs slightly parted. Every part of him wanted to join her.

I am a rank idiot.

"Jericho." Her plea tore through his heart.

He pulled his pants up as he hovered over the bed, wanting her with a passion so biting, it was all he could do to stave it off. "What did they do to you?"

She glared up at him. "Fine. If you won't help me, I'll find someone who will." She rolled off the bed.

Jericho shot to the door to block her way before she left and found Asmodeus or someone else he'd have to kill for touching her. He cupped her face in his hands. "Delphine, stop. Tell me what happened."

She fought him until she realized he wasn't budging.

"Answer me," he insisted.

Her gaze was unfocused as his voice finally reached her. "I was dreaming . . ."

"And?"

She frowned as if she couldn't recall. "Azura was there. She came after me."

"What did she do?"

Delphine paused again before she answered. "She gave me food. Food . . . Zeth told me not to eat, but I couldn't stop her. She forced me to eat it."

Jericho cursed. So that was how they were getting the Skoti. They were drugging them.

She groaned softly as she rubbed her naked body against his again. "I'm on fire, Jericho. Please help me. I can't stand how much it burns."

He let out his breath. Well, she already hated him. Obeying her wouldn't change anything.

She took his hand from her face and led it to her breast. Her puckered nipple teased his palm, making him harder than he'd ever been before. "Please."

What man could argue with that, god or otherwise? Scooping her up in his arms, he returned her to the bed. The sweet scent of her body was branded into him as he skimmed his hand over her bare stomach. But he didn't want to take from her while she was like this. This wasn't *her*.

It was the drug talking. The drug begging for him. But she was still in pain from it.

So he gently separated the folds of her body to stroke her. She cried out in relief and pulled him close so that she could kiss him senseless.

Jericho's body strained, begging for him to take her. But in spite of all that had happened to him, he wasn't an animal. He wouldn't prey on her.

He was better than that, and for the first time in centuries, he believed it.

Delphine trembled with the incredible sensation of his fingers soothing her. They teased and excited her in a way she wouldn't have thought possible.

Finally something was stamping down the fierce ache inside her.

When he pulled back from her lips, she actually whimpered. Where was he going?

She had her answer as he slid himself down between her legs and took her into his mouth. Unable to bear the sheer ecstasy of it, she cried out, burying her hand in his soft hair. Never had she imagined anything so splendid. The heat of his mouth combined with the strokes of his tongue and fingers was blinding.

She looked down to meet his gaze. The primal heat in his mismatched eyes set her on fire.

Jericho growled at the taste of her. His body was so hard and ready, but he was used to controlling those urges. Right now, it was her orgasm he was after.

And the truth was, he enjoyed the way she tasted, the sound of her pleasured murmurs as she played with his hair. He'd missed the comfort of being touched. The smell and taste of a lover. He could spend the rest of the night like this, just savoring her.

Delphine shivered at the long stroke he delivered, especially as he dragged his whiskered cheek down her cleft. It went through her with ribbons of pleasure.

Biting her lip, she felt her body clenching tighter until she couldn't stand it anymore. In one moment of supreme bliss, her body burst.

She screamed out, clutching him to her as he continued to lick and tease, making her orgasm all the more intense.

When he'd finally wrung the last spasm out of her, he moved forward to rest his chin on her stomach while he lay between her legs. He traced a small circle around her navel as his gaze held hers.

"Better?"

"Yes," she breathed as she brushed her hand through his hair. "Much better."

He nuzzled her stomach with his whiskers, adding another shiver to her.

Delphine sighed in utter contentment as she felt the fire draining out of her to be replaced by a sense of utter satisfaction. "So that's what those feel like, huh?" No wonder he'd been so calm and kind after his orgasm. She really did feel at peace right now.

Then she became aware of the fact that she was completely naked. Exposed.

He was lying between her open legs. . . .

No one had ever seen her like this. No one.

Heat crept over her face as horror filled her.

Jericho lifted himself up as he became aware of the change in her. She was tense now. Her face flushed as her eyes returned to the beautiful shade that haunted him. "What's wrong?"

She tried to cover herself. "What have I done? I'm so embarrassed."

He moved to her side before he pulled the sheet over her. "Don't be. You weren't in control."

She covered her face with the sheet. "How can I look at you after that?"

Jericho stifled a smile at her dire tone. Her reserve amused him, but he did feel bad for her. He tugged lightly at the covers until she had to look at him. "You're beautiful, Delphine. There's no shame in what we've done."

"But—"

He kissed her words away. "No buts. I don't want you to be embarrassed with me. Ever."

Delphine smiled at him, grateful for his kindness. What amazed her most was the fact that he hadn't taken advantage of her, even though she'd begged him to. He had helped her out selflessly. Even now, she felt how rigid his erection was, but he made no demands on her.

She'd been wrong about him. He did have compassion, after all. He could have walked away or taken her ruthlessly any way he wanted to. But he hadn't. Even though he was still hard, he'd withheld himself.

For her.

Her heart warm with that knowledge, she placed her hand on his scarred cheek. He nipped playfully at her thumb.

"We have to do something about this, Jericho. I don't know what Azura gave me, but it's terrible what it does."

"There's no telling what they've found, but the question is why give it to the Skoti? Why incapacitate an army that you want to fight for you?"

"Maybe they don't want them to fight. Maybe it's something else they're after."

He grimaced. "Such as?"

"I don't know. You're supposed to be the one with the Source connection and fighting expertise."

"Yeah, but that doesn't give me any insight into evil. You have to remember that Noir and Azura are cut from an entirely different bolt than I was."

Delphine was glad to hear him say that. There was nothing redeeming about either Azura or Noir.

Brushing her hands through his hair, she was amazed at how relaxed she was while lying naked with a man. His breath tickled her face, and even though his weight should have been heavy, it was comforting to have him pressing against her.

Was this what love was like?

No, maybe not love, it was too soon for that. But there was something very bonding about this shared moment. It was familiar and comforting.

"Do you think we can get the others free?"

He looked up at her with his mismatched eyes. "You calmed down rather quickly once I"—he flashed her a devilish grin—"placated you. They must be constantly feeding the others to keep them like this. Which again begs the question of why."

"We have to get them out of here."

He made a sound of disagreement. "Saving Olympians isn't my priority."

She yanked his hair.

"Ow!"

"You're lucky that's all I'm pulling on," she said sternly. "Those are my brothers and sisters you're talking about."

Jericho looked away as those words resonated inside him. They were his, too. For all the good it did them. "I'm not a god of forgiveness, Delphine."

"No, you're a god of strength, and the greatest

strength of all is being able to forgive the people who've harmed you. Even greater still is the ability to fight to defend them. Be a better person than they were. I know you can be."

Jericho shook his head. "You have more faith in me than I deserve."

Her gaze burned him with its intensity. "I disagree. I have seen the other side of you and that's the side I'm appealing to. There's more to you than hatred and fighting. You have a beautiful heart, Jericho. I know it."

The only problem was he didn't. He couldn't find forgiveness inside him. Only bitter resentment. Utter hatred. Contempt.

Until he looked at her.

She alone had made him feel something else. But the problem was he didn't understand what she stirred inside him. At least other than lust. That he knew intimately.

But the part of him that was holding her now was alien and frightening. He didn't know or understand it.

It was the same foreign place that had defied Zeus to save her life.

She owed him, and for some reason, he couldn't bring himself to force her to pay him for his sacrifice. He only wanted what she was willing to give him.

What is wrong with me?

He'd always been the type of person to take what he wanted. But it was so different with her. Closing his eyes, he savored the sensation of her flesh under his cheek. The gentle strokes of her hands in his hair.

He never wanted to leave this.

Delphine ran her finger down the stubble of his cheek. She loved the feeling of his skin. So different from hers. Most of all, she was stunned that he lay so calmly with her. She knew the violence he was capable of and yet . . .

It was like taming a ferocious beast that she knew wouldn't be so kind to another living soul.

Only she knew this side of him, and it made her treasure it all the more. Treasure him.

"Jericho?"

They both jumped at the quiet voice that whispered through the room.

Jericho covered her. "Jaden?" he asked in an equally hushed tone.

Jaden appeared in the corner as nothing more than a faint mist. He looked worse than when Jericho had seen him earlier. There were fresh bruises on his face and blood on one side of his mouth. But he seemed oblivious to the pain. "They're plotting against you."

"Who?"

Jaden gave him a "duh" stare. "Your best friends, fool, who do you think? The Easter Bunny or the assholes who brought you here? FYI, they're planning to feed you to the gallu so that they can control your powers without your fighting them. If I were you, I'd be gone five minutes ago."

Jericho tensed suspiciously. Why would Jaden help him? "How do I know you're not lying?"

"I have no reason to lie. But if you want to hang out

here and get eaten, far be it from me to stop you. As is, my ass is fertilizer if they catch me talking to you."

Still, Jericho was skeptical. People didn't help him, and he found it hard to imagine Jaden doing so without getting something in return.

"I believe him," Delphine whispered. "I don't trust Noir."

Jericho snorted. "I don't trust *anyone*." And especially not the evil who'd brought him here. He'd been suspicious of them from the moment Azura had first approached him.

"Maybe you should try trusting *me* for once," she said in a determined tone.

Jericho was torn. He really didn't know if he could trust Jaden, and yet he had no reason to doubt him. It made sense. Why give him his powers back unless they knew they had complete control over him? He wouldn't make that mistake, especially given the totality of his powers. If he'd brought him over, he would have put him under lock and key.

Just to be safe.

Look at how they treated Jaden. It was obvious fair play and kindness weren't part of their world.

But he had another problem. "Where do we go?"

Delphine frowned. "What do you mean?"

"If I go to Olympus with powers, Zeus, in spite of what he says, will attack me. I have no doubt."

She shook her head. "That's not true. He promised to give you all of your powers back."

Jericho laughed. "I think that's what you heard. I don't believe for a nanosecond it's what he said."

"I'm not lying."

"I'm not saying you are. Tell me verbatim what thunder-ass said to you."

She let out a frustrated breath. "He said that so long as you fought against Noir and the Skoti, you'd have your powers."

Jericho cast a droll look at Jaden's mist. "What does that sound like to you?"

"That you will only have your powers when you fight against Noir and the Skoti."

"Yeah, exactly."

Delphine frowned. "Isn't that what I just said?"

"No," Jericho answered. "You heard that my powers would be returned to me. What I hear is that I'm a lapdog unless I'm fighting to protect their scabbing hides."

"He's right. After what he's done to Cratus, Zeus would never take the chance of giving him unfettered powers."

"He knows what I'd do with them and more to the point, what I'd do to *him* with them."

Delphine felt sick that she'd been so easily duped. But then, as Jericho had pointed out, she'd heard what she wanted to. What they were saying made a lot more sense. "Then what do we do?"

Go to New Orleans. Jaden's voice was in their heads as if he was too afraid of being heard even in a whisper. *Find Acheron Parthenopaeus. Let him know what's happening and he can help.*

"Why would he do that?" Jericho asked.

"For the love of the Source, Jericho," Jaden snapped. "Do it. He's the only hope you have right now."

Jericho opened his mouth to argue. But before he could make a single sound, the door flew open, disintegrating Jaden's mist form.

"Knock, knock."

It was a gallu demon, and he wasn't alone.

CHAPTER 8

JERICHO DRESSED HIMSELF AND DELPHINE IMMEDI-
ately. He started to launch himself at the gallu, but Delphine caught him and pulled him back. "You can't.
One scratch or bite where your blood mingles with
their spit or blood and you're under their control. Think
about it."

But it wasn't in him not to fight.

Growling with rage, he covered himself in black
body armor. "They better be able to penetrate Kevlar."

Delphine was stunned as he went for them. He caught
the first one with a punch so hard, it lifted the gallu three
feet into the air and sent him slamming into the wall behind him. The second one tried to take a bite out of Jericho, but he caught the gallu by his shirt and flipped him
over his shoulder. In one swift move, he pulled his dagger out and went for the third.

Delphine gasped as the one on the floor got up and
rushed toward her. Without armor or her powers, she
was defenseless. She looked around but there was
nowhere to go. No way to outrun him.

She was trapped.

Just as the gallu would have reached her, he rebounded off an invisible wall. It took her a second to realize what had happened.

"Ha!" she said triumphantly as he smacked it with his fist. Jericho must have used his powers to shield her.

The gallu wasn't happy as it opened its mouth to show her two rows of serrated fangs. She lifted her chin and gave him her best "neener, neener" smile.

"Sooner or later, you're mine," he promised.

She scoffed at him. "Careful, baby, I bite back." Just not today and not without her powers. Lucky for him because when it came to fighting, she seldom had an equal.

Jericho, on the other hand, was in his glory as he beat them down. She'd never seen anyone enjoy a fight more. At least not until five more joined the first three. Undaunted, he kept going, but she wasn't so audacious.

Even the strongest of the strong could be overrun and killed when this badly outnumbered.

One bite. One scratch. He would be gone forever.

"Jericho, please!" she begged as they attacked him at once. "It's not worth the chance. I don't want you to get hurt. Please stop."

Jericho hesitated at the anguish he heard in Delphine's voice. Glancing over his shoulder, he saw the concern on her face as he punched one gallu and then scissor-kicked another. Her hand was splayed against the invisible wall he had around her. Her brow was taut as her eyes begged him to listen. She looked so upset.

Most of all, she cared . . .

For him.

Such a simple, unbelievable thing. Only Nike had ever shown that to him and never with the kind of passion that Delphine was showing now. It gave him pause.

A shadow crossed in front of him.

It was Noir.

Noir looked around at the gallu with a disgusted sneer. "Do I have to do everything for you bastards? Stupid, worthless dogs. Hold him down and bite him. How hard is that?" Noir sent a blast straight at Jericho's chest.

There was no way to avoid or deflect it. Jericho cursed as it sent him reeling and skidding across the floor. The pain of it caused him to drop the shield around Delphine.

She kicked the gallu back as it ran for her.

Jericho rolled to his feet. His instincts were to attack the gallu in front of him and then go after Noir. Instead he dodged the gallu and went for Delphine, who had no way to protect herself.

The moment he touched her, he teleported them out of the room and back to his apartment to keep her safe.

Or so he thought.

Noir and the gallu followed them and flashed into the room right behind them.

Jericho looked at Delphine's panicked expression. And he knew what he had to do. There was no other way.

Delphine's heart sank at the number of gallu at Noir's command. Where had they come from? They didn't stand a chance against them.

But she didn't have time to think about that as Jericho faced her. She was waiting for him to fight them. Instead, he pulled her closer to him. Before she could ask him what he was doing, he reached for her neck.

And pulled her collar off.

Stunned, it took her a minute to realize what he'd done and why. He didn't want her hurt. He was putting her safety above his own.

Warmth spread through her.

"Go," he said, his eyes tormented. "Get to safety."

"What about you?"

"They're just going to follow me wherever I go." He kissed her lightly on the lips. "Leave." He gently pushed her away, then turned to confront the demons.

Nothing had ever touched her more than what he was doing.

For her.

She met Noir's gaze and saw his next intent plainly. He was going to use her to get at Jericho. Every part of her wanted to stay and fight, but she knew she couldn't. She was a liability he couldn't afford to have.

There was no way to win this.

But she wasn't going to leave Jericho at their mercy. Not like this. He was way too outnumbered and even with armor, he wouldn't be able to hold them for more than a few minutes.

Rushing Jericho from behind, she wrapped her arms around his taut, muscular body and teleported him out of the room and to Olympus.

The moment he realized where he was, he turned on her, his face a mask of fury. She could tell he'd rather be eaten by the gallu than spend one second in the Oneroi hall. "What did you do?"

"I saved you."

His expression was furious. "Saved me, my ass. I can't be here. I don't *want* to be here."

"I know," she said, trying to soothe him, "but it gives us a breather from Noir. He can't come here and he damn sure can't bring the gallu into our domain."

Jericho growled at her. It was true, and he knew it. However, it didn't change the fact that this place brought back vivid memories that he wanted to keep buried.

He hated it here.

Delphine cupped his face in her hands. "It's all right, Jericho. Forget the past. Things have changed."

Had they? "We're in the hall of the Oneroi. It looks the same now as it did then."

"It might look it, but there are no Oneroi here now. It's just us."

And Phobos, who came through the door looking astonished. "I can't believe it. You're back here . . . together. I was sure I would never see you again. What the hell did you do?"

"Don't ask," Delphine said sheepishly, making Jericho wonder if she hadn't known Phobos would be here.

Jericho's open hostility didn't bother the god at all as he came forward to stop in front of Delphine. "Did you see Deimos?"

Jericho was going to refuse to answer, but he knew how close the two of them were. And while he had a grudge against Deimos, it was no reason to be a total dickhead to Phobos. "He's in bad shape, but alive."

The relief on Phobos's face was tangible. "Is there any way to get him out?"

Delphine shook her head. "I don't know. We barely made it out. And now we have gallu after us. Along with Noir."

Phobos's expression was total astonishment. "The Sumerian gallu demons?"

She nodded.

He let out a disgusted sound as he turned his attention to Jericho. "Damn, Cratus, do you have to piss off everyone you meet?"

Intending to thoroughly trounce the bastard, Jericho took a step toward him only to find Delphine in his way.

"You're not going to hurt him."

"Wanna bet?"

She planted herself firmly in his path, hands on both of his shoulders. "Yes, I do. And I *will* win."

Jericho looked down and paused. Anyone else would have been hammered for daring to stop him. The fact that she was so tiny in comparison to him just made it all the more laughable. He could crush her and not even feel it.

And yet, he wasn't about to take her on, which was probably the funniest part of all. What was wrong with him that he had no will when it came to her?

Stepping back, he narrowed his gaze at Phobos. "Say thank you to her, Dolophonos. She just kept you from getting your ass handed to you."

Phobos arched a brow and stepped forward.

"Stop it!" Delphine snapped, turning on Phobos and forcing him back a step. "One more round of Grand Testosterone and I swear I'll geld you both where you stand."

Phobos held his hands up in surrender, which made Jericho feel somewhat better. He wasn't the only one intimidated by a Chihuahua.

The Dolophonos looked over her head to meet Jericho's gaze. "Any idea how to get my brother out of there?"

"Dynamite. With any luck it might blow the bastard up, too."

Phobos wasn't amused.

Delphine let out an exasperated breath before she answered him. "Jaden told us to find someone named Acheron Parthenopaeus. Do you know him?"

Phobos choked. "Yeah, I do. I'm surprised you don't."

"Why?"

"He's an Atlantean god, known as Apostolos. He used to spend a lot of time with Artemis, but we don't talk about that. Tends to make the sour redhead even surlier than normal, and it sends Apollo off into a screaming fit."

From where Jericho stood, that could be entertaining. He wouldn't mind beating the shit out of Apollo for a few rounds.

Delphine scowled. "I don't spend much time in the hall of the gods or with Artemis. I try to avoid any nuclear fallout that comes from that entire crew."

"Yeah, well, at six foot eight, Acheron's a hard man to miss. Anyway, he's a major badass. But I don't know if even he can take on Noir and win."

Jericho shrugged. "Jaden thinks he can."

"Then let's go see my buddy and see what he thinks."

Jericho crossed his arms over his chest as Phobos took them to a small shotgun house in the French Quarter. Oddly enough, it was only a few blocks away from where he had been working at Landry's.

Delphine frowned at the well-kept, unassuming place that had pretty, white lacework trim. It blended in perfectly with all the other houses on the street. Nothing marked it as anything special. More than that, she didn't sense anything out of the ordinary. No powers or anything else. "A god lives here?"

Phobos laughed at her tone. "Believe it or not. And this is a much nicer and bigger place than the apartment he used to have here in Nawlin's."

Still, she was skeptical. She just couldn't imagine an all-powerful entity calling this . . . home.

"If you say so," she said in a singsong tone.

Phobos smiled. "And I do. I also say follow me." He walked up to the door and knocked.

"Why didn't we just pop in?" Jericho asked as he allowed Delphine to ascend the stairs first.

Phobos made an amused choking sound. "You can't. He has it shielded. Besides, he's a god and can be a nasty one if you upset him. You try popping into any place where his beloved wife is and you'll get fried faster than chicken at KFC. He doesn't have a sense of humor when it comes to her. So wipe the frown off your face before you hurt her feelings and get gutted for it."

Given that extensive warning and the passion in Phobos's voice, Delphine was expecting a goddess to answer the door. Someone who would make Aphrodite tremble in fear and shame.

So when the door opened to show her a very average-looking woman with nondescript brown hair that was pulled into pigtails, she was confused. The only thing the woman had in common with most goddesses was her tall height and beautiful hair. The rest of her appeared completely human.

Dressed in a long, beige skirt and green sweater, she gave them a bright, friendly smile. "Hey, Phobos, what are you doing here?"

Phobos returned her smile. "Hi, Tory. We're here to see the big guy. Is he around?"

"Sure." She stepped back and opened the door for them to enter.

Phobos walked in first, with Delphine two steps behind and Jericho pulling up the rear. The house was very normal. Quaint and orderly, it was decorated in neutral tones: dark browns, golds and a little rust. Again it was nothing out of the ordinary, except for maybe the Greek artifacts and statues of the Olympian gods that were sprinkled throughout nooks and crannies. There were also happy family photos scattered about and a small Bengal cat in the corner napping on the floor while a sunbeam warmed its exposed belly.

Delphine's gaze stopped dead on one picture in particular. It was a younger Tory in the ruins of an ancient

Greek temple with a blond woman and a dark-haired man. . . . A man Delphine knew very well.

"Arik?" she said in stunned surprise.

Tory cocked a brow. "You know my cousin's husband?"

"I'm not sure . . . He looks like someone I used to know."

"It's the same Arik." That had to be the deepest voice Delphine had ever heard, and it was tinged with an accent she hadn't heard in centuries.

Atlantean.

Turning in the direction it came from, she saw an extremely tall man sitting in an armchair with a black electric guitar in his lap.

His hair was dyed a deep purple shade and his eyes were a peculiar swirling silver color. Dressed as a human goth, he didn't look any older than his early twenties. But the aura of power that enveloped him set off every warning bell in her body. This wasn't a human being.

This was an extremely powerful immortal.

One who looked to be the complete polar opposite of the woman who smiled at him. And when he returned the smile to her, the look in his eyes said that Tory was his entire world.

Gods, what she wouldn't give to have a man look at her like that.

Tory moved to stand behind him with one hand on his shoulder. The god appeared relaxed, and yet Delphine had no doubt that if they made a single move he didn't like, he would snap them down to burnt toast in a heartbeat.

"What's up, Pho?" he asked Phobos.

Phobos laughed. "Like you didn't know before I knocked on the door." He turned to indicate them. "Delphine and . . ." Phobos hesitated on what he should call him.

"Jericho," Jericho said from between clenched teeth.

Phobos didn't respond to the anger in his tone. "Jericho and Delphine, meet Ash Parthenopaeus and his wife, Soteria. Tory for short."

Delphine was surprised by the introduction, especially since she knew this wasn't the same Soteria from Olympus. "You're named for the Greek goddess of safety?"

Soteria's face lit up, then quickly turned into a concerned "oh." "You're one of them, aren't you?"

"One of whom?" Delphine asked.

"Ash's"—Tory made quotes in the air with her fingers—"special friends. No one else ever knows who I'm named after. It's too obscure." She looked down at her husband and shook her head. "No wonder she knew Arik. Makes total sense now. Do all the Greek gods know each other?"

Ash laced his fingers with hers on his shoulder. "Not always and definitely not intimately. It's a rather large pantheon. Delphine is an Oneroi. Hence her acquaintance with your cousin Geary's husband. Jericho you would know better as the god Cratus."

Both of Tory's brows shot up. "*Prometheus Unbound* Cratus?"

Ash nodded.

"Oh," Tory said slowly, looking Jericho up and

down with a gaze of appreciation and fear. "I'm sure you're still a very nice . . . god, right?"

Jericho wasn't amused, but he wasn't about to pick a fight with her over it. He wasn't afraid of Ash, but he knew a god this powerful wouldn't be an easy one to fight. Win, lose or draw, it would be bloody.

And long.

Tory looked down at Ash. "Why are they here?"

"Noir is after them." The fact that Acheron knew that without them having to tell him said it all about his powers.

But it didn't answer Jericho's main question. "Why would Jaden send us to you?"

Ash grinned roguishly. "'Cause I'm a genuinely nice guy who plays a mean guitar."

Tory laughed. "Spoken only by someone who doesn't know what a grump you are in the morning."

Unamused, Jericho gave them a droll stare. "You know, that might be funny if the situation wasn't so dire. You do realize Noir could be here any minute."

Ash let go of Tory's hand to idly strum a chord as if he didn't have a care in the universe. "No, he can't. I mean, yes, he *could* in theory. But it would get bloody fast and while he may or may not be stronger than I am, he won't risk the repercussions of taking me on."

"Why not?"

"He might have the gallu. But I command the Charonte demons. If he wants a battle, I can give it to him, and in numbers that would ruin his best day."

Jericho was adequately impressed. "I thought the Charonte vanished with Atlantis."

"You were mistaken. They're alive and well, and more than eager to feast on gallu meat. For that matter, there's an entire club of them here in town."

Jericho cocked one brow. "Are you serious?"

"Like the grave."

For the first time, Jericho let out a relieved breath. Things were starting to look up for them. The Charonte were natural enemies to the gallu and best of all, they were immune to the gallu's bites. With them at their side, they at least stood a fighting chance.

At least until Ash spoke again. "The other reason Jaden sent you to me . . . I'm training the Malachai."

Jericho couldn't have been more stunned had Ash stood up and hit him with the guitar. "Are you out of your mind? Why would you train an instrument of destruction?"

Ash shrugged. "We all choose our destinies. Our birth doesn't dictate our future unless we allow it."

Jericho rolled his eyes at the laissez-faire attitude. "How naive can one god be?"

Tory smiled indulgently. "Acheron is the Harbinger for the Atlantean Destroyer. Prophecy said he would be the one to destroy the world, and yet he's one of its fiercest protectors. Even though he was conceived to be the tool his mother would use for annihilation, he's never once given in to his destiny." She looked down at him and shook her head. "And the gods know he's had more cause to wish the world to end than anyone else I know."

Acheron kissed her hand. "So you see, I know a thing or two about training a destroyer and teaching him how to fight his natural urges. We're only in trouble if we leave the Malachai on his own and then Noir gets his hands on him."

Jericho still had his doubts about that. "So say you. You have no way of knowing if, once he's trained, he'll follow you or Noir."

"True. But then again, you're here when just a few hours ago you were willing to fight to the death at Noir's side."

"The bastard betrayed and attacked me. No one turns me into a mindless supplicant. He should have known better than to try."

"And I believe when the time comes, Nick will make the same decision. He might hate me, but he doesn't follow anyone too blindly."

Since Jericho didn't know the Malachai personally, he wasn't willing to put that much faith in him. "Do you know that for sure?"

"Call me optimistic, but I'm going to say yes." Ash held his hand out to indicate the chairs behind them. "To quote my wife, cop a squat. We need to figure out a way to rescue the Oneroi and Skoti before Noir turns them into gallu."

Delphine went cold at the thought. If that were to happen . . .

Mankind would be completely doomed.

"Do you think we can free Jaden, too?" she asked as she sat down on the couch next to Jericho. Phobos sat on the other side of her.

Acheron shook his head. "Unfortunately, Jaden's lost to us, but he's still an ally when he can be."

Tory frowned as she continued to stand behind Acheron. "What about Jared?"

Delphine duplicated the expression. "Who's Jared?"

Ash's answer amazed her. "The last Sephiroth." The Sephirii had been created to fight Noir and his army of Malachai back in the time before man and recorded history.

Delphine was extremely confused. "I thought after Noir and the Source had their war that all of the Malachai and Sephirii were put down."

"They were," Ash explained. "All except for the one Sephiroth who betrayed his brethren. He was damned to an eternity of slavery. Since the universe is real big on balance, one Malachai was spared to rain death on the Sephiroth should he ever go free. That Malachai still holds all the power needed to realign the entire universe that would put Noir at the top of the food chain."

Jericho glanced at Delphine before he turned back to Acheron. "Why is the Malachai not with Noir?"

"Nick's father had a break with him. No one knows why. Centuries ago, the elder Malachai went into hiding with Noir and Azura chasing him every step of the way. A couple of decades ago, he decided to lay an egg and our current Malachai was born. As soon as Nick reached an age to replace his father, the old Malachai died."

Delphine still didn't quite understand. "So why has Noir been unable to find this Nick?"

"Nick's powers were bound to protect and shield him from Noir and give him a chance to be turned from his original purpose. It wasn't until a Source god attacked him that those powers were unlocked so that he could defend himself. I've been attempting to train him ever since."

Tory gave a scoffing laugh. " 'Attempting' is right."

Jericho narrowed his gaze as he honed in on that one word and its implications. The last thing they needed was a trained Malachai at their throats. "He's resistant to it?"

Ash shook his head. "Not to the training or his destiny. The problem is, he hates my guts. It's a personal problem we have to resolve."

Tory let out an undignified snort. "They're working on it . . . slowly."

"Great." Jericho sighed. "So where does that leave us with the Sephiroth?"

"Well, the biggest problem is his current master just happens to be the Daimon queen. Since I and my Dark-Hunter brethren hunt and execute her Daimons, she's not really inclined to be on our side or do us any favors. But who knows? We might catch her on a really good day."

Yeah, right. "Not bloody likely."

"My thoughts, too."

Delphine let out a tired breath. "We're completely ruined. My brethren are in the hands of evil, about to be turned into mindless predators, and the only hope we have is an untrained Malachai who might leave us to fight for them and a Sephiroth in the hands of the Daimons."

Daimons were a vampiric race who lived by stealing and destroying human souls. Best of all, they adamantly hated the Greek gods since Apollo was the one who'd cursed them to drink blood and die painfully and horribly at the age of twenty-seven. The only way to survive beyond that was to take human souls.

As a result, the Daimons weren't big on helping anyone except themselves. Not that she blamed them. They had been royally screwed by her pantheon.

Delphine was ill with their predicament. "It's not a good day to be human, is it?"

"It's not a good day to be us, either," Phobos added sarcastically.

Delphine couldn't agree more. "You think Noir will team up with the Daimons?"

Ash shook his head. "Stryker, while screwed up, won't fight with them. They have no code. Stryker and his people aren't fighting to kill, they're fighting to survive. We're lucky in that. He only allows his people to take the lives they need to . . . and that of any Dark-Hunter they can find since we're his biggest predators. While I'm sure he wouldn't shirk at world domination, his priority is the survival of his people. Noir, on the other hand, kills for pleasure and wants to overthrow *all* pantheons and take over. Neither Stryker nor his wife are big into following other people. They will fight him until they're dead."

Jericho scratched his cheek. "Maybe we ought to let the two of them fight it out."

Phobos snorted. "That's got pay-per-view all over it. Unfortunately, we'd get caught in the crossfire."

"I still think they might team up with Noir," Delphine insisted. It would make sense. The Daimons could take the humans while the gallu took the rest of them.

"No," Ash said adamantly. "I know Stryker, and besides, the gallu *were* with him up until a few months ago when they tried to eat him, his wife and his daughter. Being the most unforgiving of souls, he's not going to welcome them in any time soon. As a result, the Daimons are having open season on them. For now, we're safe in terms of *that*."

Jericho still wasn't fully convinced. "But screwed in terms of everything else."

"Not entirely." Ash looked at Phobos. "How many of your people do you have left?"

"Couple dozen . . . maybe."

Ash nodded thoughtfully. "We can work with that."

"What about the gallu?" Jericho asked.

"I can get the Charonte to help with them. It just leaves one thing . . ."

"The Sephiroth," Jericho said. Even though he was a Source god, Jericho couldn't handle Azura, Noir, the Skoti, *and* the gallu alone. They needed help. "I think we need to talk to the Daimons."

Ash inclined his head. "I couldn't agree more."

CHAPTER 9

JERICHO WAS DESCENDING INTO HELL. WELL, MORE
like an Atlantean hell realm called Kalosis, but still . . .
why argue tit for tat?

Hell was hell, no matter the pantheon.

Delphine had stayed behind with Phobos, after
much argument. But Acheron had agreed that the
fewer people asking, the better chance they would
have.

Stryker and his wife, Zephyra, would respect a
single emissary. Two or more, they might consider
lunch.

Tory led Jericho down a black marble hallway
holding a light stick over her head. It reflected off the
walls with an eerie luminescence that would be
haunting if he were human. As it was, he found their
distorted images fascinating.

They were heading toward Stryker's reception hall.

Since Acheron couldn't come here without starting the apocalypse, Tory had volunteered to guide
Jericho and make the introductions. Apparently part
of Acheron's duties as Harbinger was to release his

mother from her prison . . . which happened to be the realm they were in.

If Acheron so much as made a tiny appearance here, his mother would go free and destroy the world, so he could never see her.

Would have been tragic if Jericho were capable of feeling sympathy for someone else. He could appreciate it, but frankly, he didn't care.

Tory smiled at him. "It's really noble of you to risk so much for the Oneroi."

Jericho snorted. "I don't give two shits about the Oneroi. My plan was to fight against them with Noir, but he decided it would be easier to sic the gallu on me and control me that way. He declared this war, and I'll be damned if I'm going to let the gallu attack me in my sleep. I've spent enough of my life with other people in control of me. I won't spend one more moment that way. Noir wants a fight, I'm going to give him one. And I will not lose."

Tory let out a slow breath. "I forgot you're the son of Styx and Pallas."

He inclined his head to her. "Yeah, and I'm full of both their venom. Don't start no shit, won't be no shit. My goal is to get the Oneroi and Skoti back on their feet, and then take out the gallu as quickly as possible. After that, it's open season on the Olympians."

"Does that include Delphine?"

He saw red at the mention of her name. Delphine was something he had no intention of discussing with anyone. "She's none of your business."

Tory gave him a placating look. "Sorry. I wasn't

trying to offend or pry. I was just pointing out that you seem to care for her."

Yeah, but the problem was he didn't understand why. One touch, one whisper and he was undone by her.

Why Delphine, when no one else had ever made him feel like this? What was it about her that cut through his anger and made him feel . . .

Warm.

Human.

Whole.

In all these centuries, he'd never felt like he did whenever she touched him. She held more power in a single caress than any entity he'd ever known.

She alone had the power to bring him to his knees.

Unwilling to think about it, he changed the subject. "How is it you're able to come and go from this realm?" It seemed odd that Stryker would tolerate her here.

"My mother-in-law gave me total freedom to visit her whenever the urge strikes me, especially since Ash can't come. While Stryker might want to bind me in chains and feed me to his Daimons, he wouldn't dare. Apollymi can be a little hard to defeat."

"And yet Apollymi tolerates you?"

She smiled. "She hates humans, but adores her son. There's nothing she wouldn't do for Acheron."

"Except leave the humans alone."

"Well, there is that." She walked down the glistening hallway with one hand on the wall. "I know it doesn't make sense. But she declared war on the humans and refuses to back off. However, Ash and anyone he loves is supposed to be immune from the Daimons she controls."

There was a note in her voice that set off Jericho's alarms. "Supposed to be?"

Her expression turned dark and sad, letting him know that she felt deeply for all involved. "Nick's mother was very close to Ash. She died from a Daimon attack a few years ago, which is why Ash and Nick are now at war with each other. Nick blames Ash for it and won't let it go. It's very sad, really, and breaks my heart to see them fight. But I'm told they're getting better, which concerns me. If what they have now is better, I'd hate to see worse." She drew up short as a blond woman cut off their path.

Petite and lithe, and dressed in a black leather cat-suit and corset, the woman narrowed a vicious glare at them. "What are you doing here snooping around, Tory?"

Instead of reacting to the woman's angry tone, Tory cocked her head. "I didn't think I was snooping. It didn't feel like a snoop. I have snooped before and can honestly say this isn't it."

The woman glared at her.

"Relax, Medea," she said in a calm, even tone. "We've come to see your mother."

She narrowed her eyes. "Your funeral."

Tory smiled good-naturedly. "It's always so good to see you, too. You're just such a ray of happy sunshine. I so look forward to all our interactions."

Medea sneered at her. "You should be glad you

helped save my life. It's the only reason you're alive right now."

Tory snorted. "And my living has nothing to do with the fact that you'd be toast if you touched me, right?"

The glare Medea cast at her should have been lethal.

Jericho didn't speak as they followed Medea into an empty office. Decorated in dark golds and burgundy, it was obviously designed to intimidate. Not that it worked on him. There wasn't much that intimidated him.

Or more to the point, there was *nothing* that intimidated him.

Medea paused in the doorway. "Wait here. I'll get her." She shut the door and locked it, which seemed ridiculous given the fact that they could pop out of here at any minute. But far be it from him to point out the obvious.

As soon as they were alone, he faced Tory. "I take it Zephyra is her mother?"

She nodded.

"You think we stand a chance with this?"

Tory shrugged as she looked around. "We won't know until we talk to her. I think she might, and I use that word with all applicable optimism, help us."

"Help you do what?"

Tory snapped around to see Zephyra, who had flashed herself into the room behind Stryker's desk. Tory frowned intently at the demonness. "You're looking rather tan for a nocturnal creature."

Zephyra ignored her.

Almost identical in looks to Medea, she was unbelievably beautiful with lush curves that were heightened by her tight black dress. "Have you a point to this visit? Or should I just kill you now and start a war?" She looked past Tory to Jericho. "And I really resent your bringing a god into my domain."

Jericho winked at her, which only seemed to make her angrier.

Unable to see his gesture, Tory smiled. "You know I wouldn't do it without a really good reason."

"And that is?"

"We need Jared."

Zephyra laughed incredulously, then sobered so fast he wondered if he hadn't hallucinated the laugh. "You're wasting my time. Get out."

Damn, she was a surly bitch. It made him wonder how Stryker tolerated her.

"Oh, come on," Tory said, "it's not like you're using him for anything. Really, what is he doing right now?"

"One thing he's not doing is pissing me off, which is more than I can say for you."

"Children," Jericho said, stepping forward. "Let's try this again. We have a gallu problem. Led by Noir and Azura, they are planning to convert Oneroi and Skoti into gallu so they can attack unfettered in our dreams. When that happens, no one is going to be safe. No one," he reiterated coldly. "And by that I mean you. Since the gallu are just as likely to eat a Daimon as they are a human, you might want to think about it."

Zephyra narrowed her gaze threateningly. "And

people in hell want ice water. Something they're a lot more likely to get than you are my Jared."

Jericho clenched his teeth to control the urge he had to shake the stubborn woman. "We're up against Noir and Azura. Have you any idea how bloody this is going to get?"

Zephyra didn't speak.

"What do you want in exchange for him?" Tory tried.

"There's nothing you have."

Suddenly a loud crash sounded from outside the room. Zephyra went rushing past them to throw open the door that was opposite of the one they'd come in through.

Jericho's eyes widened as he saw a Daimon in the center of a large hall. Only he wasn't a Daimon any longer. He had the milky eyes and skin tone of an infected gallu victim. The other Daimons were backing off, giving him space. He would lunge, and they would run. That was the beauty of the gallu—not only could they turn people into zombies, their zombies could make more zombies.

If they were ever loose, they could kill everyone in no time.

Jericho looked at Zephyra. "You were saying?"

She exposed her fangs at him and hissed. "You brought him here?"

"Hell, no. From what I understand, the gallu have a score to settle with you guys on their own."

"You have no idea." She grabbed a sword from the wall and headed after the Daimon.

Jericho was extremely impressed as she rushed into

the fray. The Daimon-gallu went for her. She ducked his arms, spun and in one clean stroke severed his head from his body. Without stopping her flow, she held the sword out to another Daimon. "Clean that up, Davyn, and tell Stryker we have a problem."

"I noticed."

Jericho's attention went to the extremely tall, dark-haired man who joined them. From the commanding air and deadly aura, he would guess him to be Stryker.

Stryker looked down at the corpse on the floor and sighed angrily. "What are the damn gallu doing now?"

Jericho answered before Zephyra had a chance. "They're uniting with the Oneroi and Skoti to attack us in our sleep."

Stryker cursed foully. "I should have killed the gallu when I had the chance."

Zephyra gave him a knowing smile. "Oh, baby, think of the mistake that would have been."

"What mistake?" Tory asked.

Zephyra crossed her arms over her chest. "I think we need to corral the gallu. What exactly did you have in mind with Jared?"

Tory moved forward. "Is he immune to them?"

"He's immune to most everything."

Jericho was glad to hear that. "Good. Our plan is to liberate the Oneroi and Skoti from Noir."

"What if they're already infected?" Stryker asked.

Jericho didn't hesitate. "We kill them."

Stryker smiled. "I could almost like you." He stroked his chin thoughtfully as he moved closer.

"The only problem is the gallu can still infiltrate the dreams of anyone they've met."

"But our sleep is protected," Zephyra said. "With the abilities we possess, we can fight them in that realm."

"Even so, they're not as powerful in dreams as the Oneroi," Jericho added. "The combination of the two, disastrous. Even for you. One infected Oneroi or Skoti, and we're toast."

The look on Zephyra's face said that she was adamantly opposed to handing Jared over to them.

And Jericho had had enough of her indecisiveness. "Look, I'm through playing with you. We need someone who has actually fought and won against Noir. While I can fight him on my own, I want someone who knows the bastard's weakness. That would be Jared. Now hand him over."

Zephyra arched a taunting brow. "Or what?"

Jericho shot his hands out and released two god bolts that went skittering past her.

To her credit, she didn't flinch or even blink.

Jericho put his hands down. "Trust me, you don't want to find out."

Stryker curled his lip. "Those tactics don't work here. Fear is not a big motivator for us. You would do well to remember that I, too, am the son of a god and can hurl those bolts right back. . . . However, there is something *I* want."

"And that is?"

"A green amulet Jaden took from an old woman in New Orleans. I'm sure he still has it. We give you Jared, and you will bring us that amulet."

Every suspicion in Jericho's body hit overdrive. "What does this amulet do?"

"It's protection."

Now why didn't he believe it? Maybe because Stryker didn't seem like the kind of Daimon who needed protection from some piece of ancient hokum. Not that it mattered.

Promises today.

Lies tomorrow.

If Jericho didn't like what the amulet did, he wouldn't have to bring it here. Nothing said he had to fulfill his part of the bargain. The last time he'd kept his word, he'd paid dearly for it. Things were different now. *He* was different now. The most important thing was to get Jared.

"Done."

Stryker narrowed his gaze. "Don't fail me."

"You don't fail *me*," Jericho shot back.

Tory shook her head. "So do we let you two lock horns and butt each other off the mountaintop now?"

Stryker gave her a hard stare. "I have no idea what Acheron sees in you." He looked over at his wife. "Let them have Jared."

Zephyra made a loud noise of disagreement. "Not *have*, my love. Borrow. Jared is only on loan."

"Fine," Jericho said. "We'll return him as soon as we finish with him."

"You'd better. Otherwise Stryker and I will feast on your innards, bathe in your blood and I will use your eyes as earrings."

Jericho snorted. "You know, with imagery like that, you should write for Hallmark."

ASH HAD JUST RETURNED TO HIS HOUSE WHEN HE felt something strange in the air. An instant later, Phobos reappeared.

Alone.

His bad feeling intensified when Delphine didn't return with him. "What happened?"

Phobos let out a tired sigh. "We were attacked by Zelos as we gathered the Oneroi."

Ash felt ill at the news. Jericho would have a stroke when he found out his brother had taken the Oneroi. "What?"

Phobos raked his hand through his hair. "He was looking for Jericho and instead found us rounding up the others. He took both Delphine and Nike. Apparently Zelos has defected to the dark side. Noir has lost his mind."

"No. It's strategic planning on his part. He's wiping out the pantheon by using its own members. It's what makes him so insidious. With Nike and Delphine, he thinks he's castrated Jericho."

"Yeah, well, either way, we're screwed."

"How so?"

Ash stepped back as Jericho, Tory and Jared appeared. Tory, he pulled toward him just to feel her there and know that she was safe. Especially given everything that was happening. If anything ever happened to her . . .

He'd make Azura and Noir look like teddy bears.

Jericho frowned as he scanned the room and didn't find what he was looking for. "Where's Delphine?"

Phobos answered before Ash could tell him to soften the blow. "Your brother took her and Nike."

Ash winced at the god's bluntness, which he could tell by Jericho's expression went through him like an acid enema.

Jericho froze in place as a rage so potent he could taste it built inside him. Never in his existence had he been angrier. "What?"

Phobos had the good sense to look sheepish. "We were blitzed. Zelos came in and grabbed her before anyone even knew he was there."

Unable to bear it, Jericho used his powers to cover his hand in metallic claws. He grabbed Phobos by the shirt and shoved him into the wall so hard, he broke the sheetrock. "You bastard! How could you let him take her? I'll fucking kill you!"

Ash caught him and pulled him back before he could do more damage to Phobos. "Calm down."

"They have Delphine!" It took every ounce of willpower he possessed not to attack Acheron. Somehow even now his self-preservation knew attacking the Atlantean god would be a serious mistake.

"I heard that," Ash said calmly. "English may not be my native tongue, but I'm pretty good at understanding it." He released him.

Jared stepped forward. Dressed in a long black leather coat, his red hair was pulled back into a sleek ponytail. The most surprising thing was that his skin wasn't pale or freckled. Rather he was tanned with strong features.

Though he was nowhere near as tall as Ash or Jericho, his powerful aura was enough to make even the baddest of asses stand down. His eyes were hidden behind a pair of opaque sunglasses, but even so they seemed to glow. "Give us the sword Noir gave to you."

That succeeded in making Jericho pause. "How do you know about the sword?"

"It belongs to me. I hear her calling and I want her back."

Using his powers, Jericho released Phobos, who came off of the wall with a fierce growl. When Phobos took a step toward him, Ash stopped him by putting one hand on his chest.

"Let it go, Phobos. You got off easy in my book. Had that been Tory they'd taken, you'd be in pieces."

Ignoring them, Jericho summoned the sword.

The moment it appeared, Jared's entire demeanor changed. Instead of being stern and ready to battle, he was reverent and humble. Kneeling on the floor, Jared took the sword from his hand and placed it blade-down to stand before him.

He whispered in a language Jericho didn't know, which he would have thought impossible. One of the benefits of being a god was the ability to understand all languages. But this . . .

It was completely foreign to him.

The sword began to spin on the floor by itself. Faster and faster. A bright light emanated from the hilt, blinding them. Then it began to bend until it formed a tiny, beautiful woman, who stood no more than three feet tall. Her skin and eyes shimmered gold while black hair cascaded over her shoulders to her hips. Dressed in a flowing black gown, she had the long ears of an elf and her eyes slanted like a cat's. A small gold crown held her hair off her face in an intricate twining gold. Diamonds and rubies dangled from the crown around the shape of her face.

She was exquisite.

No wonder the sword had seemed alive.

It was.

"Mistress," Jared said, taking her hand. "Forgive me."

Her eyes flashed red as she removed her hand from his grasp to touch his hair. "It's been a long time, Jared."

"I am so sorry." His voice broke as if he was fighting back tears.

She knelt on the floor in front of him and removed the sunglasses to show the eerie red, orange and yellow eyes of his. "I know, *couran*. But I'm not the one you need to beg forgiveness from. Now stand, and together we will fight again."

His gaze was so tormented that it made Jericho's chest tighten. "I will not fail you again, Mistress. I swear it."

She smiled kindly. "I understand why you did what you did. There is no malice in me." She clenched his hand in hers and held them together in the center of her chest, over her heart. "You have others to save now. We need to be quick about it."

She released him and sat back. In one flash of light, she returned to being a sword again that stood before him.

Jared took the hilt in his hand, kissed it reverently and stood.

Jericho looked at Acheron, wanting to understand what had just happened.

Ash tucked his hands into his pockets. "The Sephirii had ten elite warriors called the Mimoroux. Each one chosen by the sword he or she carried."

Jared manifested a baldric and put it on so he could carry his sword. "Takara went two thousand years without a Shiori."

"A what?"

"A guide." Jared swallowed before he spoke again. "No one was allowed to wield her. Not until me."

Jericho didn't understand until Ash explained. "She was the most powerful of the swords. And whoever wielded her led all the other Sephirii."

Shit. The Sepherii had been betrayed by their leader. By the most chosen among them . . .

Jared shook his head. "I deserve what was done to me and worse. But this isn't about the past. We have to stop Noir." He looked at Acheron. "Do you have your Charonte?"

"They're ready when we are."

Phobos moved forward. "I have a handful of surviving Dolophoni and Oneroi standing by right now."

Jared inclined his head. "Then we attack. May the Source guide us true."

Jericho scoffed. "Screw the Source. This is about vengeance, and Noir is going to regret *ever* messing with me."

CHAPTER 10

TERRIFIED, DELPHINE WAS THROWN INTO A DARK CELL by one of Azura's handmaidens. The door slammed shut, sealing her inside with a sickening thud. There was no light whatsoever, and in the oppressive darkness she could hear something breathing.

Where was it?

More importantly, *what* was it?

Worse, Azura had returned the containment collar to her neck. All she had was her bare hands for protection. Never had she felt more vulnerable.

"I'm getting really tired of being grabbed and tagged." For thousands of years, she'd fought without ever failing. Now she couldn't seem to move without screwing up.

Something coughed.

Delphine spun around, ready to battle. "Who's there?"

"Me." The voice was so weak that at first she didn't recognize it.

"M'Adoc?"

"Yes."

She followed the sound of the heavy breathing to find him somewhere on the ground near her feet. Now that she was closer, she could tell that the sharp breaths weren't from anger. Rather they were gasps of pain.

Afraid of stepping on him, she paused.

Still she couldn't see even the faintest of outlines for his body. "Are you all right?"

"Just peachy," he said in a tight tone that betrayed the excruciating pain he was in.

She reached to touch him only to have him let out an agonized curse. It felt as if there was blood on her fingers and when he'd jerked, she heard some kind of heavy chain rattle.

"Don't touch me."

"I'm sorry," she apologized. "I can't see."

"Just . . . stay . . . put."

"Is there any light here?"

He coughed. "You don't want it lit."

"Why not?"

She heard something skittering across the room. Terrified, she turned, trying to see it in the darkness. But there was nothing there at all.

"Trust me, child. You don't want to see what's in here with us."

Something rattled around the door, making the hair on the back of her neck rise. She didn't like this. Not even a little. "Are you chained?"

"Yes."

"Can I free you?"

"No. They have the chains embedded through my body."

Her stomach clenched. How horrifying. Most of all, how could he stand the pain he had to be in? "Why are we here?"

"To be fed to the things that call this place home."

Raw, unmitigated terror filled her. "What?" She panicked even more.

"Calm down, Delphine. You have to."

She heard the skittering again. Turning around, she tried to locate it.

"They attack when they sense fear. You must control your emotions. I know it's hard, but concentrate."

Her heart pounded so hard, she was amazed it wasn't flying out of her chest. It didn't help when she stumbled and fell over a broken skeleton on the ground. The moment she did, something unknown touched her leg.

"What? Who's here?"

"Shhhh," M'Adoc breathed soothingly. "Calm down."

If he said that one more time, she would scream. "Why won't you tell me the answer?"

"Because I'm trying not to scare you more. Just breathe slowly. Think about something comforting."

Delphine closed her eyes. In the past, her mother would have come to her mind. But today, it was an image of Jericho smiling at her that made her feel safe. Protected.

The skittering backed away.

"That's my girl."

She pushed herself up slowly. "Is there anything I can do to help you?"

"Keep the monsters from winning this war. You have to make sure that Noir is stopped no matter what."

That's what she intended to do. "I'm trying, M'Adoc."

She heard him curse in pain before he spoke again. "You're a brave woman, Delphine. You always were."

She rubbed at the chills on her arms. "I don't feel brave, especially not right now."

"That's what bravery is, especially for a woman not used to having emotions. When you feel deep, paralyzing fear and you don't let it stop you, that is true courage. There's never bravery without fear. Just as there's no love without hate."

She wasn't sure if that was true or not. Her experience with emotions was too recent. The concept of bravery seemed beyond her understanding. "Why did they put you here?"

"I wouldn't give them what they wanted. I refused to convert and join Noir's plans. Besides, Zeus was more cruel than this when he rounded us up to punish us for his dreams. Noir and Azura have nothing on him. Beatings and torture I can take."

Delphine shivered as she remembered some of her own beatings. Though Oneroi were immune to emotions, the ability to feel and experience pain had stayed with them. For one thing, it wasn't truly an emotion, it was a physical response to being hurt, and for the other, it allowed Zeus and the other gods to punish them when they stepped over the rules. "What about the others? Did they convert?"

"M'Ordant's dead." She heard the tears in his voice as he said that, and her own heart ached at the loss. M'Ordant had been a stickler for the rules, but at the same time, he'd been a good Oneroi. And a great friend.

Any time she'd needed backup, he'd been there to help. She would miss him greatly. "They killed him days ago when he refused to eat their poison."

She didn't want to ask the next question and yet she had to know the answer. "What about D'Alerian?"

"I don't know. I haven't seen him since we were captured. Part of me hopes he's dead, too, rather than being tortured like I've been. I know they'd never get him to convert, either. May the gods help him wherever he is."

She groaned in frustration. "Why are they doing this to us? There are other pantheons out there."

"But not with the Oneroi. It's our powers they crave. More than that, Zeus banning our emotions made the Skoti an easy target. Noir was able to infiltrate our ranks by promising to return their feelings to them. Stupid, gullible bastards believing his lies."

"It's not entirely their fault. He's drugging them."

"I know. They tried to drug me, too."

"And still you didn't convert?"

"No. I'm not stupid enough to call that prick master. Better I should live out eternity in this hole being eaten alive than help him."

Delphine . . .

She gasped as a demonic voice spoke her name. It reminded her of her mother.

Help me, Delphine. Please.

"Ignore them," M'Adoc snapped.

"What are they?"

"The souls of the damned. If you answer them, you'll take their place in this hell forever, and they'll be free to wander the mortal realm."

The calls were louder now.

Delphine plugged her ears and made herself hear Jericho's voice. She closed her eyes and imagined being with him. Holding him.

That's it . . .

Laughter rang out.

Suddenly, light poured through the room. Delphine screamed as she saw the ghastly white specter in front of her. Its face was hollowed out. Its eyes sunken in darkness. Wisps of dirty gray hair floated around a bloated face as it reached for her to pull her close to it.

"I will not fear you!" she shouted. "I fear nothing. Nothing!" She prepared to battle it.

The ghoul launched itself at her.

Delphine ducked its punch, expecting it to attack her. But just as it reached her, it screamed and pulled back.

It was Jericho.

He had the creature by the neck. "Get Delphine out of here," he shouted over his shoulder. With one swift move, he cut the creature's throat and slung it away just in time to catch an assault from another one.

Phobos ran at her and pulled her toward the door. "Wait!" she said, trying to stop, "M'Adoc is here, too."

"We've got him." Phobos shoved her into the hallway.

Asmodeus was outside, waiting.

Delphine drew up short, expecting him to be against them. "What are you doing here?"

"Being counted among friends. But for the record, you guys better not lose. I don't want my ass fried over this, or any other body parts, either."

"Why would you help us?"

Asmodeus shrugged. "I hear stupidity is a fatal disease. Doing my own experimentation to see if that's true or not. If I survive, we'll know it's not. If I die . . . well, it'll suck. Bad. And I won't be happy."

Phobos came out of the room with M'Adoc leaning heavily against him. M'Adoc's face had been beaten to the point she barely recognized him. His clothes were torn and showed her a body rife with bleeding wounds. "C'mon."

She had no chance to argue before they left this realm. The next thing she knew, she was in a huge, white room with Tory and several other Oneroi. A man and a woman were tending the wounded while they lay on the floor in utter agony.

Three Charonte popped in with more wounded, whom they laid on the floor before vanishing again.

"What's going on?" she asked Tory, who was helping one of the Skoti drink a glass of water.

"Ash, Jericho, Jared and Phobos are pulling as many of the prisoners out as they can."

Still, Delphine was confused. "Why bring them here?"

"It's the safest place until we can regroup. Ash wants to count the survivors first."

Delphine looked around at the small handful who were here. It really didn't look promising. But at least they weren't fighting them. The Skoti appeared too weak to do anything other than lay on the ground and groan.

It sickened her to see them like this.

"Here. Let me help you."

She turned to find a petite woman by her side. "Help me with what?"

She smiled kindly. "Remove your collar. Relax, my name is Danger, and I'm one of Acheron's stewards. You're safe here, I promise."

Delphine lifted her hair up so that Danger could unfasten the collar and restore her powers . . . again. She was getting really tired of losing them. "Thank you."

"You're welcome." As Danger pulled it off, a sharp sting went through her.

Grimacing, she pulled back. But it took her a minute to realize it wasn't from the collar coming off.

It was her powers warning her that Jericho was in serious trouble.

JERICHO LEFT THE PIT TO RETURN TO ASH AND JARED, who were fighting demons, gallu and other creepy things, in the main hole where most of the prisoners were being kept. He couldn't take a step without being hammered by them.

But that was all right by him. He was getting a lot of pent-up aggression out. Poor them for being the recipients. If he wasn't enjoying it so much, he'd actually feel sorry for them.

As it was . . .

He cut a demon in half.

Phobos popped back in by his side. "Has anyone seen Deimos?"

Jericho caught another gallu, threw him on the ground and plunged his dagger between the creature's eyes to kill it before he answered. "He was with Jaden."

"Where?"

"Hanging on a wall."

Phobos gave him a harsh glare. "Can you show me?"

Leaving Ash and the Charonte to fight, Jericho led Phobos and Jared down the same hallway he'd taken earlier with Asmodeus. One of the best parts about his returned powers was being able to remember little details such as this. He'd missed the flawless memory of the gods.

Once they returned to the room, they had to kick the door in to enter. Something that wasn't easy, but they were determined.

Jericho paused as soon as he saw the gory remains of the Oneroi inside the room. It looked like someone had recently torn them apart. Worse was the stench of their bodies.

Damn Noir. He couldn't believe he'd ever been dumb enough to even think of following him. What an idiot he was.

Phobos made a cry deep in his throat as he ran toward his brother, who lay limply against the wall. There was no sign of life.

But it was the look on Jared's face that held Jericho completely transfixed. There were no emotions evident, and yet his yellow and orange eyes spoke of unfathomable anguish.

Without a word, Jared went to Jaden.

Jaden lashed out until he saw who had touched him. Disbelief etched itself across his battered face. "Jared? What are you doing here?"

Jared responded with a feral snarl as he slashed the

chains holding Jaden to the wall. It didn't succeed in cutting him loose, but the chain did loosen with each sword stroke. "I'm getting you out of here."

"You can't."

"Bull-fucking-shit."

Jaden grabbed him by the shoulders and gave him a harsh, penetrating stare. "You. Can't," he repeated forcefully.

Pulling away, Jared's growl of frustration echoed through the dankness.

Jaden leaned back against the wall, panting from pain, nursing his right arm. "Get the others to safety and don't worry about me."

"I won't leave you here."

"You can and you will." Jaden's snarl matched his. "For once in your life, listen to me and do as I say. Get out of here and stop wasting time arguing over inconsequentials."

Jared grabbed the cloth over Jaden's left shoulder and clenched it into a tight fist. "You're not inconsequential. Not to me."

Jaden touched his hand. "In this battle I am. They won't kill *me*. Now go. Save as many of the others as you can."

Jericho didn't know what to make of their confrontation as Jared pulled Jaden into his arms and held him close and tight. The way they held each other . . . they were either brothers or lovers . . .

Or *really* close friends.

"I will fix this," Jared said, releasing him. "Somehow, I'm going to make this right. I swear to you."

Jaden shoved him away. "Dammit, go!"

Jericho turned his attention to Phobos, who had Deimos cradled in his arms.

"He's alive," Phobos said. "Barely."

"Get him out of here."

Phobos didn't argue. He teleported out immediately.

Jared was another matter. He lingered as if he couldn't bear to leave Jaden. Guilt, fear and pain were clearly etched onto his face.

But as a rush of demons assaulted them, Jericho's attention was turned from Jared to survival. He clotheslined the first gallu to reach him, then grabbed the next one. They rolled to the ground. Jericho punched him hard in the face before he rose to catch the next one who was descending on him.

He blasted that one back with his powers, but not before the demon delivered a blast of his own. It caught him hard in the chest and sent him reeling.

Jared cut the demon down with one fierce sword stroke.

As Jericho rose to his feet, he felt a chill down his spine.

Noir was here.

He sensed it even before the god appeared in the room, three feet from him.

Noir tsked as he raked him with a repugnant glare. "You have no idea what you've started."

Jericho sneered at him. "Neither do you, asshole. All you had to do was play nice with me. But you thought it would be more fun to kick me around, drug me and turn on me. Bad move on your part."

Noir laughed. "Turning on you is what people do

best. Haven't you learned that yet? You have no friends. You have nothing."

Against his will an image of Delphine went through his mind.

"Her?" Noir said derisively as if he could read his thoughts. "Delphine doesn't care about you. She was sent by Zeus to either seduce you to their cause or kill you."

Those words slammed into him. It couldn't be. She wouldn't do that. She was above it.

"It's true," Noir insisted. "Ask Jaden."

Jericho turned to look at Jaden, who then glanced away as if he couldn't bear to tell him the truth.

Noir laughed. "You're such a gullible fool. So much for the brave Cratus. You're pathetic. You sacrificed yourself for a woman who betrayed you. One who will always betray you. She is nothing, and neither are you."

Pain shredded Jericho's abdomen. Looking down, he saw the sword that Noir had stabbed him with.

Noir grabbed his chin, holding it in a tight grip before he jerked the sword out. Jericho gasped at the raw fire that ripped through him.

"I should have known you'd be nothing but a waste of time. So much for commanding my army."

Jericho staggered back as Jared ran forward to attack.

The two of them went at each other like Titans. Jaden started for him.

"Stay out of it, maggot!" Noir warned.

Jaden didn't listen. But as soon as he reached Jericho's side, a light flashed. One that pierced Jaden, lift-

DREAM WARRIOR 191

ing him off his feet to pin him to the wall like some sort of sick lab experiment.

Jaden cried out in pain as he glared at Noir. "If I ever get this collar off, you are so fucking dead."

Those words barely registered in Jericho's mind as he tried to use his powers to heal himself.

It didn't work.

How could that be? Grimacing, he tried again, and again nothing happened.

Noir shot a blast at him that sizzled over his body. "You're pathetic."

Jericho tried to stand, but something knocked him back down. He armored his body.

Not even that helped.

Jared couldn't get to Noir—Azura had flashed in to block his way. The two of them locked swords and clashed as Noir stalked toward Jericho.

I'm not going to die like this. . . .

By all the power in the Source, he wouldn't go down in this hell hole.

Noir stabbed him through the back, pinning him to the floor. "Ah . . . did I miss your heart?"

Jericho hissed as Noir jerked the sword out of his spine. Rolling, he tried to kick him off. It was useless. He closed his eyes and summoned all the power he could from the Source.

Noir laughed at him. "You didn't really think we'd *fully* restored your powers, did you?" He stabbed him through the chest, narrowly missing his heart.

Jericho cried out in pain.

Twisting the sword, Noir yanked it out. "This time, I won't miss." He plunged it down.

Just as it would have struck him, a blur whizzed past Jericho, catching Noir about the waist and knocking him away.

It was Delphine.

She manifested a staff and used it to drive him back. Jericho was in awe of her as she engaged Noir as an equal. Every time he lunged, she parried and struck a fresh blow. Her movements were a symphony of grace and agility, and her successful hits were pissing Noir off.

She planted the staff on the ground, then used it to vault her entire weight into Noir's stomach. He grunted, falling back.

Delphine rushed back to Jericho. "Hold on, baby," she breathed before she teleported him to Ash's home in Katoteros—the Atlantean heaven realm.

He lay on the floor with Delphine above him, her brow knitted in worry. Noir's words rang in his ears.

Was everything about her a lie? Had she betrayed him?

"Why did you come back for me?"

She looked incredulous at his question. "I didn't want to see you hurt."

"You don't even know me."

She spoke to him then, but he couldn't hear her words for the pain of his body. Instead, he felt the darkness creeping in, swallowing him whole.

Delphine felt her heart clench as Jericho's eyes rolled back in his head and he expelled a long breath.

Terrified he was dead, she leaned down, trying to feel for a heartbeat. There wasn't one. . . .

No, wait. It was there. Barely. His breathing was faint, but it, too, was audible.

Thank the gods for it.

"They made one helluva mess of him."

She looked up at the blond man who worked as Acheron's steward. Alexion. That was his name. "Is there a bed I can take him to while he heals?"

Alexion scowled. "You don't want to transport him to Olympus with the others?"

She shook her head. "He hates it there. Please. I can heal him, but he needs to rest."

Alexion touched his arm and Jericho vanished.

She opened her mouth to question him about his actions, but before she could say a word, he sent her to the same room where Jericho was lying on a large, intricately carved black bed. The white linens were quickly stained by Jericho's blood.

Alexion flashed in beside her. "I don't know what to do with him in terms of those wounds. I thought he was a god." Which meant Jericho shouldn't be bleeding like this. He should have been able to heal himself.

But he was a special case and no one knew that better than she did.

"He is."

"Then why's he bleeding like that?"

She wasn't sure, but she had a sneaking suspicion it had something to do with his human heart. Maybe Zeus had kept him from healing so that he could kill Jericho off at a later date. Zeus could be cold and tricky that way.

"I don't know." Though she knew Acheron trusted this man, she didn't know him at all. The last thing she'd ever do was tell him about Jericho's weakness. No one else needed to know that, and she would guard it to her grave.

"Do you need anything?" Alexion asked.

"No, thank you. I can tend him."

He inclined his head to her. "All right. I'm going to see to the others then. Call me if you need anything."

Alone with Jericho, Delphine used her powers to remove his shirt. She grimaced at the sight of his wounds and scars. Alexion was right, Noir *had* made a terrible mess . . .

Stabbing for his heart. One of the wounds had barely missed it.

She went cold as that realization sank in.

Noir knew. Somehow, someone had told him that Jericho could be killed by piercing his heart. There was no other reason for him to have been stabbed like this.

But who would have told him that?

Why?

If they failed to stop Noir, all of them would suffer. Olympus would fall and no one would be safe.

But as Jericho had said, most people were for sale. Those who weren't were few and far between. Maybe the god involved thought he could stay on Noir's good side and avoid being the target. Or maybe he had offered Jericho up as a sign of good faith. Or maybe he just hated Jericho that badly.

Who knew?

Heartsick with the thought of someone being so cold, she used her powers to seal his wounds, then manifested water and cloth to clean the blood away. As she ran the cloth over the sharp ridges of his abdomen, she paused at the sight of the scars there.

Jagged and deep, they matched the one on his face.

She winced at the sight. Zeus. She knew those scars. They were from his lightning bolts. Sickened at the pain Jericho had been through, she sat on the bed and traced the line of the scar on his face to his lips. Even while unconscious, his power was unmistakable.

And he'd come back for her to save her.

His words to Phobos rang in her ears. Yes, he'd gone to save others, but he had made it a point to come after her, too. Even before his sister. She had taken precedence. Tears of tender gratitude made her gaze hazy.

"You are so fierce," she whispered.

Yet for her, he bled. He, who'd sworn he wouldn't cross Noir, had done so. Not just because Noir had threatened him. She didn't believe that. From the very beginning, he'd protected her in a way few people had.

Jericho hated the world, yet he'd been her self-appointed guardian.

She took his hand into hers and stared at the dark, scarred skin. Rough and calloused, it was almost twice the size of hers. These were the hands of a killer and of a lover, and they belonged to a man who captivated every part of her.

His eyes fluttered open.

"Hi," she breathed, grateful to see him awake.

Anger furrowed his brow. "Am I on Olympus?"

"No, you're in Katoteros. I wouldn't let them take you there."

Jericho tightened his grip on her hand as his gaze turned stormy. "Why are you being nice to me?"

"What do you mean?"

"I have threatened and intimidated you. We barely know each other, and yet you're being kind. Why?"

"Do I have to have a reason?"

His gaze was dark and accusatory. "Everyone lies. Everyone's for sale. What do you gain by your kindness?"

She was baffled by his hostility. "I have no motivation for it other than to repay you for saving me."

Those words seemed to anger him more. "So what you're telling me is that you didn't make a deal with Zeus to seduce me?"

CHAPTER 11

JERICHO WATCHED THE SHOCK AND PANIC PLAY across Delphine's face. He knew the look of someone having been caught red-handed and it disgusted him that he'd been so easily duped. How could he have ever believed in her?

"So it is true." Curling his lip, he jerked his hand away from her grasp. "I should have known."

As he started to get up, she shoved him back onto the bed almost roughly. He'd never seen her really fired up before, but right now her eyes smoldered. "Don't you dare take that sanctimonious high road and leave, you stubborn man. Yes, Zeus told me to seduce you. I won't deny it. And so did your sister, for that matter. But when have I ever listened to them? Zeus also told me to capture Arik, and I didn't do that, either, as you have seen."

"You did seduce *me*." He hated the note of pain in his voice that he couldn't suppress. Most of all, he hated the fact that he cared enough about her to be hurt. After all these centuries of trying to protect himself, she'd wormed her way past his defenses and had struck a blow to his heart that he wanted to hurt her over.

She looked aghast. "How? By being nice to you? Is that all it took? For some reason, I thought seduction was a lot harder than that."

That ignited his own wrath. "Don't you dare patronize me."

"I'm not the one patronizing you, Jericho. You are if you think I've seduced you. All I've done is treat you like a human."

"Then how pathetic am I that that's all it took?"

She hit his stomach. Not hard; it was more like she wanted to get his attention. But it was enough to ignite his anger.

"You're not pathetic," she growled. "You're not worthless. But you are hurt. Maybe even a little confused and probably a lot of deranged, but not pathetic."

"Deranged?"

"Well, you did barge into hell to save a woman who was dumb enough to get caught . . . how many times now? Personally I wouldn't have saved me after the first time. That to me says you're deranged."

Jericho wanted to yell at her. He wanted to deny her and be angry. To hurt and curse her very existence. Yet as he looked at her, all he saw was a perfect mouth that needed kissing and a beautiful smile that warmed his heart. He saw green eyes with flecks of gold set into a face that haunted him.

How did she do it? How could he want to strangle her one minute and then be fine the next? But her words cut straight through his anger, diminishing it until he was lost.

For the first time in centuries he didn't feel pathetic or worthless, and it wasn't because he had his powers restored. It was because she saw him as something more than that.

Most of all, he wanted to be the man she saw him as.

And before he could stop himself, he kissed her.

Delphine was stunned by his actions. How could he go from being so surly in one heartbeat to this?

"You're not right in the head, are you?" she asked as he nibbled his way to her ear.

"No. There's definitely something wrong with me." He pulled back to stare at her. "I want to hate you, but I can't even stay mad at you."

She narrowed her gaze at him. "You know, I think you're more in need of lessons on how to seduce than I am. Why don't you call me fat and ugly while you're at it?"

He laughed.

The sound caught her completely off guard. Deep and from the heart, it wasn't mocking or sarcastic. It was real. "What? Was that a laugh?"

He tried to sober. "No."

"Yes, it was. I heard it. Holy cow," she teased, "call Hermes to spread the news. I think I just started the end of the world . . . it has to be a sign of the apocalypse." Her teasing died as she caught a look of hurt that he quickly concealed. "Jericho, I was teasing you. I would never hurt you intentionally."

"Good, 'cause you live in a place inside me where only you can do me harm."

Delphine froze at the barely audible words.

His gaze locked with hers. "I hate you for that."

"You don't have to hate me. You know I'd sooner kill myself than hurt you."

He narrowed his gaze. "No, I don't know that. And you're asking me to trust in you when everyone I've ever known has betrayed me?"

"Nike hasn't betrayed you."

He scoffed. "Nike was the one who told Noir how to kill me."

Delphine was stunned. "What?"

"He projected the images of her telling him to me as he stabbed me."

She gave him a chiding glare. "Azura also told you that I was Zeus's favorite, which is absolutely not true. They're liars, Jericho. They wouldn't know the truth if it bit them in their privates. Believe me, if their lips are moving, they are lying. Guaranteed. Your sister loves you. She was adamant that you not be hurt. Why would she turn around and then tell him how to kill you?"

"Then who did?"

She shrugged. "There was a room full of gods when Zeus snarled it out. It could have been any of them."

Jericho scoffed at her blindness. It could have been Nike. It was possible. "How can you have faith in anyone after everything that's happened?"

"Because I choose to. I won't let people like Zeus and Noir ruin my life by making me suspicious of everyone around me. I won't give them that power. They're not worth it."

Jericho wanted to be like that, too, but it was so

hard. He didn't know if he had it in him any more to trust. He'd been hurt one time too many.

She pushed him back down and covered him with the sheet. "You need to rest. While I've mended your wounds, you're still sore and wounded. Give your body time to heal completely."

"There's too much to be done. I need to know—"

"No."

He blinked at her, unable to believe she'd just told him no. Forcefully and rudely. "No, you d'in'."

"Yes, I di'id," she mocked. "Don't make me use my Jedi ninja mind tricks on you. I might screw up and fry your brains."

He couldn't suppress a smile at her unfounded threats. "I appreciate the concern, but Noir is still scheming and we need to talk to Deimos and M'Adoc. Maybe they know something we can use."

She bit her lip and cringed as if she didn't care for that thought. Gods, how he loved that fretful look. "You know the only way to see them is to go to Olympus. Is that really what you want?"

"No. But I want Noir's heart in my fist and if going there is what I have to do . . ."

"You want his more than Zeus's?"

She had a point. It was hard to decide who he wanted to murder more.

Both would be preferable. "Maybe."

She rolled her eyes at him. "I think you just like being angry."

"Not really." Anger just seemed to be his main sustenance. "But Noir is after us with a personal vendetta. This is no time to be squeamish or timid. The best defense is a good offense. We need to make the lion a rabbit and run him into the ground."

"What if we can't?"

"I'm not going to think that way. Noir is ours and we're going to make him wish he'd never stuck his head out of Azmodea."

Delphine couldn't deny him the passion he felt. She just wished there was a better way. But if he was willing . . . "Then Olympus it is. But do try to behave. I know it's hard for you, but . . ."

He snorted. "I won't piss on the floor."

"It's not the floor I'm worried about. It's their corn-flakes."

With a droll glower, he dressed himself in a black top and pants before they teleported to the Vanishing Isle, where Acheron and his people had taken the remaining survivors.

Delphine followed Jericho, bracing herself for a rough showdown. The one thing she'd learned about Jericho was that his temper would always get the better of him. And from what she'd seen of Deimos and M'Adoc, they didn't need anyone else beating on them.

They entered the temple hall—where the Oneroi gathered to feast, gossip or share information. Today the hall had been turned into a large infirmary. There were a few Oneroi tending the wounded.

But it was the demigod who'd been placed in charge of them that surprised her.

Zarek of Moesia had been born human. Even worse, he'd been raised as a human slave who'd been wrong-fully convicted of raping his owner and then executed for it. For thousands of years, he'd lived as one of the Dark-Hunters who rode herd on the Daimons. At least in theory. In reality, Zarek had been one step this side of insane—and not even a full step. He'd been kept isolated from mankind for *their* protection.

A few years ago, Artemis had declared him a threat to mankind and had sent an assassin after him. But not before Acheron had petitioned the goddess Themis to judge him to see if he was worth saving. Unable to do so herself, Themis had sent her daughter, Astrid, in to judge. Astrid had not only judged Zarek sane, she'd saved his life and fallen in love with him.

Ever since then, the two of them had been inseparable.

Tall, blond and beautiful, Astrid was on the opposite side of the room with a female Oneroi she was assisting.

Zarek was directing the other attendants who were healing and moving the rest of the Oneroi and Dolophoni. Even though he was considered a god now, he still retained that feral human quality. It didn't help that his hair was short and jet black. The same color as his sharply trimmed goatee. There was just such an air of menacing power about him that it made the hair on the back of her neck rise.

He crossed the room as soon as he saw them. "Ash told me you guys wouldn't be joining us."

Afraid Jericho might say something to set Zarek off, Delphine stepped between them. "Change of plans. Why are you here?"

"I asked him to come," Astrid said as she joined them. "Not all of the Skoti are returning, so I was afraid of another attack. For some insane reason, a number of them are still siding with Noir."

Zarek inclined his head to his wife. "So if the punks come here, they're going to dance with the devil and get the short end of the horn."

Astrid smiled proudly as she wrapped her arm around his waist and squeezed him. "No one better than my Zarek to rip someone's head off." She looked at Jericho. "You two should get along famously."

Instead they were both suspicious as they sized each other up. It would be amusing if they didn't have so much riding on this.

"Where's Deimos?" Jericho asked.

Astrid pointed to the far corner. "Phobos went back to help the others and to save as many as he could."

"Thanks." Jericho led Delphine away from Zarek and Astrid over to where Deimos was resting. He looked down at Delphine as guilt consumed him. "I should be there, too, helping them."

"You can't." She patted the center of his chest, just over his heart. "Noir knows how to kill you. We have to take you out of the game or risk losing you."

"Fear doesn't control me."

She gave him a dry smirk. "I know, tough guy. But you have one hell of an off switch that I'm sure he's shared with everyone on his team."

"And the one thing I know is that everything in the universe has a weakness. He knows mine. We have to find Noir's."

Deimos scoffed as they reached him. He was bruised and still bleeding. Someone had bandaged his head and one of his eyes was covered by white gauze. "Find it, my ass. Look at me. They can't even heal me of the damage he's done. When was the last time you saw me busted up like this?"

Nonplussed by the question, Jericho shrugged. "Over a Thracian slave dancer. You and Phobos got into it until I had to separate you. You both looked like that afterward."

Deimos started to laugh, then cursed. "Only you would remember that."

"I'm sure Phobos hasn't forgotten it, either."

"Perhaps."

Delphine knelt beside him. The pain he had to be in . . . Unlike Jericho, she'd never seen him like this. "What is going on, Deimos? Why has Noir come at us like this after all of this time? I know he wants the Skoti, but why hasn't he attacked before this?"

He let out a long, tired sigh before he answered. "In short, it's because the Malachai is back. The moment the elder Malachai turned on Noir and ran, his powers began to weaken significantly."

She frowned. "I don't understand."

"You know how our powers weaken when we have no one worshiping us?"

That was the theory. However, she'd always wondered about it. "Yes, but the Oneroi powers never really have. Not like the other gods'."

"That's because Acheron started using the Dream-Hunters to help his Dark-Hunters cope and heal through the dream state. With their numbers and by needing you guys to help them heal, the Dark-Hunters helped the Oneroi to maintain the strength of their powers."

"Oh . . ." So that was why their powers had never really diminished. She was suddenly more grateful to Acheron than she'd been before.

"Well, a lot of Noir's power," Deimos continued, "is contingent on the Malachai and his loyalty. Azura was able to maintain some of her power because she feeds on Jaden, who in turn feeds from the demons and their need of him. But once Nick's father ran out, Noir began to weaken immediately. When Nick's powers were restored, it brought Noir out of a nearly coma-tose state. The more the Malachai uses his power, the stronger Noir becomes. It's why he needs the Malachai so badly, and it's why he keeps attacking us. He's hoping to draw the Malachai to him."

That made sense, and it explained where Noir had been all these centuries past. But there was one more dark power that had yet to rear its ugly head. "What about his sister, Braith?"

"Noir and Azura are looking for her. So far, they have no idea what happened to her."

Jericho answered for him. "Can they surf dreams and find Nick?"

Deimos nodded. "Plus the more gods who swear service to Noir, the more powerful he becomes off them. We're powerful when the humans believe in us, but when it's a god, it makes us twice as strong." He looked at Jericho. "You can drive him back and he knows it."

That was true except for the one fatal flaw caused

by Zeus that made Jericho just a little too easy to kill. "What is Noir's weakness?"

"Jaden."

Jericho scowled at the unexpected answer. "What do you mean?"

Deimos winced as if pain cut through him before he answered. "If we free Jaden, we can put both Noir and Azura down. He has the power, but right now he's enslaved to them and forbidden to do them harm."

And freeing him would be next to impossible. By now Noir would have clamped down on his prized pet.

Jericho looked at Delphine before he spoke again. "So the easiest thing to do to keep Noir from gaining more power is to kill the Malachai."

Deimos snorted. "You would think. But there's a major problem there. His life is tied to Acheron's. You kill him and Acheron drops right after him."

Delphine let out a frustrated breath. "If Acheron dies, the Destroyer is released and the world ends."

Deimos nodded.

Jericho cursed. "Who thought that was a good idea?"

"Ash, when he didn't know Nick was the Malachai."

Flippin' figured. Jericho would condemn him for his stupidity had he not done dumber things himself. Starting with having saved the woman next to him.

Well, maybe that wasn't so dumb after all . . .

"So what are we going to do?" Delphine asked.

"Right now the most pressing thing is to either kill or reclaim the Dolophoni, Oneroi and Skoti working with Noir. So long as a single one serves him, we're screwed."

Yeah, the last thing they needed was to be that vulnerable while they slept. No one needed a Freddy Krueger reenactment.

Jericho crossed his arms over his chest. "How many do they have on their side?"

"About a hundred."

Delphine glanced up. "But we have more. We can fight and bring them home."

"Or kill them," Jericho added. Personally, he preferred the latter. If they hadn't come over willingly, in his mind they couldn't be trusted. Better to take them out than take them in and be sorry.

Delphine gave him an irritated glare. "We need to launch another attack on them."

"You'll need a leader," Zarek said as he joined them. "One massive, concentrated attack from the hall of mirrors to catch them while they're in the dream realm, and another for those who are awake."

Jericho nodded. "It'll be bloody, but Zarek's right. We have to sober the Skoti and heal the others so that we can finish this."

Delphine shook her head as she considered it. She wasn't sure they stood a chance as the situation was currently. "But who's going to lead? M'Adoc—"

"He's not a military commander," Deimos said, interrupting her. He looked up at Jericho. "You're the best shot we have. You can monitor the Source for activity and ride herd on Noir and Azura when they draw from it. Plus you have command experience and know how to best corner enemies and execute them."

Zarek looked less than pleased. "He can't do it alone. How many Source gods do we have?"

Astrid answered. "Four. Jared, Acheron, Nike . . ." she paused as she cut a sideways glance to him, "and Jericho."

"There are two more," Deimos said.

Astrid frowned. "Who?"

"The Sumerian god Sin and his twin brother, Zakar."

Now it was Delphine's turn to be baffled. "Why would they fight with us?"

"Sin is Acheron's son-in-law."

"Oh," she said as she understood. That changed a lot. "That might work, then."

Zarek scoffed. "Or it'll blow up in our faces."

A devious glimmer lit Jericho's eyes. "Well, the other alternative is to wake a few Titans and break ass on all of them."

Zarek's evil laughter rang out as if he had a good image of that in his mind. "Zeus would shit kittens."

Jericho shrugged. "Do any of us care?"

Delphine and Astrid raised their hands.

Astrid cleared her throat. "In case you guys forgot, the Titans are just a tad upset about their eternal imprisonment. You let them out now, and I think we'll have a worse problem than just Noir. Plus there's a lot more of them."

Delphine nodded. "What she said and then some."

"I have a better idea." M'Adoc flashed in beside them.

Delphine was surprised to see him here and even more that he'd been eavesdropping on their conversation.

But he was still unsteady on his feet and didn't last long before he collapsed.

Jericho caught him before he fell and helped him sit on the floor.

M'Adoc took a second to steady himself before he explained his idea. "Our weakness was the Skoti. Noir got to them by promising to restore their emotions. Once there—"

"He's been drugging them," Delphine finished, remembering Zeth's warning to her and the biting effects of the food.

M'Adoc nodded. "So long as he keeps them like that, they can't fight him. But if you get Zeth sobered, we can reunite the Skoti with the Oneroi. With our emotions intact, the indignant fury of what's been done to us will fuel our fight. And more than that, Noir will have nothing more to offer them. Especially since he's now attacked all of us."

Jericho was still skeptical. It seemed somehow too easy. "Are you sure about that?"

M'Adoc nodded. "We need their sense of loyalty and fairness restored. With the ban lifted, we'll be back as we were."

"Can we do that?" Delphine asked. "I thought once a curse was given it was eternal."

"Not always. But it has to be removed by the god who delivered it. Besides, this one's already weakening. The emotions you have, Delphine, haven't you noticed they've grown stronger?"

"I thought it was residuals from battling the Skoti."

M'Adoc shook his head. "Zeus isn't the power he used to be. As with Noir, the fewer people who worship him, the weaker he's become."

Deimos nodded. "And unlike Apollo, he doesn't

have a race of Daimons believing in him to feed his powers."

"Exactly. He has the ability to rescind the curse. Unlike Apollo's, his isn't fatal and can be undone."

Jericho stepped back. "Then I'll go have a word with thunder-ass."

Delphine turned on him with a panicked expression that warmed him. "You can't. He'll kill you."

"Does it matter?"

"It does to me."

Jericho smiled as he cupped her cheek in the palm of his hand. No words had ever meant more to him, and it stunned him that she was so sincere. "It'll be all right." He nudged her next to Zarek. "Keep an eye on her until I'm back."

"You know," Deimos said, pushing himself up to sit. "I'm thinking she might not be too far off. You might want to have some backup before you go talk to Zeus."

Knowing the bastard, that would just piss him off more. Zeus didn't like an audience whenever he was wrong. This would take some serious finessing that would only work if there was no other witness to it. "I stood at his right-hand side for centuries. I know how to talk to the man."

Deimos snorted derisively. "You also got yourself one of the harshest punishments from him."

"Which means I know how to push him too far. Don't worry. I won't make that mistake again."

Delphine turned a worried look to M'Adoc. "M'Adoc, talk him out of it."

"I don't know if I can, Delphine. You'd have a better shot than me."

"And not even *you* can." Jericho started to leave, but Delphine stopped him.

"You be careful. Please."

Treasuring those precious words, he inclined his head before he teleported himself from the Vanishing Isle straight into Zeus's private temple.

Jericho went cold as old memories assailed him. He and his siblings had once stood guard here while the father god bathed or slept with whatever nymph or goddess had caught his fancy. Only a tiny handful of other gods had ever been admitted here.

And in all these centuries nothing had changed. It was still the same cold, marbled hall it had always been.

Closing his eyes, Jericho reached out with his powers to locate Zeus.

He was in his bath, hopefully alone.

Jericho took a moment to return the patch to his eye and manifest his body armor. He articulated the fingers of his right hand back to his metallic claws and freed his wings.

There wouldn't be any begging. He was here merely to state his case and argue it if need be.

If Zeus wanted a fight, there would be a fight.

Jericho left his hair to flow freely down his back as he made his way through the golden-and-white marble hall to the back of the temple. The bathing room was a huge atrium with a waterfall at the far side that fed the tub, which was the size of a, pardon the pun, Olympic-sized pool. Steam floated off the water, letting him know it was hot and soothing.

Zeus lay on the opposite end of the waterfall with

his eyes closed while a nymph sat on a nearby stool playing a lyre for him. From this vantage point, he looked completely relaxed and unaware of the fact that Noir was basically one step away from his throat.

Stupid bastard.

The nymph looked up and gasped at the sight of Jericho.

Zeus jerked upright. Cursing, he turned in the water to face him. "What are you doing here?"

"I've come to visit . . . Father."

Zeus curled his lip before he barked at the innocent nymph. "Peia, leave us."

The nymph vanished instantly. Her lyre fell to the ground and rang on an off-key note.

Zeus reached for his long robe and tied it around him while he was still in the pool. Using his powers, he rose straight up before he stepped on the concrete so he could approach Jericho. "Have you lost your mind?"

Jericho ignored his snarling tone. "It feels like that some days. But no. I'm sane and I'm here to talk to you."

"About what?"

"What you're going to do."

Zeus narrowed his eyes threateningly. "And that is?"

"Free the Oneroi."

CHAPTER 12

ZEUS RAKED HIM WITH A SCATHING GLARE AS HE stopped right before him and tugged the belt of the robe into a tight knot. "You are insane."

Strangely there was a calm serenity inside Jericho that didn't react to being goaded. How odd. Normally such a dressing-down would have had him going for Zeus's throat.

Maybe Delphine was rubbing off on him because he swore he could hear her telling him to calm down.

"No," he said slowly. "The only insanity would be for you to ignore me. The Skoti and Oneroi need their emotions in order to effectively fight against Noir."

Zeus shook his head. "They'll turn against us. You can trust me on that."

How stupid could one god be? Was he blind? "In case you haven't noticed, they've already done that. And they're picking apart your pantheon one god at a time. The Oneroi and Dolophoni are almost nothing more than, pardon the pun, a bad dream."

Jericho crossed his arms over his chest confidently.

"If you give them back their emotions, their loyalty to the pantheon might win out over their current lust and ambition. Plus, Noir will have nothing left to offer them. The only reason they're there now is to have the emotions you banned from them. Restoring them is the only hope you have."

Zeus curled his lip. "How do you know?"

"You're still alive right now, aren't you? Even though I have dreamed of nothing but slaughtering you for all these centuries. Even though I hate you with every piece of me. You're still alive because of the loyalty I have to being Greek. And the hatred I feel for Noir having tried to use me. That's what we need to reawaken in them."

Zeus scoffed. "None of that motivates me to spare them."

"Then tell me what will."

Zeus narrowed his eyes as he considered it. Jericho swore he could hear the gears grinding in the god's mind. "What exactly are you offering?"

Don't do it, you idiot. Tell him his life.

But he knew threats wouldn't get him what he needed. Zeus was the only one who could lift the ban. This wasn't the time or place for arrogance or bluster.

They needed this.

Do it for Delphine's future . . .

This was her freedom he was asking for. *Her* life. Somehow that made it easier for him. "Whatever it takes to end the curse you should have *never* given them."

Zeus cocked his head as if he heard Jericho's thoughts. His gaze darkened threateningly. "This is over that little Oneroi I sent after you, isn't it? You don't care about the others. You only want her to be free." He laughed mockingly. "I'll be damned. The mighty Cratus brought low by a common sleep god. Sending that hot little ass after you actually worked."

"Don't call her that," Jericho growled. It was all he could do not to attack over it. Delphine wasn't an object and be damned if he'd let even Zeus reduce her to one.

Zeus laughed again, making Jericho want to punch the arrogance right off his face. "You think if she has her emotions back she'll be able to love you, don't you? Care about you. Nike told me she'd be the one weakness you couldn't deny. And she was right. There's nothing like a pretty face to weaken a man, especially one who was banned from sex as long as you were."

That was probably the last thing Zeus should have reminded him of because right now he was holding on to his temper by a very narrow margin. "Leave her out of this."

Luckily, the god knew when to back down. "Fine. You asked me for a favor and so I'll grant it on one condition."

"And that is?"

"Once we have the Skoti reined in, you'll be my dutiful slave for the rest of eternity."

"Fuck you." Jericho's response flew out of his mouth before he could stop it. Was the bastard out of his gourd? Did Zeus really think he'd be that dumb ever again?

Zeus shrugged as if the fate of their entire pantheon didn't rest on this decision. "Then no deal. I only hope your little Oneroi is a better fighter than they are. Otherwise . . ."

Jericho was aghast at his nonchalance. "Are you completely stupid? If Noir gets his foothold on gallu ruled Skoti, you're all doomed. *We're* all doomed."

"My dreams are protected—a precaution I took long ago. My only fear is Noir, and with you out of the way, that's one less tool he'll have." Zeus smirked. "Yes, you want to spite me and fight for him, but you won't. Not now. Not after you've seen your beautiful Delphine. You won't hurt her, will you?"

"Shut up."

"Why? Does the truth offend you?"

Roaring with anger, he extended his wings and seized Zeus by his throat.

The god didn't flinch as Jericho held him against the wall. "Go ahead. Kill me," he goaded. "Release my powers back to the Source. But if you can't handle them, and we both know you can't, they'll go to Noir and make him all the more powerful. Or worse, they'll rupture the universe and kill every living thing. Is that what you want?"

Jericho tightened his grip, wanting to kill the bastard. He wanted to bathe in his blood and taste his entrails. . . . "I hate you."

"Hate me all you want. But it's your decision in the end. You can help them by agreeing to my demands, or refusing and then watching them all fall to Noir and Azura. Which will it be?"

Jericho shook his head, trying to understand Zeus's rationale and selfishness. "How can you not care about what happens to them?"

"I'm not without a degree of compassion, but I've never shirked at what needed to be done. Ever. I slaughtered my own father to rule this pantheon. Do you think for one minute I'd hesitate at killing the rest of this pantheon to guard my place as king?"

Jericho squeezed his throat as he imagined Zeus lying dead at his feet. But in the end, he knew Zeus was right. With his human heart, he wouldn't be able to absorb those powers. It would kill them both and empower Noir.

Or it would destroy them all.

"So what's it to be, Cratus?"

DELPHINE FROZE AS SOMETHING PAINFUL RUPTURED inside her. It felt as if her heart had burst open and was sending fire throughout her veins. Crying out, she fell to her knees, clutching her chest. Every breath cut through her. Every agonizing heartbeat.

What on earth was happening to her?

Terrified it was a new attack from Noir and his army, she looked about the hall where the other Oneroi and Skoti were also writhing in pain. None of the Dolophoni seemed to be affected by it.

"What's happening?" she asked M'Adoc.

M'Adoc was gasping and groaning. "He did it. It's our emotions being unlocked."

Could it be . . . ?

It was only when the burning stopped and her unlocked emotions swept through her that she realized exactly how hollow she'd always been. Everything around her was more vibrant and sharp. Every sound, every taste. The light was blinding as emotions flooded through her. Hate. Love. Sympathy. Fear. Sadness. Happiness. She was laughing and crying. Cringing yet wanting to shout in joy.

"Breathe," M'Adoc said in her ear. "Let it settle down."

She tried her best, but it was so difficult. So much for Azura having unlocked them—that was nothing compared to what she felt now. The goddess must have only unlocked the human part, because that was no comparison to this. "How do humans handle them?"

"Some handle them better than others, and they're more used to it since they have them from birth. You'll get used to them, too . . . eventually."

He seemed to have recovered.

She was another matter. It was all too raw.

Until Jericho showed up. A shout rang out from the Oneroi and Skoti who welcomed him back. But he paid them no attention. His gaze was only for her as he made his way straight to her.

Tears blurred her vision as he scooped her up in his arms. "Thank you," she breathed.

He inclined his head before he flashed them out of the hall to where her room was.

She put her hand on his face, resting her thumb on the eye patch that he'd replaced. The joy and love she felt for him were unbelievable. Never in her life had she felt the like.

"How did you talk him into it?"

"Don't worry about it, it's not important."

Yes, it was. He had no idea what it meant to her to finally understand the part of her that had always been blocked. No wonder the Oneroi had gone Skoti. The sensation was so heady and intoxicating. She wanted to experience everything. To feel all emotions as deeply as possible.

"You are amazing, my Jericho."

Jericho froze at the words, which cut deep into his heart. "What did you say?"

"You are amazing."

"No, what did you call me?"

She smiled up at him. "My Jericho."

Strange how the thought of belonging to Zeus disgusted him on a level of pissed-off he could barely comprehend. But being owned by her . . .

It would be heaven.

Closing his eyes, he kissed her deeply, needing to feel her in his arms. For her he had twice bartered his freedom. But at least now he knew the one single truth.

She *was* worth it.

NOIR WENT RAMROD STIFF AS HE FELT THE POWERFUL wave piercing his realm. It stank of Olympian. Most of all, it reeked of Zeus.

What was that bastard up to?

It wasn't until he looked at the Skotos beside him that he understood. Zeus had freed them all. Their emotions were coming back to them.

A jubilant shout rang out as they embraced each other like long-lost siblings.

Azura popped in beside him. "What the hell is this?"

Noir curled his lip in repugnance. "The Olympians.

They're trying a new tactic." He moved past her to where his demons glanced around, dazed. "Gallu! Convert *any* Olympian you can find. Now!"

The gallu attacked, but the Skoti, who were now in full control of themselves, fought back with unprecedented skill. The drugs they'd used to numb them had vanished from their systems the instant their emotions came back.

Azura turned toward him with fear in her eyes. "This isn't good."

"Don't panic. It's a temporary setback and nothing we can't overcome." Noir used his powers to seal their realm. While he couldn't stop the Skoti from leaving, he could prevent anyone or anything else from coming in.

For now that would keep them from being attacked until he found a way to counteract this latest twist. Jericho was resourceful, he'd give him that. But he was no match for Noir. Noir knew how to motivate people.

And now that he had Kessar and his gallu . . .

He was going to win this no matter who he had to kill.

"SO THE PROPHECY IS TRUE."

Dressed in navy slacks and a dark blue top, Zeus turned at the sound of Hera's echoing voice. He'd been planning to return to the hall where the other gods would be dining by now, but this stopped him dead in his tracks. "What are you doing here, Hera?"

His wife manifested just inside the doorway that led from his bedroom to the main hallway. Tall with dark auburn hair, she was one of the most beautiful of all goddesses. And even though he cheated on her from time to time, he knew that she had no equal. Truly, she was exquisite and bold.

His perfect match.

"I just wanted to say how surprised I am that you're blithely acquiescing to a prophecy you once fought so hard to avoid."

"I don't know what you're talking about."

"Oh, come now, love. You know exactly what I'm talking about. It's the very thing that you've been fighting against since the day you banished the emotions from all the Oneroi. We both know there was no dream. No Oneroi who played in your sleep. They wouldn't have dared, no matter how angry you made them. It was Tiresias's words that caused you to slaughter and subjugate them all."

His breathing ragged, he glared at her. How dare she bring this up? It was something he'd relegated to the far past. Something he'd more than taken care of centuries ago. The prophecy had been averted and the world set to rights.

Still Hera went on, oblivious to his mounting anger. "On the fifth of June, a child born of man and of the heavenly gods will summon forth the greatest of Titans and lay the mighty Zeus low. In her hand spins the will of the Fates, and the great Kosmetas of the Olympians will be no more. For she will wield the ultimate power and she will walk in the world of man and in the world of dreams. Her love, her compassion will be the end of the Olympian order and a Titan will again rule them all." It was the curse his father had bestowed on him after Zeus had castrated him.

You will be ruined, and I will laugh as you fall . . .

Zeus's fury exploded. "Stop it," he snarled, ready to blast her.

Hera was relentless. "You know it's true. The very day Tiresias told you about the Oneroi baby that had been born—the one who would one day dethrone you, you called out the Furies and the others to pursue them all by claiming you'd been assaulted in your sleep. You especially made sure those half-blooded daughters who were prophesied to be the ones to replace us were brutally slaughtered. What was it you said, 'Leave none alive,' and so the Dolophoni and others drenched the earth red with the blood of half-breed infants. No one dared to question the great Zeus, whose word is law. But we both know the truth. You didn't want their emotions banished and their daughters slain because of a dream that never occurred. You wanted to maintain your place as the king of the gods."

He sneered at her. "I didn't see you standing up for them then."

"How could I have stopped you? You were a god possessed, and I wasn't stupid enough to stand in your way. Only Cratus was, and that baby that you sent everyone out to kill . . . did you know it survived?"

Zeus went cold at the question. "What? It's impossible. Dolor swore to me that he'd killed the baby. He tortured Leta with tales of how her daughter had died. How he'd gladly massacred it."

"Dolor wanted to cause her pain and he slaughtered a child, all right. But it wasn't hers. Her baby lived."

In that moment, he wanted to kill his wife. "Why didn't you tell me? How could you have kept this a secret?"

"I didn't know about it until now."

"What do you mean?"

"The demon they returned with, Asmodeus. I was having a nice, long chat with him about Noir's plans and the demon's future here among us Olympians. He told me that he overheard Jaden tell Cratus Delphine is the daughter of Leta and her human husband. She is the baby Cratus was sent to kill. The baby he refused to harm."

No . . .

Zeus staggered back as the implications hit him fully. How could he not have seen it?

Because prophecy was never meant to be thwarted.

I am the king of the gods . . .

No one was more powerful than he. Not even those three bitches called Fate. He would not be overthrown by some half-blooded human abomination.

He was Zeus. The king of all the Olympian gods, and all the power that went with it belonged to him.

But what set his fury roaring was the knowledge that he'd unknowingly put Delphine together with Cratus. He had sown the seeds of his own destruction.

Because of Nike. That little bitch would pay for her part in this. If he survived.

It's not too late.

No, he could still stop them all. Cratus had a human heart and had bound himself to Zeus. Nike was already trapped and in Noir's hands. They could easily leave her there to die.

As for Delphine . . .

He met Hera's dark gaze. "They both need to be put down."

"Agreed."

He arched his brow, surprised by her backing. Normally she fought against his edicts. "You agree?"

"I certainly don't want to be replaced by a half-human byblow. We are the rulers of Olympus, and by the Source and all its power, we will remain so. No matter what it takes."

A slow smile spread across his face. It was good to have his wife on his side of an argument for once. "Then summon the Phonoi." Murder, Killing and Slaughter, they were triplet goddesses who thrived on taking lives. Without conscience or mercy, they would attack. And best of all, they knew how to kill a god and not rupture the universe.

Zeus laughed at the thought of unleashing their destruction. "I have a new victim for them."

CHAPTER 13

DELPHINE LAID HER HAND AGAINST JERICHO'S FACE, letting his whiskers tease her palm as she stroked his lips with her thumb. "Have you any idea how much you mean to me?"

Jericho swallowed at her question. He hoped the answer was at the very least equal to what he felt for her. Otherwise it was going to really suck. "No."

She reached down to take his hand in hers. "More than any words can ever express."

Those syllables were still ringing in his ears when she used her powers to dissolve her clothes. Completely naked, she led his hand to her breast. "Make love to me, Jericho. Show me what it's like to experience you with all of my emotions intact."

His body reacted instantly to her request as his internal voice shouted in jubilation. "Are you sure?"

"Absolutely."

She dissolved his clothes before he even had a chance to think about it.

Jericho slid himself into bed with her so that he

could gather her into his arms. Oh, the sensation of her velvety skin rubbing against his . . .

If he died right now, he could ask for no greater send-off.

Her lips met his as he inhaled the warm scent of her body. He'd spent eternity alone. But somehow her touch eliminated all of his past. It was as if he'd known her forever. As if he couldn't imagine a world without her in it.

He never wanted to be away from her. If only he could have that one dream.

Delphine shivered at his hardness as he pressed against her. His body was ripped with taut muscles. Hard and smooth. Oh, he felt so incredibly good on top of her. She reveled in running her hands down his back to his lean waist and tight hips. Even though he was so much larger than she, he fit her perfectly as his soft white hair fell forward onto her face.

She sank her hands into his hair, pulling it back as their tongues danced together. He was so hungry with his kisses, she half-feared he'd devour her. She wrapped her legs around his hips, cradling him with her body. Chills spread over her as he left her lips to kiss a hot trail to her neck and ear.

Delphine gasped at the sensation of his tongue swirling around her earlobe. She should feel vulnerable and exposed, yet she didn't. All she could feel was Jericho. She wanted to possess him and keep him with her forever.

Her love for him burned white-hot through her heart, spreading out to every inch of her body. She alone knew this part of him. Saw the side of him that was kind and giving.

To the rest of the world he was brutal, but to her he was tame and sweet.

She almost laughed at the thought of his being sweet. Yet it was true. Where she was concerned, he was. And it made her wonder what he'd be like with a child of his own. She could so easily imagine it.

She wanted to be the one to give him that legacy and peace. To hold him close, away from the world that would harm him. She didn't want him to fight anymore. He'd had more than his share of that. She wanted to show him a world where he could trust and be gentle. A world where no one would hurt or betray him. Ever.

"Stay with me, Jericho," she whispered in his ear.

"As long as you hold me like this, I'm not going anywhere."

She smiled at his husky words. At the emotion that deepened his tone and touched her heart. "You will always be safe with me."

Jericho breathed her in as he lost himself to her touch and to her promise. Never one to believe in such bullshit, he couldn't suppress the part of him that caved to it now. The part of him that would walk through the fires of hell just to touch her cheek.

Against all of his armor, she'd wormed her way into his soul. And he was lost to her now. There was no hope for him. All he could do was trust in her to keep her promises. Trust in her not to be one more person he should have never believed.

Don't hurt me, Delphine. The silent plea lodged in his throat, making him ache even while her touch set him on fire.

Her hands skimmed over his skin, teasing and delighting him. It'd been so long since anyone had held him like this.

No. No one had ever held him like this. For the first time, he was in the arms of someone who cared for him. Not a goddess out to make her other lovers jealous. Or a nymph who wanted to scratch an itch.

Most of all, he was being held by someone *he* cared about. Someone who meant something more to him other than a quick tumble.

Delphine touched more than his body. She touched his heart and his soul. And he would die to protect her.

Why not? You've already sold your freedom for her. Twice.

He should be angry over that. But he wasn't. The thought that she would be whole was enough for him.

You won't be saying that when Zeus is torturing you.

Actually, he would. The memory of this moment would carry him through Zeus's worst and there would never be a single regret. He knew it. His own life no longer mattered to him as much as hers did.

She *was* his life and he was safeguarding it by giving up his freedom. It was a small price, really, and one he was glad to pay.

Pulling back, he stared down at her face. He traced the line of her cheek while his gaze was locked to hers. "You are so beautiful."

She reached up and fingered his eye patch before

she lifted it off and dropped it to the floor. He'd always been so self-conscious over the scar and white eye, but not with her. He wanted her to see him as he was.

And she did see him for all his faults and strengths, and it didn't matter to her.

Smiling so sweetly that it made his breath catch, she cupped his cheek in her soft hand. Tilting his head, he kissed the inside of her wrist.

"I'm so sorry for what Zeus did to you."

"It's all right. It was worth it." Part of him wanted to tell her why he felt that way—because it had been for her—but the other part didn't want to shatter her memories of her childhood. What good would it do to tell her that he was the reason she'd been spared?

It wouldn't help her. Telling her that would only serve him, and he didn't want her to love him for what he'd done back then.

He wanted her to love him for himself. For what they shared together now. Not out of gratitude or debt. He wanted her love untainted.

I can't believe you said that. More than that, he couldn't believe that he wanted her love or anyone's. He was a god of hatred and strength. He'd always been disdainful of love and all tender emotions. He'd scorned anyone and everyone for acting a fool over something as transitory as love.

Yet as he lay here, naked with her, there was nothing inside him except a gentle peace he never wanted to end. She knew him. Had seen him at his worst, and yet she weathered it with grace and kindness, all the while never giving in to him.

She was the best part of him and he knew it.

Never in his life had he begged anyone for anything. But for her, he would gladly sacrifice his dignity and life.

Something you will be giving up as soon as Zeus has his hands on you. But that was all right, too.

He could live with that.

"What are you thinking about?" she asked. "You look so sad."

He kissed her brow. "Only that I wish we could stay like this forever. That we never had to get out of this bed."

"It would be nice, wouldn't it?"

Jericho nodded before he rolled over, putting her on top of him and cupping her breasts in his hands. Though they were on the small side, they were still the most perfect breasts he'd ever seen.

Delphine sucked her breath in sharply as Jericho rose up to suckle her right breast. Every flick of his tongue made her stomach flutter in response. She was on fire now, craving him with a madness she barely understood. It was as if she held an emptiness that only he could fill and until he did, she was going to ache for it.

She cupped his head in her hands while he teased her. His hard erection pressed against her stomach. She wished she had more experience to know how to please him. What it would take to make it special.

"What should I do for you?"

He looked up with a frown. "What?"

"I want to please you. I'm just not sure how."

His smile touched her deep inside. "Baby, I'm happy

just to taste you. But . . ." He took her hand and showed her how to cup him.

His groan of pleasure made her smile. At least until she squeezed too hard and he hissed. "Gentle, love, gentle."

"I'm sorry."

Jericho laughed at her fearful tone. It thrilled him that she was so concerned about him and his pleasure. Most of all, he wanted to bathe in her scent until it was branded into his senses. Until he was coated with her.

Laying her back on the bed, he pulled back to stare at her there in the dim light. Her pale skin was gorgeous, her legs slightly parted in open invitation. And he was going to love her so thoroughly that she'd never forget this moment.

Zeus could put him in chains any minute now. But before he went, he wanted this one last memory to take with him. She would be the only balm he'd ever know.

Delphine was stunned by the ferocity of his kiss as he returned to her lips. But he didn't stop there. He moved over her body slowly, thoroughly, kissing and licking every inch of her. From her throat to her breasts, then lower to her hips. He worked his way down her legs to her feet and toes. Squealing in pleasure, she had to force herself not to kick as he suckled each of her toes in turn.

But it was when he came up between her legs to taste the part of her that craved him the most that her real pleasure began. He lifted her hips from the bed as his tongue delved deep inside her.

Delphine couldn't breathe at the intensity of the heat that cut through her body. She buried her hand in his hair as he tasted her fully.

"Come for me, Delphine," he growled. "Let me taste your pleasure."

But she didn't give in until he sank his fingers deep inside her. The moment he did, she screamed out in release as her body burst into ribbons of ecstasy.

Jericho smiled at the sound of her orgasm. Finally it was time for what he wanted most. Her body was still convulsing as he lay over her and slid himself inside.

Delphine gasped at the sudden fullness inside her body. At the sensation of Jericho full and hard. Never in her life had she imagined just how good this would feel. And when he slowly began to rock himself against her, she honestly thought she'd die from the bliss.

He held himself up on one arm to look down at her. "Are you all right?"

She wrapped her legs around his, drawing him in even deeper. "Absolutely. I couldn't be more so."

His smile made her heart flutter. She cupped his scarred cheek, staring into his dual-colored eyes as she watched the pleasure play across his face. He drove himself deep inside her, then paused. Gathering her in his arms, he rolled, putting her on top of him.

She gasped as he lifted his hips.

"Ride me, Delphine. I want to see you take your pleasure from me."

Unsure, she was timid at first, afraid she might somehow harm him. But as she moved and he growled tenderly, she grew more bold. Honestly, she loved being able to look down at him. To see the way the muscles of his abdomen moved.

His gaze locked with hers, he reached down between their bodies to where they were joined. She had no idea what he intended to do until his fingers stroked her cleft.

The moment he touched her, she jumped in pleasure. "Oh, my goodness."

He smiled again. "Like that, do you?"

Unable to speak, she nodded.

Jericho laughed as he stroked her in time to her thrusts. He loved the sight of her biting her lip as she quickened her strokes. He wanted to come so badly he could taste it, but he didn't want this to end. He wanted to stay inside her forever.

Why did sex have to be so short?

He ground his teeth, trying to stave off his climax, but as she found her own release while he was inside her, he was lost to it. Throwing his head back, he roared with the ferocity of his orgasm.

Damn . . .

He drove himself as deep as he could while his body exploded with pleasure. Oh, yeah, she was worth hell and then some. And he'd sell his soul to the lowest bidder if he could stay here with her like this for eternity.

Damn you, Zeus. But he'd made his bed and he would lie in it.

For Delphine. He could never lose sight of why he'd made his pact. It was for her and her alone. . . .

She'd been right all along. Sometimes people did

do things for others without expecting anything in return.

Love was real and he felt it with every part of him. All he needed was to know she was happy, and it was enough for him.

I am the worst sort of fool.

But even with his conscience yelling at him, he couldn't regret what he'd done. This was exactly what she'd tried to explain to him, and it was only by experiencing it that he finally understood.

His mother was wrong. Hatred wasn't the strongest emotion. What he felt for Delphine gave him more courage and more determination than all the hatred that had corrupted him. This was the reason to live.

Not for revenge and definitely not for hatred.

He lived for her love.

Sighing, Delphine sank down over him. She laid her head against his chest so that she could hear his heart beating as her body settled down. His arms held her close, making her feel protected, and as far-fetched as it was . . . loved. She knew better than to hope for that where he was concerned.

He thought of love as a weakness to be spurned. If only she could make him understand what she felt for him.

But it wasn't meant to be. She could only dream of having Jericho love her the way her parents had loved each other. Even now she remembered the way her mother had wept when her father had died.

She'd been thirteen when he'd caught an infection. For weeks he'd suffered while her mother did everything she could to heal him.

He'd left them in the middle of the night. Her mother's anguished screams had awakened her in the morning. It'd taken three men to pull her mother away from her father's body, and there had been no consoling her.

Her mother had only lived six months before she'd succumbed to an illness herself. At least that's what they told Delphine. But she'd known the truth. Unable to live without her father, her mother had willed herself dead. Nothing Delphine had done had been able to cheer her mother.

"You will find love one day, daughter. And you will understand. I only hope that when it comes for you, you're able to grow old and have decades together." Those had been the last words her mother had spoken to her.

Arik had brought her here three days later.

Since the day of her arrival on the Vanishing Isle, Delphine had given up on ever understanding what her mother had tried so desperately to explain.

And when it had finally come for her, she'd found it in the most unlikely of places. In the arms of a god of hatred . . .

Who would have ever imagined?

She propped her head up on her hand to stare up at his beautiful eyes. "That was incredible."

He laughed gently as he brushed his fingers through her tangled hair. "I'm pretty sure you broke me."

She jerked up, concerned over what he meant. "What? Did I hurt you?"

"No. I'm just too content now to move."

She returned his smile. "You're so wrong."

Jericho wrapped his arms around her and held her tight against him until she protested. Never in his life had he felt like this about another being.

No anger. No pain.

Just her.

At least until a sharp crash sounded outside their doors. He could hear angry voices and something that sounded like breaking glass.

Anger destroyed his hard-won peace. "I should have known it was too soon to be feeling satisfied," he groused, dressing himself.

"Let's at least hope it's not a gallu."

He scowled at her, and the tone of her voice that said it was the worst thing she could imagine. "Why? They're not all bad, in a smelly, skanky, need-to-be-killed kind of way."

"My point exactly." She dressed and joined him by the bed.

Jericho took her hand and led her from the room, making sure to keep himself between her and the possible threat they were heading toward.

By the time they reached the hall, three Oneroi were holding Zeth back while M'Adoc brushed at his clothes. It appeared that Zeth must have attacked him.

But at least M'Adoc was looking better. Some of the bruises had healed, and he wasn't nearly as pale as he'd been earlier.

"I want his heart in my fist," Zeth snarled.

M'Adoc gave him a patient stare. "As do we all. But for now, we're blocked out of Azmodea. The best we can do is prepare to fight until we find a way in."

Zeth struggled against the men holding him. He let loose a battle cry that echoed around them.

"Easy, tiger," Jericho said, letting go of Delphine to join their small group. "I don't want that shit ringing in my ears. If it does, you've got a much worse problem than Noir. I'll be the one beating your ass."

Zeth shook the others off him. He straightened up to give Jericho a knowing once-over. "I remember you. You tried to get through the drugs to talk to me."

Jericho inclined his head. "You were definitely out of it." He looked around at the Skoti and Oneroi . . . and remembered a time when the two groups had seldom interacted. "You guys all good now?"

M'Adoc shrugged. "Depends. Now that we have emotions again, some of us are harboring grudges and hard feelings." He passed a meaningful look at Zeth. "While others just want to kill because they can't handle their anger."

Jericho scoffed. "Sounds like a regular walk in the park for me."

M'Adoc gave a sarcastic laugh. "We're trying to restructure our duties, and some of us are in disagreement about who the new leaders should be."

Zeth curled his lip. "The Skoti need their own rep. We don't trust you assholes. Too many centuries of you killing and stalking us."

M'Adoc growled low in his throat. "Excuse me? You were the ones who provoked *us*. None of you could behave, and you were one step away from bringing the wrath of Zeus down on *all* of us. Having been one of the original ones he tortured, I can tell you we were kinder on you than he would have been on us."

Zeth rolled his eyes. "Whatever."

Jericho cast a sideways glance to Delphine, who seemed as bemused by their argument as he was. Not to mention he really resented being pulled out of her arms for something so stupid. They were lucky he was feeling a bit mellow right now.

Delphine looked about the room of gathered Oneroi and Skoti. "You all appear a lot more clear-headed than you were earlier. What else have you decided?"

M'Adoc indicated several of the Oneroi around him. "We're getting rid of the nomenclature Zeus forced on us."

Jericho scowled, not understanding. "The what?"

"M, V and D apostrophe names. Zeus gave them to us as a punishment and to strip out our individuality. Our real names were forbidden, and he used those letters to further humiliate us by reminding us that we were his obedient servants and not our own entities."

Zeth's blue eyes glowed with hatred. "Each letter designated a job we were supposed to perform. M were those who policed the Oneroi and Skoti—basically the narcs of the group. The V's helped humans through sleep and the D's helped the gods and the Dark-Hunters. It's why one of the first things Skoti do when they rebel is to revert to the names we were given at birth. In most cases. There have been a few such as V'Aiden who didn't. But I've always thought he was an idiot anyway."

Madoc glanced to Zeth. "And we're now one force reunited. Right, Zeth?"

"Bite me, asshole."

The Oneroi standing behind him popped him on the back of the head. Zeth turned to attack, but didn't manage more than a step before Madoc had him in a headlock. "Don't try my patience, Zeth. It's running perilously thin." He let out a deep sigh as he glanced back to Jericho. "It really makes you wonder how Ash manages to handle the Dark-Hunters, doesn't it?"

Jericho laughed. "So what name do we call you?"

He released Zeth, who snarled, but thought better of attacking him again. "I'm sticking with Madoc. It'll remind me of why we can never let Zeus or anyone else ever subjugate us again."

"I can respect that. And I think I know how Ash handles his crew." Jericho pulled off the whip that Azura had given him and handed it to Madoc.

But as he did so, a thought struck him.

"Sonofa . . . I know how we can get inside Azmodea."

Madoc's eyes lit up with the same excitement he felt. "How?"

"Asmodeus!" he shouted, summoning the demon to him.

The demon appeared instantly. "You rang, Mino— well, you're not really the Minor Master anymore, are you? What should I call you?"

Jericho narrowed his gaze threateningly. "Think of a polite term, demon."

Asmodeus's eyes widened. "Mister Master it is. What can I do for you?"

"Get us into Azmodea."

The demon sputtered in disbelief. "Why in the name

of smelly feet would you want to go there again? What good could possibly come from that?"

"We need to get Jaden out."

"You can't."

Jericho turned as Jared approached them. He must have teleported in right after the demon. Still dressed in black, he looked remarkably fresh and undamaged given the fight they'd all been through.

"What do you mean?" Jericho asked.

Jared's eerie eyes were sad. "Jaden willingly consigned himself to their service. You take him out of there without their permission, and he dies. Believe me, if I could have carried him out of there, I would have."

Delphine sighed. This was getting worse. Thanks to Zeus they couldn't send Jericho in and now they couldn't even use Jaden. "Then how do we stop Noir and Azura if we can't get to Jaden?"

"You'd have to send in Cam and Rezar. Only they have the power to imprison Noir and Azura."

Delphine glanced around, grateful to see she wasn't the only one who thought Jared had lost his mind. "Who?"

Jericho answered in a cold, dead tone. "The original gods of the sun and of fire. They are said to be the most powerful of all the creation gods."

Jared inclined his head to him. "Exactly. They alone have the powers to negate Azura and Noir." Air and darkness. Those could only be extinguished by sun and fire.

That at least gave Delphine a degree of hope. "Where are they?"

Jared shrugged. "No one knows. After the first war, they, disgusted by what they'd seen from the gods and humanity, withdrew into hiding."

Jericho cursed foully at the news. "You've got to be kidding me."

Jared shook his head. "The only person who could find them or even identify them is Jaden. Or Noir and Azura. Since I'm relatively sure they don't want them found, I wouldn't put money on the two of them helping us."

Jericho expelled an agitated breath. "So there's no way to completely defeat them."

"They're gods, Jericho. You've already fought that war, and how many centuries did you and the Olympians fight? Taking out a god isn't easy. The best you can do is trap them, but that takes stealth, and since they're both on guard now . . ."

"So what do we do?" Madoc asked.

"You'll have to negate the gallu threat. Protect the humans and wait for the Malachai to mature his powers—praying the whole time he doesn't join ranks with Noir." Jared looked around at the Oneroi gathered. "And keep them out of our dreams. I'm sure with the gallu, they'll be attacking on that front. Zarek's plan is the best bet you have. Reclaim, neutralize or kill every Olympian who stands with them. Show them no mercy."

Zeth frowned. "But you're still saying that we can't win this."

"No—we can . . . eventually. It won't be this week or this year and definitely not today. But if we assemble the right team and make no mistakes, we can defeat them and put them in a place where they'll never be able to harm another person or god again."

Delphine swallowed at the dire prediction. "And if we fail?"

Madoc sighed. "It'll suck to be human."

"It'll suck more to be us," Zeth said in a surly tone.

Jared nodded.

"I can't believe I was ever stupid enough to trust Noir. Come to the dark side. We have cookies," Zeth grumbled.

Jericho clapped him on the back. "Don't be so hard on yourself. It wasn't the cookies that tempted you."

"No. When you're denied basic necessities, you're willing to do anything to get them."

Jericho met Delphine's gaze. "Believe me, I know and I almost made the same mistake you did. Evil is seductive. It's what makes the two of them so dangerous."

"No," Jared said, his tone dire. "It's our willingness to believe their lies and to see what we want to see that makes it so dangerous. Even when we know better, we lie to ourselves and that's where the true betrayal is."

Zeth nodded. "As the great poet once wrote, 'To thine own self be true.'"

They all stared at him aghast.

"What?" he asked in an offended tone. "You don't think a Skotos can be literate? I happen to love Shakespeare. *Hamlet* is one of my faves."

Jericho snorted. "I'm not touching that one with tongs and a gas mask." He looked back at Madoc. "What other changes have you guys decided on?"

Madoc indicated him and Zeth. "We don't know if D'Alerian lives or not. I'm going to keep hoping, but until we know for sure, we have to have someone to lead the Oneroi and help them adjust to what's going on." His eyes sad, he hesitated before he spoke again. "M'Ordant's dead, and our hierarchy is in shambles. As much as it pains me to admit it, I think Zeth is right and it'll help to have him in as a commander. He's been leading the Skoti for a while now and they tend to listen to him."

Zeth scoffed. "For the record, I was his third choice behind Solin and Xypher."

Madoc gave him an unamused stare. "And all things considered, you're probably the more sensible one anyway. Xypher's more demon than Skotos, and Solin . . . he'd only be interested in monitoring and helping our women."

Deimos gave a short laugh of agreement. "Phobos and I are still in charge of the Dolophoni. Nothing changes there, except we'll be assisting the Oneroi more now than we have in the past."

It all sounded great to Jericho except for one minor concerning detail. "Have you run this by Zeus?"

Madoc shook his head. "Not yet, but I don't think he'll oppose it. So long as we keep his dreams clear, he should be all right with it."

Zeth didn't look as convinced. "What if he takes our emotions again?"

"He won't," Jericho said with total confidence.

Still, Zeth was skeptical. "How can you be so sure?"

Jericho wasn't about to tell them of his bargain

with the asshole. No one needed to know what he'd relegated himself to for their benefit. "I put a safeguard in. If he goes back on his word, it won't go well for him."

Asmodeus wrinkled his brow as he looked back and forth between the group. "So where does my demon self fit into all this?"

Deimos draped an arm around his shoulder. "Technical advisor. Since you know our enemies so well, we're going to pick your brain."

Asmodeus's eyes widened. "I'll tell you what you want to know. There's no need to torture me for it."

Deimos looked around, his face a mask of befuddlement. "Huh?"

Delphine laughed before she explained. "Pick your brain is an idiomatic expression, Asmodeus. It means we'll have you tell us things. We're not actually going in there to mess with your head."

He let out a long, relieved breath. "Oh, thank the Source. I can't stand it when someone opens my skull. It really hurts."

Deimos screwed his face up in sympathy. "I'm glad I'm not a demon."

Asmodeus looked eager again. "So where do we start?"

Madoc glanced to Jericho and Deimos. "With Azura and Noir—we need to be attacking them and weakening them. So long as they're defending, they won't be able to plot. The more we use our Oneroi to hit them, the better. They have to sleep sometime."

"And I can help," Jared offered. "So long as my lady

allows me to. By the way," he looked at Jericho, "you can never allow them to have Jaden's medallion."

"Why?"

"When placed over the heart of a god, it renders the god powerless."

Jericho gaped as a brilliant idea went through him. "Can we use it on Noir?"

"I'm rather sure that's why Jaden wanted it."

"Then why hasn't he used it?" Zeth asked.

Jared gave him a wry stare. "Have you ever tried to put something like that around the throat of a god who hates you? It's not the easiest thing. I'm sure if it were simple, Jaden would have done it."

"Okay, good point, but still . . ."

"We need that amulet," Jericho finished.

Jared nodded. "But once Zephyra learns you don't have it, she's going to recall me."

"Maybe, maybe not. We might be able to negotiate with her again."

Jared scoffed. "Negotiating with her isn't the easiest thing to do. More often than not, it involves bloodletting. And by that I mean mine."

"Delphine?"

Delphine frowned as she saw an Oneroi woman calling her from across the room.

"Do you know her?" Jericho asked.

"No, but she obviously knows me." She smiled at him. "I'll be right back."

Jericho watched her leave, his heart heavy. The one thing he regretted most out of all this was that as Zeus's slave, he'd never see her again.

She would be lost to him.

Unwilling to think about it, he returned to their conversation. He wouldn't regret what he'd done. Only the future that the two of them would be denied.

DELPHINE FOLLOWED THE ONEROI WHO MOTIONED her out of the hall. What could the woman possibly want? And why couldn't they speak in the large room with the others?

Curious, she approached the goddess, who had finally stopped walking away from her. "Did you need something?"

Raven-haired and petite, the woman reminded her of someone, but she couldn't think of who. She turned toward Delphine with a smile. "Yes, there is something I need."

"And that is?"

The woman split from one into three identical goddesses. Before Delphine could even move, they had her bound.

"Your death," the first one snarled an instant before she slashed her throat.

CHAPTER 14

JERICHO PAUSED IN FRONT OF THE LARGE WINDOWS that looked out onto the serene beach far below. It was beautiful here, and he wondered how many times Delphine had stood in this spot unable to appreciate how lovely it was because of what Zeus had done to her.

That would no longer be her problem.

Madoc joined him. "You know, I've been faking not having emotions for so long that I'm not really sure how to show them now. I still want to be completely stoic. Weird, huh?"

Jericho shrugged. "Makes sense to me. When you live a lie long enough, it has a way of becoming the truth." Although after all the centuries he'd spent living as a mute, it was hard to believe how easily he'd adapted to speaking again.

It made him wonder if anyone other than Delphine could have opened him up the same way.

No. No one had ever had her effect on him. She was unique, and without her, he would have been lost for all eternity.

Madoc stepped closer and lowered his voice. "I

didn't want to say anything in front of the others, but Zeth and I talked it over. We'd like to offer you the third position as Oneroi leader. We think you'd be great at it."

Jericho frowned. "I'm not an Oneroi."

"No, but you're a warrior with practical experience outside of dreams. We need someone to teach us new tactics against the demons."

What a nice world that would have been. But his new reality would never allow him that kind of luxury. "Yeah, well, I'd love to, but I have to decline."

"Why?"

Jericho glanced to the door where Delphine had vanished. "My time is spoken for and there's no way to get out of it. Sorry. But I can think of someone else who would be great at it. Someone who can move entire mountain ranges with nothing more than the sheer force of her obstinate will."

Madoc smiled as if he understood perfectly. "Delphine?"

Before Jericho could answer, the door crashed open to show him Delphine battling three identical women. Clad in black, they came at her with swords even as she danced around them, blocking their moves with her staff and thrusting back with a skill most men lacked.

Jericho knew those lethal bitches in an instant—at one time they had been his allies on ancient battlefields.

The Phonoi.

Rage consumed him at the sight. How dare they attack her! Without any rational thought, he flashed himself to Delphine's back so that he could protect her while she fought. But the moment he did, the Phonoi vanished.

"Cowards!" he shouted. "What? Are you too afraid to fight someone you know can kick your ass?" But then that was how they operated. They never attacked in the open. They moved like wraiths. Out of the darkness to kill and withdraw.

Scared for Delphine, he turned to face her. There was a vicious cut on the side of her neck that made his anger rise even higher.

"What did they do?"

She grimaced as she dissolved her staff. "They tried to cut my throat. But unless my powers are bound, I'm not helpless."

Thank the gods for that because he still wanted blood over the attack.

She hissed as she wiped at the wound. "It hurts, though."

Jericho looked past her to where Madoc had paused near them. "Madoc, can you heal her?"

The Oneroi wasted no time. He placed his hand over the wound and sealed it shut. But his eyes were as worried as Jericho's. "Who do you think sent them?"

Delphine wiped her hand over her neck and clothes, removing the blood from both. "*Why* would they send them?"

Jericho stared at her. "Who have you made mad?"

"Just you and Noir. With everyone else I tend to keep a low profile to avoid events such as this."

"Well, you obviously pissed off someone with some pull." The Phonoi only served a handful of gods. And he was determined to find out who was behind this.

Jericho summoned Jared to him. The Sephiroth came instantly, but there was a trace of blood at the corner of his lips that he wiped away with one knuckle. Whether it was his or someone else's Jared didn't say.

"Is there something you needed?" Jared asked.

Jericho nodded. "While I draw my powers from the Source, I know that you are more in tune with it. I need you to listen and tell me who sent the Phonoi after Delphine."

"Will that knowledge help you?"

Jericho looked at Delphine. "Absolutely."

Jared stiffened his arms out by his body and splayed his hands as if he was connecting with something none of them could see or hear. His eyes dilated to solid black and then turned completely red. Even the pupils. His skin turned so pale that he looked dead. The veins on his forehead protruded as he whispered in the language of the most ancient of gods.

Then his voice changed to that of the Source. Neither male nor female, it was a soft whisper and spoke in a language they could understand.

"You have summoned us from our slumber. Tell us what you seek."

Jericho crossed his arms over his chest. "The name of the god who is controlling the Phonoi."

"You know the answer, dear Cratus. There is no need to bother us with something so trivial."

"I know my suspicions, but I need to know the truth."

"Zeus." The name echoed throughout the hall.

Jericho growled low in his throat as his fury snapped hard. "Why?"

A single tear of blood ran down Jared's white cheek. "She is the one who can destroy him. Fathered by a mortal man and from the womb of a goddess she was born. It was why you were sent all those centuries ago to kill her. Why her mother fought so hard to protect her."

Delphine froze as she tried to understand what the Source was telling them. "My mother was human."

"No," the Source whispered. "Madoc was there the night they came for you. He fought by your mother's side."

"I fought with Leta, but Jericho wasn't there," Madoc said.

"You had already been taken into custody when he joined Dolor in their small hut. Though you didn't see him, he was there, and he saved the life of the one child Zeus was trying most to kill."

"I don't . . ." Madoc paused. "No, Zeus punished us for a dream he had."

"You knew the truth then as you know it now. No Oneroi ever came forward or was punished as the one who gave Zeus his dream. You even suspected it then, but never dared to breathe your suspicion out loud for fear of what more they'd do to you. Had any Oneroi dared to humiliate him, Zeus would have taken the one responsible and displayed his remains as a warning to all the others."

Madoc cursed. "He's right. I always wondered why Zeus failed to point out the one responsible. Why we were banned from ever mating again . . ."

Jared looked to Delphine. "A prophecy is only as powerful as the one who believes it. Now that you know the truth, it is only you who can command it." Jared hissed as his eyes and skin tone returned to normal.

He had broken his connection to the Source.

Delphine still hadn't moved as she tried to sort through everything. "My mother wasn't my mother?" She looked at Madoc. "Why didn't you tell me?"

"I didn't know. I mean, I knew you favored Leta in your looks, but never in my wildest hallucinations would I have dreamed you were her supposedly dead daughter. Thank the gods that I never told Zeus about you."

Indeed. And thank the gods she had made it a point to avoid the others. Had any ever suspected . . .

But it made her wonder about the woman who'd borne her. The woman she'd never met. "Is my mother still alive?"

"Yes. She lives in the human realm with her husband."

Delphine let out a happy yet sad cry as tears filled her eyes. Her mother was alive.

She turned to look at Jericho.

He wasn't there.

"Jericho?" Frowning, she glanced around the room but he was nowhere to be found.

Madoc scowled as he looked about, too. "He was right here."

The same thought went through them at the same time.

"Zeus."

Jericho had gone after the father god . . .

CHAPTER 15

ZEUS WAS LAUGHING AT HERMES WHEN HE FELT A rush of malevolence. It was so potent, it was tangible and it cut through him like a barbed knife.

Glancing around the hall, he tried to find the god or goddess who would dare feel that toward him. But he saw nothing. No one was even paying attention to him.

Was he hallucinating?

"Is something wrong?" Hera asked from her throne on the right side of his.

"Do you not feel that?"

"Feel what?"

Before he could answer, the door to the temple was shouldered open. Dressed in his full battle regalia, Jericho shoved the doors wide. The long black duster clung to his body, outlining every muscle that had been honed to kill. Sharp spikes stood up on each shoulder, curving in toward his face like a lethal frame.

His wings were wide as his long white hair flowed over his shoulders and down his back. Both of his hands were covered with sharp metallic claws that scraped against the gold of the door like nails on a chalkboard.

His black, silver-studded boots tapped an evil staccato as he walked across the marbled floor with a look of hell-wrath and merciless vengeance carved into his eerily perfect features.

No one moved.

No one dared. Only Zeus knew who his target was. The rest held their collective breaths in anxious fear lest Cratus call them out and they have to face him.

Undoubtedly they all remembered the last time he had boldly strode into this hall.

But today was different . . .

"Ares!" Zeus barked at his son, who was the god of war. "Protect your father! Take that dog down! Now!"

Ares covered himself with his armor, then jumped from his table into Jericho's path. Without hesitating, Jericho summoned his shield and sword before he lunged at the god. Their shields clanged loudly as Jericho used his to drive the god back.

Ares dug his feet in and leaned with all of his weight against the shield, but it wasn't enough to block Jericho. He was like a steamroller with only one destination in mind.

Zeus.

"Your blood won't appease me, Ares. Stand down or feel a wrath the likes of which you can't imagine."

Ares stabbed at him over the shield.

Growling, Jericho lifted the edge of his shield to deflect the strike, then returned it with a thrust of his own. His short sword curled around the back of his opponent's shield and opened a gash in Ares's upper arm.

Sick of the obstacle, Jericho threw his shield down and used his sword to pound against Ares's shield. Faster than the god could counter, Jericho delivered slash and stroke after slash and stroke down on the gold shield, bending it fast and furious until it was melded to Ares's arm. The god cried out as the gold pinched and bit into his flesh.

Jericho kicked him back, sending him sprawling across the floor.

He used his powers to wrench the sword from Ares's hand and brought it into the grasp of his left claw.

Crossing the swords in an arc before he brought them down to rest at his sides, Jericho turned around, looking at all the gods and goddesses gathered. "Anyone else want to bleed for this bastard?"

Zeus hurled a lightning bolt at him.

Jericho deflected it with his sword. "I will submit to you no more."

Another one came at him. This time, he dropped Ares's sword and caught the bolt in his hand. It sizzled against the silver claws, humming and throbbing. But it didn't hurt him through his armor. "Are you mentally defective, Olympian? You *never* defeated *me*. I submitted to you, but never again."

Zeus pulled forth another bolt. "You have a human's heart. You *can* be killed!"

Jericho threw the lighting bolt back at Zeus, who barely dodged it. "Then do it. If you or one of the blind fools who follows you honestly believe you can . . . bring it on. I'm in the mood for Slaughter. Killing and Murder, too."

Zeus's eyes widened as he caught Jericho's meaning and the source of his fury.

Athena, Apollo, Dionysus and several others stood up as if they would fight on Zeus's behalf.

But before they could, Jericho felt a powerful presence at his back. Expecting an attack, he turned, ready to battle.

Then froze in place.

There behind him was Delphine, with Madoc, Zeth, Zarek, Astrid, Jared, Deimos, Phobos, Asmodeus and two dozen Oneroi. And they looked open for business and ready to defend.

He could barely comprehend what he was seeing.

The other gods backed down immediately.

Delphine and her group moved forward until they surrounded him in a protective arc. She gave him a mischievous wink. "You didn't really think you'd be standing alone, did you?"

"Yeah, I did." Jericho was still aghast at their unfounded show of support. Never in his wildest imaginings would he have seen this coming.

Never would he have asked or expected it.

Madoc snorted. "It's a new world, brother. And we, the downtrodden, are taking it back." He looked at Zeus with a feral snarl. "We won't be tools for you or anyone else ever again. Consider yourself deposed."

Zeus growled low in his throat as he glared at each of them. "How dare you! Do you really think such a puny number scares us?"

Zeth snorted. "We scared you enough that you had our daughters slaughtered. What kind of god fears an infant?"

The Olympian gods whispered among themselves.

"It's true," Jared said. "He has twice commissioned the death of Delphine, and yet she lives."

Zeus sneered at Jericho. "By your own words, I own you. You swore that if I released the Oneroi's emotions you would bow down to me forever."

Jericho shrugged. "Yeah, I did say that, didn't I? You should have made me swear by my mother an unbreakable oath . . . oops. Sucks to be on your side today."

Zeus blustered angrily. "You can't renege."

"And I never would have, had you not come after the only reason I made the bargain to begin with." Jericho retracted the claws on his left hand to take Delphine's. "Had you not lied to me and gone after her, I would have left you to live in peace while I upheld my oath. But I will not serve someone who tried to kill the only person I've ever cared about. I will not bind myself to you and leave her vulnerable for you and your subjects to attack."

Delphine's grip tightened on his hand.

Ares pushed himself up from the floor. His shield gone, he cradled his broken arm to his chest. "We can fight them, Father."

"You can fight," Jericho mocked, "but you will never win."

"Father?" Ares asked uncertainly.

Zeus glared at them. "I will not be your prisoner."

"You won't have to be." Madoc moved to stand in front of Zeus. "We don't want your position or your authority. The gods know, we definitely don't want to have to deal with the whiny, petty bullshit the rest of you mess with on a daily basis."

Deimos snorted. "I don't know. I thought it was kind of funny when Dionysus ran a Dark-Hunter over with a Mardi Gras float a couple of years ago. That amused me for days on end." He laughed like an evil cartoon villain.

Jericho rolled his eyes. His old friend had always been a bit off. It was why the two of them had once gotten along so well.

Eros and Psyche stood up from their table to Jericho's left. With white wings and blond hair, Eros was the epitome of beauty. He was also dressed in a pair of black leather pants, a black shirt and boots like a human biker. Psyche's red hair was pulled back from her face, and she was dressed like a biker's moll. She tucked her hand into Eros's.

Jericho tensed as they made their way over to him and his group.

But what stunned him most was when Eros extended his hand to him in friendship. "We're not all assholes here. And right now, I'm thinking we have a lot more to be concerned about with Noir and his crew. Consider us allies."

Zeus bellowed in rage.

"Don't have an aneurysm, old man," Madoc said snidely. "What I propose is a truce. You and your court remain as you are, plotting and scheming against each other, while we are left alone to handle our affairs."

Zeus was aghast. "You would split this pantheon?"

Madoc shook his head in denial. "This pantheon was split a long time ago. We're through being your lap dogs and living in fear of angering you. We have much more important things to focus on than your petty intrigues and dalliances." He looked at Jericho. "And with a Titan behind us, we now have the power to tell you to shove it where even Helios doesn't shine."

Zeth lifted his head high to address the gods around them. "Any of you who are willing to fight Noir and Azura, we will welcome to our team. The rest of you can carry on business as usual."

Athena and Hades stepped forward. As always, Athena stood tall in a flowing red dress and black hair. The goddess of war and wisdom, she carried herself with all the fluidity of a Grace.

Hades, on the other hand, was dark and sinister. The god of the Underworld, he only had patience for his wife, who was notably absent. "We're with you."

Zeus let out a deep sound of disgust. "Have you lost your mind, Hades?"

"No. Rather I've found my soul. Noir and Azura declared war on us. The least we can do is offer a resistance they won't soon forget . . . brother."

"Then welcome." Madoc turned back to Zeus. "We will leave you in peace, and you *will* return the favor to us."

"Yeah!" Asmodeus shouted, puffing his chest out.

Zarek leaned forward and whispered, "You might not want to do that, big guy. The angry man on the throne doesn't have much of a sense of humor."

"Oh." Asmodeus hid himself behind Jared.

Zarek laughed until he realized other people were looking at him. He immediately sobered back to an "I'll kill you and dance on your grave" stance.

"Do we have an accord?" Jericho asked.

Zeus glared at them, but in the end, he knew it was the best offer he would get without a war. A war he might very well lose. "We have an accord."

Could he have said that with less enthusiasm? But the point was he had said it.

Madoc inclined his head to Zeus and the other gods before he turned and led their group out of the room.

Jericho released Delphine and retrieved his shield from where it had landed at Artemis's feet.

Slender and elegant with vibrant red hair, she looked over to Delphine, who was waiting for his return. "If you really love her, Cratus, let her know it every day. And always put her before you and your wants just as you've done here today. Take it from someone who knows. Love lost is the hardest burden to shoulder, and it's one you can never get under." Those words spoken, she manifested his bow and quiver of arrows that he'd given to her all those centuries ago. He was amazed she'd kept them. "My gift to you. Your aim will always be true and your quiver will never be empty so long as you carry them."

"Thank you."

She inclined her head to him and stepped back.

Jericho returned to Delphine's side and followed the others back to the Vanishing Isle.

As soon as they materialized, Delphine cornered him outside the hall. "Were you really willing to give up your freedom for me?"

He looked away sheepishly.

"Jericho." She turned his face back toward hers. "Why would you do that?"

Her question irritated him. He didn't like to be

questioned and definitely not over something so . . . personal. "Why do you think?"

She glared at him. "Because I'm a bossy hag and you'd rather be enslaved to a man you hate than deal with me."

That made his anger snap even harder. "You know . . ." He paused as he realized she was teasing him. His anger turned into aggravation. "You're not funny."

"I think I'm hysterical and I want to hear from you why you would have made such a bargain."

Jericho tried to move past her, but she wouldn't allow it. *She needs to hear it.*

She cupped his mouth in her soft hand. "C'mon, sweetie, you can say it." She moved his mouth playfully. "You don't suck, Delphine," she said in a faked deep voice. "I . . . you. C'mon, Jericho. I only bite in the bedroom. You can do this. I know you're not really mute."

But why did he have to say it? Wasn't it obvious? What more would he have to do to show her how much she meant to him?

But he knew she wouldn't give him a reprieve.

Not until he put into words what she wanted to hear.

"Because I love you . . . hag and all."

"Hag!" She went for him, but instead of hurting him, she tickled his ribs.

Jericho laughed, amazed at her play. No one had ever been so cavalier with him. He caught her against him and kissed her solidly. "Thank you for coming in to back me."

"No," she said, sobering instantly, "thank you for

defending me." She poked him sharply in the chest. "But don't you *ever* do that again. I never want you to put yourself at risk on my account."

"Why?"

She met his gaze, and the sincerity in those hazel eyes scorched him. "Because I love you, too, and I couldn't stand being the reason you were hurt or killed."

He lifted his hand to her lips. "Don't worry. I won't ever leave you alone. You get into too much trouble without me."

She growled at him. "Oh, please. I never got into trouble *until* you."

"Uh-huh."

"Um, guys," Phobos said, sticking his head out of the door, "I hate to interrupt whatever weirdness you two are partaking in, but we have a situation in here you might want to check on."

Frowning, Jericho led the way into the room to find a new group of Skoti.

Baffled by their appearance, he looked at Madoc for an explanation. "What's going on?"

Madoc held his hands up and shrugged. "We're not sure. They just appeared."

Another burst of light startled them as Nike flashed into the middle of the Skoti. Her back to him, she stood at an awkward angle with her wings drooping.

Jericho took a step toward her, then froze as she turned to face him and he met her gaze.

Nike was gallu.

Madoc and Phobos cursed as they manifested swords to attack.

"No!" Jericho snarled, shoving them away from her. "She's my sister."

Madoc looked at him as if he were one pint shy of a gallon. "She's infected. She'll kill all of us."

"I don't care." She was still his sister. Jericho armored himself before he approached her.

Snarling, she came at him like a wild animal, slashing at him with her hands and trying to bite him. Her wings fluttered out, but he managed to catch her from behind and hold her there even while her wings slapped at him. She screamed and kicked, then tried to head-butt him.

Even though he was armored, he could still feel her kicks against his shins.

"I need a cage," he grunted.

Delphine made one the size of a small closet. But it was large enough to hold Nike until they could find some way to help her. "Here."

Jericho shoved his sister into it and winced at the sight of her white eyes and serrated teeth. Bubbles foamed from her mouth as she reached through the bars to get to them.

Eros and Zarek exchanged a concerned look before they glanced to the Skoti.

Eros scratched his chin. "I'm thinking we should cage them, too, before they go Linda Blair on us."

One of the younger Skoti stood up. "We're infected. But with us, it's slow-acting."

Jericho scowled. "What?"

"They're testing a new venom on us to see if they can infect one of us during a fight without our knowing we're infected. So that once we return home, we can spread it to others."

How insidious—plus it would make them all suspicious of each other even after they'd fought.

Zarek cursed. "How do we fight this?"

"You have to kill the one who infected them."

They turned to Jared, who'd spoken in the most deadpan of tones.

"What?" Madoc asked incredulously.

"Zephyra discovered it," Jared explained. "If you kill the gallu who sired the zombie, the zombie reverts to normal."

Eros sputtered. "Well, that's just stupid. Who would have done that?"

"The Egyptian goddess Ma'at. The gallu invaded her domain centuries ago, and she modified them to give her people a fighting chance."

Madoc shook his head in disgust. "Peachy, just peachy."

"Yeah," Eros agreed. "By the way, no one here better tell Ma'at I said it was stupid. She has a nasty temper, and I don't need a smack-down from her."

Jericho ignored his random paranoia. "So how do we determine who infected her?"

Zarek shrugged. "Let's kill them all and let Hades figure it out."

Crossing his arms over his chest, Hades gave him an unamused glare. "For the record, I don't clean up after you bastards. And no gallu is coming near *my* domain. That's all I need is a realm full of infected dead. That has Cesar Romero all over it."

Eros held his hand up. "Uh, Hades, that's George

Romero. Cesar's the one who used to play the Joker on the 'Batman' TV show."

Hades gave him a flat stare. "Do I look like I care? And how do you know that?"

"Psyche and I go to the movies with Acheron. He's a major zombie junkie."

Ignoring their sniping, Asmodeus stepped forward sheepishly. "I'll find out who infected her."

Jericho frowned at Asmodeus's offer. "What?"

"I can get in there without any suspicion. Hopefully, I'll find the gallu and kill it."

Delphine shook her head. "Asmodeus—"

"Look, it's all right," the demon said, interrupting her. "I know it sounds corny as hell, but all of you have made me feel like part of a team. I've never had that before. And I want to do my part to help. If any of the rest of you go in, Noir will kill you. Me . . . he'll only torture. Maybe gut and insult. Maybe even some bitch-slapping. But I'm the only hope you've got."

Delphine passed a worried look to Jericho before she returned her gaze to Asmodeus. "We can't send you in there alone."

"Eh, I'll be all right. Noir hates me anyway."

"But if he suspects you, he'll kill you."

The demon shrugged. "Who wants to live forever? Well, for the record, I do, but I want to do this for you."

Jericho stopped him before he left. He slid the ring off his finger and handed it to him. "Take this."

Asmodeus curled his lip as he shrank back from it. "I'm not about to marry your ugly ass, boy. No offense, but you ain't my type. I like my dates with less

body hair . . . and with female parts attached by nature."

Jericho let out an aggravated growl. "It's not a
wedding ring, asshole. It's Berith's ring. You get into
trouble, you can summon him to help you get out of
there."

That completely changed his attitude. "Oh, hey,
that could be worth an engagement to you." Asmodeus
grinned as he palmed it. "If I'm not back in a few
hours . . . well, I don't want to think about that. I might
change my mind about doing this. I'm thinking happy
thoughts. Creamed dog innards and rotten steak. Yeah.
Yum." He vanished.

Delphine wrapped her arm around Jericho's and
did her best not to think about Asmodeus's parting imagery or the fact that he might really call that cuisine.
She didn't know why, but she strangely liked the demon. He was like their socially stunted illegitimate . . .
cousin. "You think he'll be all right?"

"He's not the one we should be worried about."

They turned toward Hades. "How so?"

"You're not done with Zeus. I'm sure of it. He
won't attack today, but you guys have publicly embarrassed him and if there's one thing I know about
my brother . . . he doesn't deal well with that."

"It's all right," Madoc said. "We're going to solid-
ify our place here."

"And you will need to cage us," another of the Skoti
said. "We've done enough damage on Noir's behalf. We
don't want to do any more."

Jared and Madoc caged them while Delphine considered everything that was happening. She wanted it to slow down, but there was nothing she could do.

It was getting scarier by the minute.

"I'm so sorry about Nike."

Jericho stared at her, his eyes sad. "Me, too. Dammit, I shouldn't have been distracted. I should have stayed in Azmodea until I located her."

"You can't blame yourself."

"Then who do I blame? I was the one who left her there."

"Because you were worried about me," Delphine whispered. "Had I not been there, you wouldn't have gotten sidetracked."

He pulled her against him. "This is definitely not your fault, baby. I made the decision and I abandoned her. I have to have faith in Asmodeus."

Hades approached them. "I'm returning to the Underworld. Let me know if you need me."

"We will. Thanks."

Hades inclined his head before he vanished.

Jericho watched as the others set about cleaning the hall and restoring it to its former beauty. But it was the sadness in Madoc's eyes that bothered him.

Releasing Delphine, he went to check on the Oneroi. "You okay?"

Madoc started to nod, then shook his head. "I miss my brothers. I've never been here without them and I keep wondering what D'Alerian would do if he were here. What he'll say when he comes back."

If *he comes back*. But Delphine had taught him not to be callous enough to say that out loud.

"You're doing a great job." Delphine came over and patted Madoc's arm. "Really. No one could do better, and I know D'Alerian would be proud of you and what you've done to protect us."

"Thanks." He looked down at her and smiled sadly. "By the way, I spoke to Zeth about what Jericho suggested. We'd like for you to be our third leader."

Delphine was surprised by his offer. "Me?"

Madoc nodded. "But for you, none of us would be here now. You're the one who saved Jericho and helped to liberate us. Without you, I'd still be chained to the floor."

Maybe, but Delphine wasn't used to being a leader of any kind. "I don't know."

"You'd be great at it," Jericho said with a confidence she definitely didn't feel.

She didn't know why, but coming from him, the praise meant more than anything. "All right. I'll try it. But if I screw something up, one of you better help me fix it."

Madoc laughed. "And we're going to try something else a little different."

"What?"

Madoc looked over to Zarek. "We're going to add two generals. Zarek and Jericho."

"Oh, goodie," Eros said sarcastically. "Could you have chosen two surlier people?"

"That's why they'll be in charge of our army. May the gods have mercy on whoever pisses them off, because Zarek and Jericho will have none for them."

Zarek cleared his throat. "You'd better be glad I'm flattered by that. Otherwise I'd gut you."

Jericho agreed with an angry glower. "Ditto."

Delphine was smiling as Astrid appeared with a crying toddler. He had eyes so bright a blue she would have thought him a Dream-Hunter had he not had Astrid's blond hair and looked just like his father . . . minus the goatee.

Her face distressed, Astrid handed him off to Zarek. "Menoeceus wants his father."

Zarek glared at her. "Bob is crying because he wants his mother to stop calling him that crap-ass name." Zarek cuddled the small boy to him as he rocked him gently against his shoulder while he continued to wail. Loudly. "It's all right, Bob. Daddy's got you now. I'm saving you from Mommy's bad naming taste. I'd be crying, too, if my mom named me after an idiot."

"Menoeceus is a great name," Astrid said defensively.

Zarek snorted. "For an old man or a feminine hygiene product. Not for my son. And next time *I* get to name the kid and it won't be something that sounds like meningitis."

Astrid stood with her hands on her hips, toe to toe with her husband. "You keep that up and next time you'll be the one birthing it, and don't mess with me, bucko, I have connections in that department. A pregnant man is not an impossibility in my neighborhood."

She started away from him.

"Yeah, well, I'll be glad to birth it if it means I can name him something normal," Zarek called after her.

"Yeah, yeah. This from a man who whines like a two-year-old when he stubs his toe. I'd like to see you survive ten hours of childbirth."

"I am not a wimp!" Zarek cast a menacing glare at all of them. "I have the damn scars to prove it."

"You the man," Eros said. "Not that whining over a stubbed toe is anything to be unmanned about. I do it myself."

Still the boy cried as if his heart was broken.

Bob? Delphine mouthed the name to Jericho, trying not to laugh at something that was obviously a sore spot for Zarek and Astrid. The name was as unlikely for the small golden-haired cherub as the gentleness of the fierce man holding him while he rocked him.

"I want my fluff-fluff!" Bob wailed.

Zarek looked panicked. "Fluff-fluff . . ." He handed the toddler to Jericho. "Hold him for a sec."

"I don't think—" Jericho paused as Zarek literally tossed the kid at him. Terrified, he had no choice but to take it.

Holding the toddler out in front of him, he wasn't sure what to do with it. He hadn't held an infant in centuries. Eyes wide, he stared at the little guy, who was as startled by him as Jericho was by Bob. The kid was absolutely silent.

"Look what you did," he snapped at Zarek. "I broke it."

Delphine laughed. "You didn't break him. He likes you."

Jericho wasn't so sure about that. Swallowing hard, he brought it in a little closer and tried to duplicate Zarek's rocking motion.

Bob pulled his hand out of his mouth and slapped it against Jericho's scarred cheek.

Jericho made an awful face. "Oh, gah, I've been slimed."

Bob laughed.

Laughing, too, Delphine reached up to wipe his cheek dry. "It's not slime. It's a baby kiss."

"It's slime," Zarek said as he returned with a light blue blanket that had the head of a lamb on one corner of it. He angled the head toward Bob. "Hello, little Bobby," he said in falsetto. "I'm the big bad lamb come to get a hug from you. Mwah!" He made a kissing noise.

Squealing happily, Bob grabbed the blanket and kissed it.

Delphine was aghast at the sight of two huge, fierce men coddling such a tiny child.

"We need that for YouTube," Astrid said with a wink.

"Most definitely."

Zarek took Bob back so that his son could cuddle the blanket. The little guy tucked the blanket under his cheek, which he rested on his father's shoulder. "See, he just needed his fluff." Zarek gave Astrid a teasing once-over. "I'll be needing some of mine later, too."

Astrid gave Delphine a dry stare. "I'm really going to strangle him."

Zarek kissed his son on the top of his head as he handed him back to Astrid. "Any time you need an expert parental hand—"

"I'll find Jericho."

Jericho looked horrified. "Um, could you at least wait until that thing's housebroken?"

Zarek laughed. "You know, that's how I felt, too. You should have seen my face when she told me she was pregnant. I honestly had a moment of total hara-kiri, but once the shock passed and after a few months went by, I actually got used to the concept. Believe it or not, they actually grow on you. Slime and all."

Delphine wrapped her arms around Jericho's waist. "Oh, come on, Jericho. Don't you want a little miniature you running around?"

"Not really, and I can't imagine you'd want another one of me, either."

She shoved at his back playfully before she went to join Madoc.

Zarek and Astrid left him to tend to Bob.

Alone, Jericho went back to Nike. "We're getting help for you, Nike. I promise."

She hissed at him.

"C'mon, Asmodeus," he whispered. "Don't fail me."

"Oh, little brother, that incompetent demon is the least of your concerns."

Jericho started at the sound of Zelos's voice behind him. He turned, intending to greet his brother. But the moment he did so, Zelos buried a dagger deep into his chest. All the way to the hilt . . .

Through his human heart.

Gasping, he staggered back, into Nike's arms.

CHAPTER 16

"NO!" DELPHINE SCREAMED AS SHE SAW ZELOS STAB his brother quicker than she could react. Her heart wrenched at the sight of Jericho falling as Nike seized him and attacked him from behind. An unimaginable fury took hold of her. One she could neither explain nor temper.

All she could taste was the need for blood.

Zelos's blood.

Before she even realized she'd moved, she had him on the ground, pounding his head against the floor as her fury rode her hard.

"Delphine, stop! You're going to kill him."

Somewhere through the haze of her anger, she recognized Madoc's voice as he tried to pull her away from Zelos. She wrenched her hand from Zelos's black hair. Rising, she kicked him hard in the ribs. "Hold him. Because if Jericho dies, I'm going to tear his heart out of his chest and feed it to him."

Zeth's eyes were wide. "Given the ass-whipping you just gave him, I'm sure you will." He looked at Madoc. "Remind me to *never* upset that woman."

Delphine barely heard him as she ran to Jericho. Deimos had pulled him away from Nike, but not before she'd bitten him.

He was panting and shaking as he lay on the floor.

Kneeling beside him, she choked from the wave of agony tearing through her. Her gaze swam with tears. "Baby?" Her voice broke as pain overwhelmed her.

He took her hand in his and held it while Deimos pressed a cloth to the wound in his chest. "What do we do?" Deimos asked. "I've never seen a god bleed like this."

"He has a human heart . . . but he can be resuscitated. The Oneroi and Dolophoni killed him every night for centuries, and every morning he was brought back to life."

"By Zeus," Deimos reminded her. "And no offense, but I don't think he's going to be overly accommodating given what we just did to him."

Tears flowed down her cheeks as she watched Jericho's face grow paler. His breathing more shallow.

"Don't leave me, Jericho," she whispered, cupping his scarred cheek in her hand. "Please. I can't cope with these emotions you gave me. I can't. And I don't want to be here without you. I need you with me."

He lifted her hand to his lips for a gentle kiss. "In all this time, whenever I died, I never wanted to wake up again. I prayed every night for it to be the last death. And now . . ." He choked and sputtered a mouthful of blood.

Delphine sobbed aloud as she tried to help him not choke on his own blood. She was covered in it, and it rammed home the fact that he was dying. Her entire body shaking, she knew she was losing him, and she couldn't bear the thought of it.

She would *not* lose him.

"He needs an immortal heart!" she shouted to Madoc, looking at him over her shoulder. Her gaze went from him to his prisoner.

She froze as the solution hit her like a fist in the stomach. It was harsh, but . . . .

Who better to give up his life to save Jericho than the traitor among them? The brother who'd betrayed him. The brother who had always betrayed him and everyone the selfish god came into contact with.

Zelos.

She met Deimos's gaze over Jericho's body and knew that he had the same exact thought she did.

"Stay with him." Deimos got up and crossed the room.

Delphine brushed the hair back from Jericho's face. "Breathe, baby, breathe. Hold on. We're not going to let you go."

Jericho's grip weakened on her hand. "At least I had you for a time."

"No!" she snapped at him. "You've been stubborn since the moment I met you. Don't you dare get complacent now. You fight this for me. You hear me?"

He nodded as he sputtered through more blood.

Delphine heard a struggle behind her, but she didn't turn to look. Honestly, she didn't care. Anyone who could do this to their own brother deserved no mercy.

Let him die.

Deimos returned with Zelos's heart in his hand.

Repulsed by the sight, Delphine cringed. Madoc

appeared by her side. He turned her in his arms to shield her face while Deimos exchanged their hearts. Madoc's steady, deep, rhythmic heartbeat helped to focus her while she kept her hand wrapped around Jericho's. There was no way she was going to let him go.

Not ever.

After what seemed like an eternity, she heard Jericho gasp. His grip on her hand strengthened.

Her heart hammering, she pulled back from Madoc to see him staring at them.

He coughed and narrowed an angry grimace at Madoc. "If you're going to snake on my girl, Madoc, you could at least wait until I'm cold."

Holding his hands up in surrender, Madoc laughed. "I would never snake your woman. You're the only man I know who would come back from Tartarus just to slaughter me for it."

Deimos met her gaze. "Delphine, you might want to turn your head again. I've got to cauterize that bite wound before it infects him."

Delphine did, but she still heard Jericho's curse as Deimos burned the gallu bite. And even though Jericho must have been in excruciating pain, his grip on her hand never turned painful.

As soon as Deimos was finished, she scooted closer to Jericho. "My poor baby," she breathed, kissing his cheek. "Don't you ever scare me like that again. I swear if you do I will beat you senseless."

Jericho pulled her into his arms and held her tight. Honestly, he never wanted to come that close to leaving her again, either. He kissed the top of her head, and out of the corner of his eye, he saw his brother's body. He probably should have felt bad or guilty, but he didn't. Zelos had always been a jealous bastard, and he'd made their childhoods unbearable.

"Who took his powers?"

Madoc indicated himself and Zeth. "We split them."

Zeth came forward. "You want us to dump him?"

"No. In spite of everything, he is my brother. Take his body to my mother and let her do with it as she will."

Deimos scoffed at his concern. "Do you think he'd be that kind to you?"

Jericho pushed himself up. "No. But someone," he gave a meaningful look to Delphine, "taught me to be a better person than that."

"All right," Zeth said with a sigh. "Time for more clean-up." He sighed. "I'm thinking maybe we should hire a full-time crew for this."

Madoc shoved him playfully. "Since most of it was caused by your team, I don't want to hear you bitching."

Jared hissed as he started toward them.

Jericho stiffened, afraid of what was attacking them now. Damn, couldn't they have one minute of peace? "What's wrong?"

Jared looked ill and pale. "I'm being summoned home. I have to go. Zephyra doesn't like for me to resist her."

Jericho tucked his wings in and cleaned his clothes. "You want me to talk to her?"

"It won't do any good. She's out of patience with my absence, and unless you have what she wants . . ."

He looked around with an agonized expression that said he was going to miss their company. No doubt he'd miss not being tortured most of all. "Good luck to you." Bowing his head, Jared vanished.

Delphine scowled as he left. "I feel so bad for him."

"So do I. I wish there was some way to get him free."

She sighed heavily. "I'm sure no one wishes that more than he does." She glanced back at Nike. "Do you think we should be worried about Asmodeus?"

"Yeah," Deimos said sarcastically. "Given the luck we've had, he's probably being disemboweled even as we speak."

ASMODEUS CREPT THROUGH THE BACK HALL WHERE only rodents normally scurried. He was doing his best to stay out of sight, sound and smell range. Noir and Azura were raw with their fury right now, beating everything that came near them.

No wonder he'd left here. But that wouldn't save him if they happened upon him now. They would gut him and make him pay for leaving them.

"What are you doing?"

He jumped and almost screamed at the deep voice coming out of the darkness. "Dammit, Jaden," he whispered angrily, "who unchained you?"

"Noir. He was afraid someone might free me while they were rescuing and fighting the Skoti. So I'm banished to the hallway where outsiders can't walk."

Asmodeus screwed his face up as he saw the damage they'd done to Jaden. How could he even speak with the way his lips were swollen? But the most amazing part was how Jaden could use his powers to camouflage those wounds when demons summoned him to the outside world.

No one on the outside knew what horrors lived here in this hell realm.

Jaden leaned forward to gaze into the room where Asmodeus had been looking for a possible lead. "The gallu you seek is the one in the back of the room."

"I hate it when you read my thoughts."

"I know. Trust me, it's no privilege for me, either. I don't need to know how screwed up you are. I have my own issues."

"Yeah . . . so any bright ideas on how I'm going to get to that gallu, kill it without getting bitten, and not get caught?"

"You won't have to."

Asmodeus cocked his head as a wave of fear went through him. Was Jaden planning to kill him? "What do you mean?"

Jaden pulled a sparkling green amulet out of his pocket. "Take that to Jericho and tell him to free my . . . to free Jared from his master, and I'll take care of your gallu for you."

Stunned, Asmodeus couldn't move. Dare he even hope for it? "Are you sure? Can you do that?"

Nodding, Jaden put the amulet in his hand. "Swear to me you won't keep it for yourself. 'Cause if you do, so help me—"

"I know, I know. You'll gut me. Don't worry, I won't betray you."

"Thank you." Jaden started away from him.

"Hey, Jaden?"

He paused and turned back to face him.

"Why is it so important to you that Jared goes free?"

"Because . . ." When he finished the sentence, his tone was so low that Asmodeus wasn't even sure he'd heard it correctly. "I'm the reason he was damned. Now go before the others find you."

Asmodeus inclined his head to him before he used his powers to teleport out of the dismal hole back into the light hall where his friends were waiting for him.

Friends.

Who would have ever dreamed a demon like him could have something like that?

Delphine stood up from her chair as soon as she saw Asmodeus return. She looked to Nike, but the goddess was unchanged from her gallu form. "What happened?"

Asmodeus closed the distance between them. "Jaden said he'd take care of the gallu for us." He handed the necklace over to Jericho. "And he told me to give you this so that you could buy Jared's freedom."

Jericho gaped in disbelief as he held the expensive antique. "Are you serious?"

Asmodeus nodded.

And before Jericho could speak again, he heard Nike scream out in pain. She fell to her knees on the floor, where she rocked back and forth as if she were on fire. The other Skoti reacted the same way.

By the time Jericho reached the cage, Nike looked up at him, her eyes normal again. She was bewildered and scared. "Cratus?"

Jericho nodded as joy coursed though him. It'd

worked. He couldn't believe it. Opening the door, he pulled his sister into his arms and held her close. "Are you all right?"

"I'm confused. I was in a hole and Zelos came to me with a demon. He was so angry. He told me to join them, but I refused. I don't trust Noir or Azura, and I will not forsake my people." She shook her head. "Zelos called me a fool and then he made the demon bite me." She wept against his shoulder.

Jericho soothed her. "Don't worry, Nike. Zelos is gone."

"Gone where?"

"Deimos killed him."

She gasped, then winced. "I wish I could be as sad for him as I was for Bia when she died. But there wasn't much about Zelos worth mourning. I only hope that by dying, he's finally found some peace."

Her features stricken, Nike turned and saw Delphine standing off to the side. Her gaze narrowed thoughtfully as she looked back and forth between them. "I was right about my brother, wasn't I?"

Delphine smiled. "Absolutely, and I can't thank you enough."

Nike cut a devious look to Jericho. "I have a feeling that's mutual."

"It is. But that's all I'm saying on the matter." Jericho stepped back from them. "Now, if you ladies don't mind, I have something I need to take care of."

JERICHO HESITATED IN THE GLASSY DARK HALLWAY he'd visited earlier with Tory. Maybe he shouldn't be doing this.

Jared had been emphatic that Zephyra should never have the amulet. But after all Jaden and Jared had done for them, it seemed wrong to leave Jared enslaved. Having served that sentence in hell, he had a hard time delivering it up to anyone else. Especially when he didn't deserve it.

"What are you doing here?"

He paused at Medea's dangerous tone. "Do you always haunt the hallway?"

"No, but I can sense whenever a stranger is here and I don't like uninvited people in my domain."

He shrugged nonchalantly. "You can stand down. I'm not staying long. I'm only here to see your mother."

"Mum?" she called, not bothering to take him to the study this time.

Zephyra came in hot and flustered. "I thought I told you not to—" Her voice broke off as she saw Jericho. "What are *you* doing here?"

Damn, could she have added any more loathing to that single word? A lesser man would have had to scrape himself up off the floor.

"I've come to get Jared."

She snorted derisively. "Hell, no. He's back where he . . ." Her voice faded off as he pulled the amulet from his pocket and let it dangle from his fingers so that she could see it.

Her eyes eager and hungry, she reached for it.

Jericho pulled it back. "Not until you release Jared to me."

She hissed. "Fine."

"And," he said quickly before she could act, "I want one promise from you."

She looked at him as if he were the most repugnant creature ever made. "Are you insane? You're lucky you're still alive."

"Believe me, I know," he said with a bitter laugh. "But I'm not going to provide you with the means to hurt someone who's helped me. I will give you this on the condition that it's never used against Acheron or his mother. Ever."

She rolled her eyes. "As if I'd be that stupid. With my luck it wouldn't work on them anyway and they'd kill me for the insult. Now give us the medallion."

He pulled it back again. "Jared first."

"Jared!" she snapped.

He appeared instantly by her side, his features drawn and tight. As soon as he saw Jericho, he narrowed his gaze suspiciously. "What have you done, Jericho?"

"A favor for a favor."

Zephyra shoved him at Jericho. "I voluntarily release you from my service into his. Now go."

Jared shook his head and panicked as he saw the medallion. "You can't do this!"

Jericho hesitated. The last thing he wanted to do was make a mistake in this. But surely Jaden wouldn't have sent this to him if it would kill them all. "Why?"

"Because I'd rather Jaden use it to barter his freedom. Please." His voice was filled with agony.

"It's too late." Zephyra snatched it from Jericho's hand. "Now get out before I feed you both to my Daimons."

Jared winced as she and Medea vanished. A muscle worked in his jaw as if he wanted to curse.

Jericho felt bad for him. It had to be awful for Jared to find no joy in being free. "I'm sorry."

"So am I," he said wistfully.

"At least you're free now."

Jared flicked at the thin containment collar around his neck. "Hardly."

"I can remove it."

He gave Jericho a flat, dead stare. "And I'll die when you do. Only the Source can free me from my punishment."

"I don't need a slave, Jared. You'll have all the freedom you want."

Jared nodded glumly.

Strange, Jericho would have thought he'd be happier than this. But then his freedom had been bought at the expense of Jaden's. Since he didn't know what they were to each other, he had no way of knowing how harsh that was.

Jared let out a deep breath. "Do I have to reside on the Isle with the others?"

"No. You can live wherever you want."

Jared appeared relieved by that. "If you need me, call. I'm now yours to command in any way you see fit." There was no missing the underlying venom in his tone. It was obvious others had used him well and left him bitter over it. "Now if I may take my leave . . . Master?"

"I'm not your master, Jared. Your life is yours to do with as *you* see fit. I have no need of a slave. But I'll always welcome a friend and an ally." He held his hand out to him.

Jared hesitated as if afraid to take it. He frowned at Jericho before he finally shook his hand. "Thank you."

"You're welcome. Now you better go before Zephyra makes good on her threat."

Jericho waited until Jared was safely on his way before he returned to Delphine.

NOIR SLAMMED INTO THE WAR ROOM, WITH FURY streaming through his blood. "We've been routed."

Azura looked up, aghast. "By whom?"

"Who do you think?"

"Jaden," she sneered. "I'll have him skinned for this!"

Noir had had the same thought himself. "There's nothing more to be done about it. The Skoti we'd taken have defected back to the Oneroi. Zelos is dead, killed by Madoc. Nike has been freed and Cratus restored."

Azura cursed. With Cratus back at full strength, he could break Jaden free from them . . . or worse, find Cam and Rezar. That would be disastrous for them. "We have got to find Braith." Everything in the universe was balance.

Their sister Braith was theirs. She was a necessary counterbalance, and no matter what, they needed her.

Noir growled low in his throat, "And the Malachai. We have to make sure we either kill him or convert him." Because he alone held the power to overthrow all of the Source gods and wipe them out. If he ever absorbed their powers, not even Jared could stop him.

He would be able to destroy all creation and set the universe back to nil.

Those powers needed to be Noir's. With them, there was no pantheon or power who could stand against him.

Azura narrowed her gaze. "At least we have the gallu. They might be more effective than the Skoti for now anyway."

He nodded. "But this will take much more careful planning on our part. The Greeks are more resourceful than I'd given them credit for."

"No. Cratus was more resourceful. But that's all right. This is only one battle. The war will be ours."

Noir inclined his head to her. "Yes, it will. As for Jaden . . ."

Azura laughed. "He's going to be a very sorry intermediary."

"Yes, he will be, and I'm going to have fun with our new friends."

She arched a brow at that. "What new friends?"

"The Greeks. It's time to let them know we will have no mercy on them. Besides, we have an ally they don't even know about . . . yet."

Azura laughed. "True. And it's one they'll *never* suspect."

DELPHINE SAT IN A SMALL ROOM WITH MADOC, ZAREK and Zeth. By their dour expressions, Jericho knew something had happened while he was gone.

"What?"

Zeth shoved a brittle piece of parchment at him.

As soon as he looked at it, words wrote themselves across it.

"Noir has officially declared war on us and on the Dark-Hunters. If we surrender his Malachai, he'll let us live. If we don't . . ."

Jericho laughed. "He's going to make our lives hell."

"It's not funny," Zeth snapped.

Undaunted, Jericho shrugged. "No, it isn't, but we knew this was coming."

Zarek sat back in his chair and tucked his hands behind his head. "We have to find Cam and Rezar."

Jericho agreed. "And train that damned Malachai."

Zarek snorted. "Good luck on that."

"Why?"

"He's a nasty little bastard. I wanted to kill him years ago, but Ash wouldn't let me. After all is said and done, Ash may be wishing he'd not held me back."

After all was said and done, they might all be wishing that.

Jericho moved to stand beside Delphine's chair. "Well, there's nothing more to be done tonight. I, for one, am exhausted. I've been threatened, beaten, bitten and killed, and that was just in the last hour."

Delphine shook her head at him. "You need someone to tuck you in, sweetie?"

"For that, my goddess, I would worship you forever."

Laughing, she got up and followed him to her room.

He looked around at all the white lace and other frilly things that made this room uniquely hers. "You know this place is *really* girly."

She hesitated. "You want me to redecorate?"

"No," he said, dissolving his clothes and concealing his wings into his back so that he could slide into bed. "I love the fact that everything in here smells like you."

She picked up a corner of her comforter and sniffed it. "No, it doesn't. I don't smell."

He smiled at her offended tone. "You don't stink, but your scent is all over everything, and that's why I don't want anything changed. I love the way you smell. It comforts me. Now come to bed and let me hold you."

She stiffened and so did he. "Is that an order?"

"No," he said with a tired yawn, "it's the sound of me begging."

"You're really out of practice with that."

He smiled. "True."

Naked, Delphine snuggled up to his back and wrapped her arms around him. In all his life no one had ever held him like this. Even as tired as he was, he reveled in the comfort of her love.

"I'm scared, Jericho," she whispered in his ear, "and I'm not used to coping with fear."

"It's all right. I'm not used to coping with love and trust." He took her hand into his and kissed her pale, unscarred knuckles. "We can be the blind leading the blind."

Delphine squeezed his hand. "But as long as we're together . . ."

"Nothing will ever touch us. You are all that matters to me, my angel, and I would walk through hell just to touch your face."

"And I would walk through hell just to bring you food."

Jericho laughed. "Good, 'cause when I wake up, I'm going to be starving."

"I'll have something waiting for you. What would you like?"

He rolled over and pulled her against him. "You naked in my bed. That's all the sustenance I'll ever need."

CHAPTER 17

JERICHO STOOD ON TOP OF THE MOUNTAIN WHERE he'd once looked out, expecting to die. He remembered that day so clearly. The sunset was still the same shade of fire opal.

For Delphine, he'd laid down his arms and resigned himself to Zeus's punishment. Today, he could think of no better place to declare himself hers than here where it had all begun.

He turned to find her by his side, dressed in a white flowing gown with flowers in her pale hair. Even though gods and goddesses didn't have weddings the way humans did, he wanted to do something special for her.

"You have given me my life back," he said as he took her hand.

She kissed his scarred knuckles. "It seems only fair since I wouldn't have had one at all had you not found your heart and spared me."

Who would have ever thought that one single act of kindness would lead him to this path?

Lead him to her?

Unable to tell her what was inside him, he went down on one knee.

Delphine was stunned by Jericho's actions. Dressed in his black armor, he looked up at her with those dual-colored eyes. His white hair ruffled by the breeze, he was breathtakingly handsome.

"I haven't much to offer you, my lady. But I pledge myself to you. Always."

Tears clouded her eyes. "That's not true, Jericho. You have a lot to offer."

"And that is?"

"All that is good in my life is because of you. And I swear by your mother Styx, that I will *never* harm you. That I will *never* betray you."

"And I swear on my mother that every day you live you will know just how much you mean to me."

Delphine smiled. "Good, because it was hard enough to survive this courtship. I shudder at what I'd have to endure to fall in love with someone else."

He arched a brow at that. "Excuse me?"

"You heard me." She knelt down in front of him. "Now give me a kiss and show me your sincerity."

He laughed deep in his throat. "Lady, take me to your bed and I'll show you a lot more than just my sincerity."

"Well, in that case . . ." She flashed them back to her room where they could lie naked in her bed.

After all, vows meant nothing without consummation.

NIKE PAUSED AS SHE ENTERED MADOC'S OFFICE. THE Oneroi was alone, staring out the windows, to the sea.

"Is there something you need?" he asked without turning toward her.

"Yes. I remembered something that I heard while I was in Azmodea."

That succeeded in making him swivel around to face her. "And that was?"

"One of our gods feeding Noir information about us."

"Your brother Zelos."

"No," she said with conviction. "I know his voice and I know the one I heard. But I couldn't place it."

"Then how do you know it's one of us?"

"Because he wanted to take Zeus's place and have Aphrodite as his bride."

Madoc frowned. "But you can't recall who it was?"

"No, and I've tried repeatedly. Noir isn't giving up on us, and I can't shake this terrible feeling that something bad is headed our way."

Madoc laughed. "Something bad is always headed our way." He offered her a kind smile. "Don't worry, Nike. We have victory on our side."

A chill went down her spine at that. Madoc was hiding something. She could feel it. "Then I'll leave you to your duties."

Madoc watched as she left him alone. They had won this round. The Skoti and Zeth were returned to their fold. He was freed and they had Jared once again in their corner and Jericho hadn't been turned.

But like Nike, he felt the rift and it chilled him. They had established a new order, but for how long?

Zeus and the others would be plotting along with Noir and Azura.

Sighing, he looked back out at the raging sea. Right now, he had no doubt it was going to get bloodier before all the wounds were healed. His only question was who, if any of them, would survive?

CHAPTER 18

JERICHO PAUSED ON THE CORNER OF ST. ANN AND Royal as he and Delphine waited for Acheron to join them. What the hell was going on?

It'd been eerily quiet for days now as they waited for Noir's next attack. They knew it was coming, and it hung over all of them like a pall.

But even so, he took comfort in knowing that Delphine was willing to stand by his side and meet whatever came his way.

"What are you doing here?"

He turned at the sound of Jared's voice, surprised to see him in New Orleans. It'd been the first time he'd seen the Sephiroth since they left Kalosis.

"We're waiting on Ash," Delphine answered. "What are *you* doing here?"

Jared indicated a couple over his shoulder. "Demon-sitting."

Delphine frowned as she saw a Charonte female with long black hair dressed as a human goth in a short skirt, corset and striped leggings, with another demon dressed as a steampunk. The female would almost pass for human except for the small pair of red horns on top of her head.

Like the Charonte, the male demon's hair was black—a mop of dreads with a pair of goggles buried deep in them. He had a small goatee and black finger-less gloves that jutted out from the sleeves of his over-sized coat. But the most peculiar thing was a pink bunny strapped to one hip by his belt and a mutated teddy bear strapped to the other.

Yeah, they were odd-looking, no doubt.

And they were eating double-scoop ice cream and window shopping like two college students who didn't have a care in the world. At least until the male got a dab of ice cream on his nose. Laughing, the fe-male wiped it off, then licked her fingers.

"Do I want to know?" Delphine asked.

"Not really. But as long as they're not eating the tourists or natives, it's a good thing and I'm not com-plaining." Jared inclined his head to the street behind them. "There's Ash."

Delphine turned to see him striding alone down the dark street with a black leather backpack slung over his shoulder. His long black coat billowed out from his black jeans and "Raised by Bats" T-shirt to show off his burgundy Doc Martens. Yes, Delphine was in love with her husband and considered him the best-looking man in the universe, but there was something about Ash that made a woman take note.

Ash pulled a pocket watch out to check the time as he joined them.

"What are we doing here?" Jericho asked.

Ash tucked the watch back into his pocket. "We're waiting."

That didn't seem to appease Jericho. "For?"

A liquid-silver Jaguar XKR came flying up the street to make a sharp turn. It slammed on the brakes and skidded into a parking space behind a black truck on the side of the street a few feet in front of them.

Now that was impressive. It landed in a perfect position, just inches off the truck's bumper. The only way Delphine could have duplicated that would have been to use her powers.

As if on cue, the door opened. A tall, insanely handsome dark-haired man with jet-black eyes rolled out of the car into the street. But that wasn't what made her take notice of him. It was the double bow and arrow mark on his cheek.

That was the sign of a Dark-Hunter.

And as the man joined them, Delphine felt the power and the hatred that was ingrained in him. Rarely had she felt its equal. This man . . . held some of the rawest abilities she'd ever come across.

He cast a barely tolerant glare at Acheron before he gave Jared a nasty once-over.

"Why am I here, Rex?" His voice thick with a Cajun drawl, he rolled the last word out like a barbed insult.

Ignoring it, Acheron scowled at the car. "Damn, boy, how lazy are you? Why didn't you walk? We're only a few blocks from your house."

He rolled his shoulders in a casual, yet irritating, shrug. "I like my car."

Ash rolled his eyes. "Jericho. Delphine. I thought

you might want to meet the asshole you're helping to protect. Nick Gautier, this is Jericho and his wife, Delphine."

Jericho choked in surprise. "*This* is the Malachai?"

Ash grinned wickedly. "In all his pain in the ass glory."

Nick glowered at Ash. "Are we through now, Dad? Can I go play with my friends if I promise to be a good boy? I'll even try and make it home by curfew."

Ash laughed evilly. "Oh, absolutely, son. In fact, here come your new playmates now."

Delphine turned as a deep-throated Hayabusa roared down the street with a sound that was all power and speed. It parked just in front of the truck, blocking it in, followed by a Lamborghini Muerciélago, and another Gixxer Hayabusa parked in front of it.

Delphine crossed her arms over her chest as the helmets came off to show one incredibly sexy woman with insanely curly brown hair. Granted, Delphine wasn't attracted to other women, but she had to admit the woman was absolutely stunning. Her biker outfit only accentuated her long, slender limbs, and she had a walk that said she'd kick the ass of anyone dumb enough to cross her path in the wrong direction.

After unzipping her jacket to show off her blood-red tank top, she put on a pair of opaque Versace sunglasses.

The other bike was ridden by a man with short black hair and a thin beard trimmed in sharp angles that reminded Delphine of Tony Stark's in *Iron Man*. Bulging with muscles, he had a swagger that said he took no shit from anyone over anything. A small row of hoops ran up his left ear and his arms were covered with colorful tattoos.

The Lamborghini was driven by a lethal-looking man with long, straight blond hair that he wore scraped back into a ponytail. Much leaner than the brunette, he still had an aura that said he was willing to take out anyone he viewed as an enemy.

Delphine had been around warriors and gods all of her life, but never had she seen anything to equal the badass attitudes of this group.

They joined rank like a pack of feral lions ready to patrol the jungle. No, not patrol . . .

Conquer.

Ash introduced them as they joined their small group. "Guys, meet Samia, the fiercest Amazon warrior in her tribe."

The woman inclined her head to them.

"The huge mountain is Blade. He was the most bloodthirsty warlord in Mercia."

Blade didn't acknowledge them in the least. He looked more like he was sizing them up for body bags.

Ash indicated the tall blond. "Ethon is from ancient Athens. He single-handedly fought off an entire Spartan brigade. For a thousand years after he died, his name was the equivalent to the bogeyman in ancient Sparta."

Ethon flashed a charming smile. "All in a good day's work. So who am I here to kill now?"

"Down, boy. I have other plans for you."

Ethon curled his lip as if he were in pain. "Damn it, Acheron. Don't tell me you've finally released me from hell to not kill something. That's just wrong."

Ash patted him on the arm. "Don't worry. I'm sure you'll get your chance to maim and slay soon." He jerked his chin toward another man headed their way.

Delphine turned and sucked her breath in sharply at the latest warrior to join them. A bit shorter than the others, he was Asian and every bit as devastating and lethal.

"Raden," Ash said as he joined them. "A trained Shinobi who never quite learned how to come down from a blood high."

"Why should I? Blood always tastes best when it's warm."

Delphine arched her brow at that. By his tone and the way he licked his fangs, she didn't think he was joking.

Ash ignored his comment. "Tafari, Roman, Cabeza and Kalidas will be joining us later."

"Roman," Samia spat. "Are you out of your mind?"

Ash went cold and cast a look at her that was even deadlier than the assembled crew. "You will play nice and stay back from him or so help me, Sam . . . you won't like the repercussion."

"Fucking Roman scum."

Nick let out a bored sigh as he rolled his eyes. "You know, I'm having a freaky deja vu here. And honestly, I'm unimpressed. Should I know these—"

"Don't say it, Nick," Ash said sharply, cutting off his next insult. "In the land of badass, you've just been trumped. If Dark-Hunters had inmates, these would be they. Known as the Dogs of War because that's what they thrive on, they're cold-blooded and intolerant." He clapped Nick on the back. "Congratu-

lations, bud, these are your new protectors. And unlike the other Dark-Hunters, they don't drain each
other's powers."

Nick scowled. "How can that be?"

Blade grabbed Ethon and head-butted him. Normally when one Dark-Hunter assaulted another, they
felt the blow ten times worse than the person they delivered it to. But Blade showed no signs of it. "Pain is
my best friend."

Ethon slugged him hard in response. His own nose
exploded with blood, but the look on his face said
he really didn't care how much he hurt himself. He
brushed the blood aside while Blade did the same.

Ash sighed as he shook his head. "It's not that their
powers don't drain. It's that they're so powerful to begin with that it's not really noticeable the way it is
with others. And as you've just seen, they have a deep
masochistic streak much like Zarek."

Nick was aghast. "You're turning seven—"

"Eight," Ash corrected.

Nick cursed foully. "Eight of these loose on New
Orleans? Are you out of your mind? How are you going to control them?"

Ash shrugged nonchalantly. "That's why I have
Jericho, Jared and Zarek."

Nick sputtered. "Psycho-ass? You're bringing
Psycho-ass back?"

"That's Mister Psycho-ass to you, punk," Zarek
said as he materialized behind Nick and put a hostile
hand on his neck. He squeezed it hard enough to
wring a groan out of Nick. "Now who's babysitting
who?"

Jericho snorted. "Looks like I'll be the one babysitting you all."

Delphine laughed at his dire tone. "It's okay, sweetie. I make a mean Band-aid."

EPILOGUE

Knob Creek, Tennessee

DELPHINE WAS EXTREMELY NERVOUS AS THEY WALKED up the small set of stairs that led to a log cabin on top of a huge mountain, out in the middle of nowhere. It was cold and snowy, but the scenery was breathtaking.

Even so, it couldn't calm her down. "Maybe we should have called first."

Jericho made a sound of chiding deep in his throat. "You can't be serious. This is all you've talked about for the last two weeks."

"Yeah, but how do I introduce myself? What if she doesn't remember me?"

He rolled his eyes. "You're her daughter, Delphine. Believe me, that's not something she's going to forget."

Maybe, but she was the daughter her mother had thought dead. Maybe she'd pushed her out of her mind completely and gone on with her life. "What if—"

He picked her up and carried her.

"Jericho!" she snapped, afraid he'd slip on the snow and stones and hurt them both. "Put me down. I don't want to meet her like this."

He gave her a stern look before he obliged and set her down just in front of the red wood door.

Delphine was still trying to get used to her emotions, which were completely out of whack over this. She was scared and happy. Apprehensive and nervous.

None of it felt good.

But Jericho was right. Once she'd acclimated herself to the reality that she had a mother who was alive, she'd been obsessed with meeting her.

Yet now that she was here . . . it wasn't as easy as she'd thought it would be.

"I'm right here, baby," Jericho said softly, placing a steady hand on her shoulder to comfort her. "Knock on the door."

"Okay." She took a deep, long breath.

Clenching her fists, she stared at the door, which was somehow intimidating in a not-intimidating kind of way. She'd fought gods and demons, Daimons and gallu. So why was this so damned hard?

Just knock . . .

Her hand trembled as she lifted it and knocked timidly. Turning to Jericho, she shrugged. "Well, guess they're not home. I'll try again later."

She started for the stairs only to have Jericho catch her and drag her back to the door. With a stern glower, he reached around her and pounded on the wood so hard it rattled the hinges.

"I hate you," she hissed.

"You love me," he said with a tender smile. "Even when I piss you off."

She was just about to correct him when she heard the sound of someone unlocking the door. Her heart pounded furiously in fear and expectation.

Jericho turned her around at the same time the door opened to show her a woman who was almost identical in looks to her, except for her black hair and vivid blue eyes.

Dressed in a winter white sweater and jeans, her mother stared at her as if she were a ghost. Her breathing intensified. "Is this a sick prank?"

Her gaze went from Delphine to Jericho, and then it narrowed in hatred. She screeched in outrage. "You bastard! Haven't you done enough to me!"

Delphine caught her as she lunged at Jericho. "Mom?"

Her mother fought her until that one syllable registered in her mind past her fury. Tears filled her blue eyes as she stepped back to look at Delphine again. "Iole?" she breathed in disbelief. "Is it really you? Can it be?"

Delphine sobbed as she nodded. "It's me, Mom. Cratus didn't kill me like Zeus ordered. He hid me away to protect me."

Leta pulled her into a hug so tight that she could barely breathe, but Delphine didn't care.

This was her mother. Her *real* mother. She was alive and here . . . and she remembered her.

It was such a silly thing, and yet up until now she had honestly been afraid of her mother rejecting her. Of her having forgotten her.

"I loved you so much," Leta sobbed, stroking her hair. "I've hated all of them for so long. . . . Never a day has passed that I didn't think about and wonder what you would have been like had you lived." She kissed Delphine's hair, then her cheek. Shaking her head, she cupped her face and stared at her with pride shining deep in her blue eyes. "Look at you! You have your father's beautiful eyes and you're so grown."

Delphine laughed through her tears. "You look like my sister."

Leta laughed until her gaze returned to Jericho. It was condemning once more. "Why didn't you tell me she lived? How could you have kept that from me?"

"Zeus punished him mercilessly," Delphine explained.

Jericho met Leta's gaze levelly, wanting her to know that he hadn't hurt her on purpose. "If there had been a way to get word to you, I would have. I swear. But had they known she lived, Zeus would have killed her."

Leta reached up and touched his scarred cheek. "Was that . . ."

"From saving her? Yes."

Leta's tears fell even harder as she pulled him into her arms and kissed his scarred cheek. "Thank you, Cratus. Thank you for saving my baby and for bringing her back to me."

Delphine saw his own eyes mist as he looked at her. "Believe me, I'm the one who owes gratitude here."

Leta pulled back with a frown. "What do you mean?"

Delphine sniffed as she reached out to take Jericho's hand. "He's my husband, Mom."

"You're married?" Leta returned to hug her. "Oh this is . . . this is . . . wonderful!"

"Leta? Are you all right?"

Delphine wiped at her tears as a tall blond man came through the door. But what surprised her most was that she knew him.

Aidan O'Conner. The famous actor. She didn't know how many dreams she'd been in with women who fantasized about him.

How very odd.

Yet the most shocking thing was the black-headed toddler swathed in a pink jumper in Aidan's arms.

Laughing, Leta took the little girl and held her close. "I couldn't be better, Aidan."

"Then why are you crying and standing out here where it's freezing without a coat on?"

She kissed his cheek before she turned back to Delphine. "Kari, meet your big sister, Iole."

Delphine laughed as the baby waved at her and said a very shy hi.

"I have a sister?" she asked, delighted by the news.

"I have another daughter?" Aidan gasped.

Leta nodded. "Aidan, meet Cratus—"

"Jericho," he corrected.

Leta scowled in confusion. "Jericho?"

He nodded. "Cratus died a long time ago."

She inclined her head as if she understood completely. "Jericho saved my baby from Dolor when he attacked us and raised her."

"Uh, no," Jericho corrected with a nervous laugh. "I gave her to peasants who raised her, otherwise that would be really creepy."

Delphine shook her head at him and his paranoia. "And I go by Delphine."

Leta looked surprised by that.

Jericho gave a sheepish shrug. "I didn't know what name she had, and you weren't exactly being helpful to us that night. Not that I blame you. I just handed her off and went back before anyone realized what I'd done with her. They gave her their own name. Sorry."

Leta waved his words away. "Never apologize for what you did. I would never question you on that topic." She stroked the baby's back as the girl sneezed. "But Aidan's right. It's really cold out here, and we have a nice fire inside. Please come in and join us."

Jericho followed them into a quaint cabin that was decorated in navy and green with country bears. The view of the mountains through the picture windows was incredible. "Nice place you have."

"Thanks," Aidan said.

Leta set Kari down so that she could stand by the coffee table where her toys were scattered. "Can I get you something to drink?"

"No, we're fine." Delphine sat on the couch.

Her mother sat down beside her at the same time her sister left her toys to slap at Delphine's knees. Delighted by her, Delphine picked her up and placed her in her lap so that she could cuddle her.

Aidan and Jericho hung back in tough-guy poses. "So when did you guys get married?"

Jericho shrugged. "A few weeks ago."

Aidan frowned. "I wish we'd known. We'd have definitely been there."

Leta smiled at him. "Actually, that's not how the

gods do it, sweetie. You merely declare yourselves married and you are."

"Kind of anti-climatic, isn't it?"

Jericho shook his head. "Maybe, but in marriage it's more about the commitment than it is the vows."

"No," Leta said as she hugged both Delphine and Kari. "Marriage is about the love more than anything else."

Delphine looked up at Jericho and smiled. Her mother was definitely right. And she was grateful that she had the people in her life who made up her family. Both those related to her by blood and those related to her by choice.

Vanishing Isle

MADOC SAT ALONE IN HIS OFFICE, WATCHING THE scene with Delphine and her family. Yes, he was prying, but she'd talked about it so much that he was afraid of it turning out bad for her. Luckily it hadn't.

But then Leta had always been kind-hearted and loving. Too much so at times.

And in truth, he envied her that happiness. There had been a time when he'd craved that kind of domesticity, but too much had happened to change him.

Now he had much more pressing things to deal with.

The winds of change were blistering as they gathered force, and soon they would be rolling in.

He felt a sudden shift in the air behind him.

It was Jared.

Madoc glanced at him over his shoulder. "What are you doing here?"

"I'm helping to train the new Malachai and I just wanted to know something."

"That is?"

"Does anyone else know you're related to him?"

Do you love fiction with a supernatural twist?

Want the chance to hear news about your favourite authors (and the chance to win free books)?

Keri Arthur
S. G. Browne
P.C. Cast
Christine Feehan
Jacquelyn Frank
Larissa Ione
Darynda Jones
Sherrilyn Kenyon
Jackie Kessler
Jayne Ann Krentz and Jayne Castle
Martin Millar
Kat Richardson
J.R. Ward
David Wellington
Laura Wright

Then visit the Piatkus website and blog
www.piatkus.co.uk | www.piatkusbooks.net

And follow us on Facebook and Twitter
www.facebook.com/piatkusfiction | www.twitter.com/piatkusbooks

piatkus